NIGHTFALL

Lee Driver

Full Moon Publishing

Library of Congress Control Number: 2015931901

ISBN 978-0-9888683-7-3

Published May 2015

Printed in the United States of America

Full Moon Publishing LLC
433 Mystic Point Drive
Bluffton, SC 29909

www.fullmoonpub.com

Praise for the Chase Dagger Series

"Lee Driver has written an exciting paranormal mystery that has excellent plotting, brilliant characterizations and an enthralling storyline."   — *Midwest Book Review*

"Lee Driver's Chase Dagger/Sara Morningsky series is one of the few truly dependable mystery series being published today. You always know what to expect with Driver: the unexpected."
                — Craig Clarke, Top 1000 Reviewer

"The appeal of cross-genre novels is sometimes difficult to target, but this one should have no trouble attracting readers from either the mystery or the fantasy side of the fence."
                — *Booklist*

"In Driver's novels it is impossible to separate the lure of the plot and the magnetism of the characters. The chance to catch a hell of a mystery and the growing, unfolding enigma of such characters as these is exceedingly rare. Don't miss the opportunity."
                — Lisa DuMond, www.sfsite.com

"This is a delightfully nontraditional mystery that should appeal to a wide variety of readers. Let the series continue."
                — *Booklist*

"The attendant breezy sex, violence, and action, coupled with bits of Indian lore and Einstein the talking macaw, should have readers clamoring for the projected next novel."
                — *Library Journal*

Also by Lee Driver

Chase Dagger Series

Vaporizer
Fatal Storm
Chasing Ghosts
The Unseen
Full Moon-Bloody Moon
The Good Die Twice

Short Stories

Sara Morningsky, *Mystery in Mind Anthology*
The Thirteenth Hole, *Mystery in Mind Anthology*

Written as S.D. Tooley

Sam Casey Series

The Tunnel
Destiny Kills
What Lies Within
Echoes from the Grave
Restless Spirit
Nothing Else Matters
When the Dead Speak

Short Stories

Mysteries to Die For, a short story collection on Kindle

For Middle School/Young Adult Readers

Remy and Roadkill Series

The Skull

Some of the above titles are also available in large print, audio and eBook formats

NIGHTFALL

NIGHTFALL
7th Chase Dagger Mystery

PROLOGUE

"Open your eyes." He shook her like a rag doll, long dark hair tangled in his fingers. All she did was cry. That incessant whining and "please please don't hurt me please please I'll do anything you want." The pleading only made him angrier, made him want to shut her up. He wasn't sure why the eyes were important, but they were. HE told him so.

"You are beginning to piss me off," he screamed. But he wasn't talking to her. He was talking to HIM, the voice that gave cryptic suggestions as though he was supposed to fill in the blanks. And when he didn't, the voice became more incessant, until he couldn't take it anymore.

"Please please please." She could barely form an intelligible word she was so scared. He had seen her at the mall and followed her from store to store, keeping a safe distance, studying her every detail. He reduced it to a game, sleuthing out her address, spending weeks following her, getting to know where she worked, ate, and shopped. Whether she had a husband or boyfriend. The bars she frequented were more sports bars with testosterone-laden, sweaty youth flashing their latest tattooed biceps and guzzling cheap beer. He preferred wine bistros and soft music, and he detested cigarettes. But tonight he loved them because she would step outside alone to light up. This time he was waiting for her. This time she couldn't find her cigarettes because he'd swiped them from the bar when she turned her back. And even though he didn't smoke, he offered her one of his special-made ones. As he lit it, he saw her eyes glance appreciatively at the gold lighter. It only took three puffs for her to feel dizzy, for the drug to get into her system. She blamed it on one too many drinks, so he offered to let her sit in his car until she felt better.

And now, here they were in an Iowa cornfield, not a star in sight, his hands suddenly wrapped around her beautiful neck, tears streaming down her face, a whisper of "why" on her lips, and a voice in his head urging, "KILL HER."

1 "I feel special that you finally opened your front gate for me." Simon tossed a stack of mail on Dagger's desk and stood in the middle of the living room. Whenever he visited, he gawked as though it was the first time he had ever walked into the converted car showroom. Years ago, after a company built the facility, it was discovered it was sitting on reservation land. The CEO abandoned the building and Sara's grandparents converted it into their home. The floor to ceiling windows in the living room looked out onto three hundred acres of forest and wildflowers, a pond where jonquils, crocuses and other spring flowers bloomed, and a garden that wasn't much more than tilled soil waiting for planting. Stairs led up to Sara's bedroom and to a metal catwalk. Skylights overhead bathed the room in sunlight.

Simon hobbled over to the Florida room, a project Dagger had completed last year. The room was five hundred square feet of lush plants and tropical furniture. Dagger's penchant for black and gray did not bode well with Sara's love of flowers. Set between the jalousie windows was a flagstone fireplace. "That's what you've been doing. Adds a nice touch to the room."

Sara grabbed Simon's arm and pulled him closer. "It's gas so we don't have to mess with logs."

"It's one of those that vents out the back, I see." Simon swiped his hand along the top layer of flagstone. "You do good work."

Dagger studied his handiwork as he raked his hair back into a ponytail. "I was hesitant at first. But Sara assured me if we kept the French doors closed to this room while Einstein is out of his aviary, he won't be tempted to get near the fireplace or the ceiling fan."

He wrapped an arm around Sara's waist and pulled her close. "Like it?" That beam of a smile which lit up her eyes told him all he needed to know.

"Love it." She kissed him full on the mouth. "I have coffee ready. Want some?"

"Sure, babe."

"Simon? I have cookies, too." Sara saw a puzzled look on the mail carrier's face as he nodded.

Simon cocked his head as he watched her leave, then jerked his head to his friend. Dagger was busy studying Sara's attributes, the curve of her calves in her leggings, the outline of her firm ass under a floral shirt which hit her mid-thigh. Her hair fell past her waist. All she needed was a lei around her neck to complete the picture.

"Aw, hell. Eunie was right. I hate it when I lose a bet to her."

"What bet is that?" Dagger plopped down on the rattan sofa and stretched his long legs across the coffee table.

"She said you two haven't surfaced for air or answered your calls for months 'cause you wuz knockin' boots."

Dagger's dark eyes glared, trying not to give away the truth, but the smile forming on his lips betrayed him. "It's what you've been pushing for the past few years, old man. Thought you'd be happy."

"Oh, I'm happy. Just takes all the fun out of it, is all." Simon carefully took a seat in one of the chairs, not sure if such a dainty structure could hold his weight.

Sara stood in the doorway smiling. "How much was the bet?" She set a tray on the coffee table and let the men fend for themselves.

"Four hundred dollars." Simon grabbed a chocolate chip cookie before the coffee. He knew his priorities. "She's been salivating over a new watch. But I told her, nah. You two were laying low after that last case. Seeing that I haven't been able to get a response at your gate, and your mail's been piling up, Eunie was afraid you wouldn't see the invite to our anniversary party. She'd be real hurt if you didn't come."

"She finally learned how to send a text message which is how I found out about the party. Of course we'll be there." Sara tucked one leg under her and sat next to Dagger. "Any hints what Eunie would like for a gift?"

"I'd like a new fishing pole, but I guess only the wives get presents." Simon added more sugar to his coffee and took another cookie.

"How about membership to a weight loss program." Dagger nodded at the paunch hanging over Simon's belt. He was barrel-chested and tottered on spindly shaped legs when he walked. Eunie always said he looked like a Black Santa when he laughed because his belly shook.

"Really? That's the best you can do?"

"You are taking her on a trip, right?" Sara vaguely remembered Eunie always wanted to go on a cruise.

"Oh, yeah. We're flying to Hawaii and cruising the islands for two weeks. I'll probably get claustrophobic in the tiny stateroom since it will be our hotel for the entire time."

"Why don't you reserve a suite?" Sara asked.

Simon chuckled. "I'm a postal worker, honey, not a politician. Those suites cost a bundle. I've already checked that out."

"I think it's sweet that you two are renewing your vows."

"Thirty years went by fast. Too fast." He watched as Dagger's fingers stroked Sara's shoulder. How her right hand rested on the top of his thigh. If she sat any closer, she may as well give him a lap dance. "The all-consuming hots don't last long. You two best slow it down. You need a bucket of ice water moment."

"A what?" Sara was never sure what would pop out of Simon's mouth next. As usual, he didn't pause to explain.

"Stopped by Skizzy's place a few times to see if he heard from you. Said something about that BettaTec satellite moving. What's with that?"

BettaTec was a shadow corporation Dagger used to work for. After their last case where he was instrumental in stealing laser weapons out of the hands of the wrong people, Dagger noticed on a monitor he kept in his vault that one of the two satellites BettaTec controlled changed its trajectory. It was now in a path directly over Cedar Point, Indiana. Dagger had no doubt they were searching for whoever or whatever interrupted a multi-billion dollar sale.

"Connie said she was checking on it. Other than the satellite moving, there was nothing else to report. No news is good news, I suppose."

"When's the last time you talked to that freaky robot?"

"Not a robot...a computer." Dagger took a large gulp of coffee while attempting to remember the last time he was in his other office. "Maybe six or eight weeks ago. Besides, I'm sure someone would get in touch with me if anything new popped up."

Simon swiped a beefy hand across his face and studied his friend. "You may say no news is good news, but I say it's never a good sign when things have been too quiet for far too long."

2 Sheila paused in front of a business called Logan's Galleria located in a renovated strip mall that was near completion. She pressed her face to the glass and shielded the glare from the sun. Her mother taught her the appreciation of fine art. Finally, Cedar Point was getting some culture back into this melting pot of a town. She entered the shop and was immediately struck by the starkness of the décor. Everything was white, from the walls to the crown molding and thick wainscoting. The vaulted ceiling made the room look cavernous. Light fixtures dotted the walls while paintings were propped up waiting to be hung under each light.

She stepped back to get a better view of a design in the center of the tile floor. What looked like a two-headed bird in purple and gold was silhouetted against several images of the moon. The colors were vibrant, the detail intricate. Sheila caught a movement in another doorway.

"A mosaic replica of the Logan crest. Beautiful, isn't it?" The man standing before her appeared delicate. She didn't know any other way to put it. Skin more like alabaster, fingers long and bony, eyes inset as though he could press a button and they would recede into his skull. He was dressed in a black suit, white shirt buttoned tight against his scrawny neck. Perhaps they should have named the place Logan's Funeral and Crematorium.

She could tell by the way his eyes assessed her that he

definitely appreciated fine art. Hers were classic looks honed by the finest finishing schools. From her platinum hair to the best breast enhancements Daddy's money could buy to the finest clothing specialty boutiques could offer, Sheila was a society page headline every week. Everyone in town knew the Monroes. Leyton Monroe owned a string of newspapers and Sheila was their ace reporter. But today she came as a shopper, not to get a story. After all, she worked the crime beat, homicides, stories with teeth in them, so to speak.

"Carlton Abrams at your service." The bony fingers reached out to her. Sheila felt as though she were shaking the hand of a mortician, but his grip was surprisingly strong.

"Sheila Monroe." She released the grip as fast as possible. His skin was cold to the touch. "Why haven't I seen your gallery here before?"

There was a slow cadence to his voice, almost hypnotic. Instead of a mortician, he might be better suited as a hypnotist in a carnival. "It was in San Francisco and Chicago for years until the two became too costly to operate. With so much open land in Indiana, and so many high-end communities cropping up with new home owners who would appreciate fine art, I felt we could afford a much larger store. So I convinced Mark to close the two galleries and open this one in Indiana. You have a much lower tax rate here."

"So you just opened?"

"Actually, not until our grand opening. I usually don't lock the entrance. I'm still moving pieces from the warehouse." He walked over to the front entrance and turned the lock.

Sheila felt queasy and hoped she remembered to pack her mace. "I'm sorry. I didn't mean to intrude. I saw the sign and thought you were open." She noticed several arched doorways and made her way to the first one on her right. Paintings of farmlands and rural America leaned against the walls. "You plan to have a different theme for each room?"

"Yes. We have Americana in this room, landscapes in another, seashores, wildlife. The main lobby will have a collage, the best of all the themes that Mister Logan wants to showcase. As you can tell, he has an excellent eye for talent."

Sheila crossed the lobby to the only room with doors. The floor was black marble so shiny she was afraid to step on it. The French doors were painted white with black accents. Even the wainscoting in the room was a black lacquer, a sharp contrast from the rest of the shop. "Something tells me this room has been set aside for a reason."

"Mister Logan has found a new talent, and he is giving this artist his own room. Even after all of the paintings are hung, the doors are to be kept closed. Viewing will be by appointment only."

"Really." Perhaps that was the reasoning behind it, Sheila thought. The more mystery, the more the gallery could raise its prices. "And when do we get to meet this fabulous artist?"

Carlton gave a shrug of one bony shoulder. "Probably never. Mister Logan says the man is a recluse, someone with strange proclivities, not unlike highly talented artists. I understand he doesn't even like daylight. Does his best work at night. Shipped his first piece to the San Francisco gallery Mark was intrigued and agreed to see the rest of his work. The paintings started showing up at the Chicago gallery. The artist called, and that was when Mark told him he wanted to wait for the entire collection before displaying them. He still didn't give a name and an attempt to return the call revealed the number wasn't valid. Highly unusual, but it adds a bit of intrigue, don't you think?"

The skateboarder wove in and out of the shoppers
clotting the sidewalk, some moving out of his way,
others yelling expletives. He had cruised up and
down sidewalks for the past month, ever since the
weather broke. Prior to that he'd ridden a bicycle around
town, going nowhere in particular. Always looking, always
watching, always waiting. He'd been dressed differently when
he was a bike rider, sporting a baseball cap with fake gray hair
attached, a gray beard, tattered clothing from a Goodwill shop
with padding underneath to add bulk to his frame. He would
stop every so often to search through waste cans sitting by
the curb outside of the shops or huddle with fellow homeless
around a fire erupting from a fifty gallon drum. But while
his head was down, while his gloved hands pawed through
debris, his eyes were always watching, searching, looking for
her.

Sometimes he thought he saw her and tried to pin down a
routine. For one thing, her appearance never changed making
her easy to spot, yet she still found a way to slip around
buildings and out the back door of shops. Did she suspect
him? Did she know she was a target? Or was vigilance just
second nature?

In and out he wove, dressed today in torn jeans, sneakers,
a tee shirt and hoodie. The knife was tucked in his right hand.
All he had to do was zip past and slice her carotid artery. He
would be down the sidewalk and around the corner before

her body hit the pavement. Lampposts lined the curb, their bulbs casting a scant amount of light. The local stores and restaurants cast more light onto the outside world than the Victorian lanterns, which appeared to be more for decoration.

He recently started noticing a slight pattern to her routine. At one in the afternoon she would be somewhere near a restaurant handing out flowers like a garden Jehovah Witness, spreading good cheer, blah blah blah. On weekends she would hit the dinner hour, the late night people, mainly men, who needed an apology bouquet to soften the wife after spending too much time at happy hour. The trick was determining which restaurant and what part of town.

Just when he thought he should move his search to the mall, he saw her on the next block, a floral hat on her head, one arm looped under a basket handle. He picked up speed, one foot pushing off the pavement. A green light timed just right, very little traffic. Or so he thought. He didn't see the black cargo van barreling through the intersection, nor did he notice it was going the wrong way down a one-way street. The pain registered last. He felt his body floating above the street, sailing toward one of the Victorian light poles with such force he was sure all of his organs had realigned. He saw her turn toward him as the impact with the pole almost severed his head. And he'd never forget the slight smile on her face as his remains slid down the pole to the street. She knew, and he had underestimated her.

Within the hour the black cargo van would be crushed at the scrap yard outside of town. Ten minutes later the driver would be behind the wheel of a brown SUV.

4 Sergeant Jerry Martinez took a sniff of the murky contents solidifying in his coffee cup. Could something be so old it thickened into syrup? He spilled the contents into the sink. "I swear they wait for me to make a pot of coffee." He dumped the old grounds into the garbage, pushed up his sleeves, and let the hot water run to rinse out the glass decanter.

"That's what you get for coming in early, Padre." Chief Wozniak stood with his empty cup watching his former seminary classmate finish sanitizing the carafe.

"Seven in the morning isn't that early. Thought the cleaning crew washes this thing out." Padre placed a new filter in the basket, ripped open a bag of grounds, and emptied the contents. "We should pop for one of those coffeemakers that makes one cup at a time. That way you always have a fresh cup. No fuss, no muss."

Wozniak shrugged. "Sounds good. Why don't you look into that?" His beet red face wasn't an indication of his temperament. It was the chief of detective's natural color. Red hair, red face, freckles, and a bulbous nose his grandmother once said could put out candles in church.

"Am I going to be reimbursed, John?"

Coffee started dripping into the clean carafe. Like moths to light, soon the day shift would start showing up, cups in hand. Some did bring their own mocha latte whipped wonders that cost more than a gallon of gas, but soon they would be sniffing toward the break room for a refill.

"Sure, why not? We should have enough in the slush fund. Course, those have a reservoir to hold water so these idiots probably will wait for you or me to fill it. Maybe I should just start bringing a thermos from home." He watched his top homicide detective wipe the countertop and straighten the containers of cream and sugar. Wisps of gray hair sparsely covered Padre's receding hairline, and his shirt could have used a few swipes with the iron. His disheveled appearance was in sharp contrast to his kitchen hygiene. "What's on your plate today?"

"Count your blessings. Temps may be reaching the sixties in the day time, but the forties at night keep the thugs indoors. We wrapped up the drive-by yesterday so I'm just one happy camper."

"Maybe they found religion and wanna be on their best behavior."

"Hey, Martinez," a voice yelled from the front of the office. Louise's gravelly voice carried through the walls. "Doc Jamison is on one."

"Tell him I'm not in," Padre yelled back.

"He said to stop by. He's gonna make your day."

Padre handed his full cup of coffee to Wozniak. "Great. Doc better have fresh coffee made."

"I left a perfectly fresh pot of coffee back at the precinct." Padre let the door swing shut behind him as he searched the counters in the examining room. "And obviously nothing hot and fresh in this room."

"Nope, only cold and dead. Coffee can wait." Luther Jamison rolled the gurney from the steel drawer, maneuvered it in front of Padre, and carefully pulled the sheet down.

exposing the Y incision which could have been made by a machine. Luther was that meticulous. "Hit and run. Vehicle was going a good fifty miles an hour through the intersection. The victim's head was almost removed by the impact with the light pole."

Padre winced as Luther carefully positioned the head. Bruising started to appear, turning most of the skin on the body into dark blue blotches. "At least this one wasn't in the crosshairs of a gang shooting or a victim of a drug overdose." Padre hated it when kids died before they could live life to its fullest. "But this happened late yesterday, not my shift, and not my territory. Besides, shouldn't Traffic handle this one?"

Luther flicked a finger toward the cop in a *follow me* motion. The M.E.'s hair was more pepper than salt and his smooth, dark skin was unusual for someone close to sixty years of age. His staff jokingly accused him of drinking formaldehyde for breakfast. Padre trailed him to a back counter where a large silver tray contained the victim's belongings. Luther lifted the torn and bloody jeans. "No wallet, no money, no I.D. We processed his prints, but the lab didn't come up with a hit."

Padre crossed his arms and stifled a yawn. The sterile white walls and floors made the frosty temps in the morgue feel even colder. He regretted leaving his trench coat in the car. "Sure could use a cup of hot coffee."

"In good time." Luther handed Padre a copy of the autopsy report, which the detective reluctantly took.

"I trust there is a moral to this story." He perused the forensic details and noticed the police report attached. "Witnesses saw a van, navy blue, brown, maroon. No one saw the driver or a license plate." Padre snapped his eyes to Luther and exhaled audibly.

"Patience." He nodded toward the report. "As you can

tell, massive hemorrhaging, lacerated spleen, kidney and just about every other organ as well as multiple broken bones and crushed ribs."

"Someone wanted to make sure the kid didn't live."

"That's just it. He wasn't a teen. I estimate his age between thirty and thirty-five. No plastic surgery. He's one of those guys who can change his appearance with ease."

"Like a hitman."

"My thoughts exactly." Luther dumped the contents of a brown evidence bag into the tray. "This was found in his hand." He held up a nine-inch long knife with a hole at the bottom of the curved handle. "It's a karambit. The hole serves as a finger ring. Just stick your pinkie in it."

"Damn." Padre picked it up and lightly touched his finger to the blade. He immediately drew blood.

"Very lethal cutting tool."

"If it was in his hand, my guess would be he had a victim in mind."

"Agree. The second item is even more interesting." Luther picked up a petri dish from the tray and carried it to a microscope. He tapped a few keys and an image appeared on the monitor. "It's about a quarter of an inch in size." Luther enlarged the image.

Padre leaned closer, as if that alone would help him decipher what he was seeing. "What the hell is that? A computer chip?" He straightened and looked at the medical examiner. "Where did you find that?"

"In his head. Didn't even show up in the X-ray. Not made of metal, and if his head hadn't been almost detached, I would have never found it."

Padre took a step back. "This isn't one of those clones with the bomb in his head, is it? You remember that case where we found remains in the quarry, right?"

"Not the same. This seems to only be a tracker of some sort, like the ones they put under the skin of animals so they can be returned to their owners." He picked up the object with tweezers. "Lab wasn't able to decipher a serial number or trace it back to whoever or whatever put it there."

Whatever. Padre shivered at that word.

"Which brings us to the *piece de resistance*." Luther picked up a sneaker and tipped it over. A card fell out. "Take a look."

Padre hesitated. Luther's all business, clinical disposition, appeared to have morphed in seconds. The look in Doc's eyes was almost amusement. Or was it anticipation of Padre's reaction? The cop carefully picked up the card, grumbled when he saw the slight smile on the M.E.'s lips, then turned it over. It was a business card for Dagger Investigations.

"You don't recognize him?" Padre asked.

"Nope." And Dagger didn't. When Padre called all he said was that they found his business card on a hit-and-run victim.

"What about you?"

Sara shook her head as she stared at the body, its head just a bit off kilter, stitches on the chest fresh. "No fingerprints?"

"Nothing in the system. I'm running him through facial recognition."

Luther shoved the body back into the drawer and closed the door. "This is what I removed from his head. X-ray didn't pick it up. All parts appear to be a plastic of some sort." They followed him over to a monitor. Luther punched a few buttons and the object under the microscope became enlarged on the screen.

"A computer chip?" The only phrase that came to Dagger's mind was Simon's: *Things have been too quiet for far too long.* "Where was it placed?"

"Bottom right side, back of the head."

"Was it attached to anything?" *Like his brain,* Dagger thought to himself.

"Like what? A countdown dial?" Padre remembered all too well the case with the clone whose head was embedded with a remote detonation. "Thank you, no."

"No serial numbers?" Sara avoided her partner's eyes. The chip in Dagger's head displayed numbers that referred to satellite coordinates. Those numbers had led Dagger to a remote city in Nebraska, one mile below the surface, a city where he had been trained.

BettaTec was using even more advanced technology. Dagger's chip was the size of a postage stamp. The one Luther showed them was one-fourth the size. Dagger nodded at the monitor. "I need a photocopy of the chip and the deceased to show to some people."

"No please, no asking politely?" Padre prompted. "And exactly what people are you talking about?"

"Did the cameras near the hit and run pick up anything?" Sara asked. "And what about witnesses?"

Like a cyborg, Padre's eyes moved from Dagger to Sara. How like her to deflect any suspicion away from her partner. "Witnesses just saw a speeding dark blue, brown, black van, SUV, truck, semi. You know witnesses. Got twenty of them with twenty different versions. Good thing we have a traffic cam at the light."

"Whose is this?" Sara pointed at a curved knife lying next to a bloody tee shirt.

"It was in John Doe's hand."

Dagger picked it up gingerly, aware of the sharpness of the blade. "A karambit. This isn't exactly what one would use to clean his nails."

"Actually, it was popular among women in Indonesia. It was easy to hide in their hair should they ever need it for self defense. Today it is used in Filipino martial arts." Sara pointed at the ring at the end of the handle. "The ring guard makes it difficult to disarm the attacker."

Luther said, "If you ask me, she knows way too much."

"Tell me about it."

"My cop nose tells me he planned to use it on someone." Padre pointed in the direction of Luther's office. "Can I access the police database from your laptop?"

Once assembled in Luther's office, Padre accessed the case file on John Doe and found footage from a traffic camera. They saw the skateboarder zipping between pedestrians, saw the black van building speed and barreling through the intersection as John Doe zipped across the street. The impact sent the body hurtling in the air.

"Can you back that up?" There was something about the way the skateboarder kept looking ahead. It wasn't that he was trying to avoid hitting someone. Instead, it looked as though he were trying to keep up with someone. "Fast forward to impact."

Sara saw it before Dagger did. Her keen eyesight detected exactly where John Doe's attention was riveted. And she could peel away the layers of the dark tinted windows and see a small portion of the driver's face. More importantly, she saw the target, saw the hint of a smile that formed on the lips of the flower lady, a woman they referred to as Violet, and the barely perceptible nod to the driver, as though saying, "Good job."

Dagger straightened and she could tell by the deep intake of breath that he saw Violet, too. "All those people around and not one person can identify the driver or plate number."

"No plates on the vehicle." Padre slapped Dagger on the back. "The only person I have to connect to John Doe is you, my friend. Now, why don't you tell me why he needed your services."

6 When Dagger first arrived in Cedar Point he'd found a landlord who would accept cash payments, no questions asked, no lease. Casey, the owner, stayed out of his hair, especially since Dagger paid six months rent in advance. Although the Hideaway was a dive, Casey was a nice enough guy. The apartment at the time was adequate. It was located upstairs with the entrance via a rusting flight of metal stairs accessible in the back by the alley. A living room, bathroom and bedroom were all Dagger needed. He furnished it with a secondhand desk and a couple chairs in the living room. One day Einstein was handed to him in a cage, a baby of a bird that soon proved to be more bothersome than he was worth. But Dagger liked the idea of an unconventional pet that proved to be invaluable. He discovered the macaw had a photographic memory. Who needed a secretary or a rolodex with Einstein around? It was Sara who convinced him that a bird that size needed more room. How convenient that Sara's house was the perfect place, seeing that the converted showroom had an attached service area complete with drains. A perfect space to convert to an aviary. Dagger moved in with Sara, but he kept his old office as a place to meet clients rather than have strangers traipsing through Sara's house.

With the added revenue, Casey started to spruce up the Hideaway. He purchased a new pool table, tables, and barstools. Although he couldn't afford to replace the chipped wood on the bar top, he did sand it down and refinish it. Dagger cautioned Casey to cut down on the lemon wax. Shining the tables and bar top was one thing, but when patrons started sliding off the barstools, Dagger saw a ton of lawsuits waiting in the wing.

Things changed several months ago. Someone came in and redecorated Dagger's office. Everything high end, the latest in electronics, and a privacy shield that no surveillance, audio or visual, could penetrate. This was the work of BettaTec, not the radical arm of the shadow corporation led by Jonathan Keyes, also known as Director, also known as Father, but the offshoot headed by Mother and the computer Dagger only knew as Connie. Sara referred to Mother and her entourage as AlphaTec. They needed his expertise to intervene whenever Keyes decided assassinating some world leader fit into his ideological agenda, or, as in Dagger's last case, to remove a laser weapon that could evaporate brains instantly. Keyes tried to sell the weapon to the highest bidder until Dagger intercepted the sale. That was Dagger's mistake. Now Keyes suspected an enemy of BettaTec was somewhere in Cedar Point, Indiana. This was confirmed when the satellite's trajectory was repositioned.

"Nothing appears out of place." Sara circled slowly, her eyes looking for any deviation in décor, a new wall hanging, a hole in the wall that hadn't been there before. Although Dagger changed all of the locks, he knew he wasn't working with a second-rate organization. If they wanted in, they'd find a way.

Dagger pushed open the door to the bedroom. The wall unit was dusty but there wasn't a book out of place. The platform bed was covered with a gray and black geometric design bedspread, which complemented the charcoal gray area rug. They knew his likes and dislikes; unfortunately, they also knew his weakness. Mother was aware of Sara's shapeshifting abilities. They kept the video from the clone's imbedded chip when he fell from the hotel window. It recorded Sara in a red wig shifting into a gray hawk. Mother had to bring Dagger back into the fold in her war against the man whose hunger for power knew no limits. She held that video over Dagger's head, hinted that she would try her best to keep it out of the Director's hands as long as Dagger agreed to assist in anything Mother needed done. He could only imagine what Keyes would do if he were to ever witness Sara's abilities. He would find a way to create an army of shapeshifters.

The bar refrigerator in the corner of the living room hummed softly. Dagger took a seat behind a dark cherry wood desk angled in the corner of the room. Two plush barrel chairs sat in front. Although he would have left the walls bare, black and white prints of landscapes hung on either side of a bookcase. The apartment had a new car smell, which was strange since the building appeared to have been constructed at the turn of the century.

At first glance, nothing marred the surface of the desk, not a monitor or even a noticeable keyboard. But once Dagger pressed his thumb into a slight indentation in the wood, a virtual keyboard appeared. He tapped in the password and a monitor appeared before him as though suspended from the ceiling.

He pulled a flash drive from his pocket and set it on the desk. Immediately a robotic face appeared on the screen. The features appeared human, minus the hair, although its movements and speech were mechanical.

"Good afternoon Six-One-Seven."

Dagger gave up trying to get the computer to stop using his BettaTec I.D. number. "Connie, I need to speak to Mother."

"We are all here."

We. Connie never did explain who all "we" comprised. "I need you to tell me who this is." He waited for the memory stick to download the images, then selected the photo of John Doe.

"Explain."

"He was the victim of a hit and run late yesterday. A black van practically jumped the curb to kill him. No plate number on the vehicle, no identification on the victim. I believe he was an assassin." He pressed a key and the image from the street camera came to life. He played the feed in slow motion. "Do you see how he is following Violet?"

"Violet?"

"The flower lady. You are going to deny she keeps tabs on us? Watch her expression as she locks eyes with John Doe. Watch how she nods to the driver of the SUV, as though she knows him." There was silence so he plodded on. "The cops found my business card on his body. I don't know him nor do I know how he got my business card, but now the police are curious." Still silence. Dagger punched another key, and zoomed in on the chip found in John Doe's head. "Does that look familiar? Quite a bit smaller than the older version, wouldn't you say?" Dagger's cell phone rang. He dug it out of his pocket, saw the call was from Padre, and punched the power off button. "Connie, tell me something."

Now Sara's cell phone started ringing. She saw it was from Padre and took the call, stepping outside onto the wrought iron staircase.

Dagger drummed his fingers on the desk and waited. He figured they were conferring as to how much information to reveal, but he was getting tired of constantly having to drag information out of Connie. At first he thought Mother and Father were his parents. He had vague memories of living in their house, the one he'd found in the remote city one mile below the surface in the middle of Nebraska. He'd since learned that all of the orphans and street kids selected by BettaTec called the Director and his wife Mother and Father. Dagger knew next to nothing about his life before BettaTec. All he knew was that Mother altered the chip in Dagger's neck before he escaped, although Connie claims they let him escape.

Sara returned and announced, "Padre says someone stole John Doe's body from the morgue."

7 "Cameras were blacked out, alarm on the back door compromised," Sara said.

"Plot thickens, Connie. What gives? Either Mother had the body stolen or the Director's henchmen did."

Another picture of John Doe appeared on the monitor. This one was obviously not a morgue photo.

"He is just a number, as are you. The Director has certainly improved the computer chips. Those and the nanobots are completely invisible to metal detectors and electronic scanners. He is using 3-D imagers to make them. Our contact on the inside would pass us information Unfortunately, we haven't heard from him since the Director's failed attempt to sell the laser weapon. We think his position was compromised. The last message we received was that the Director sent four operatives to Cedar Point. He believed our operative, the person you call Violet, to have been responsible for interfering with the sale of the weapons. We are in the process of extracting her from your area. Unfortunately, we have no way to identify the other three operatives."

Dagger was silent while scenarios played in his head. Did Violet know she was being followed? Did she draw out the operative in some way so he could be assassinated? If he wasn't working alone, how did stealing his body help the police discover the name of his accomplices? Who would benefit by not having the death investigated?

"Very clever, Mother. YOU had my business card placed in John Doe's shoe so I would get involved in finding the accomplices. However, you failed to anticipate one possible consequence. Now the police think I knew him. How do I explain that?"

"I'm sure you can come up with an acceptable explanation. The card was placed in his shoe by Violet while the onlookers crowded around the body."

"If she is leaving town, why would the Director's operatives stick around? I'm sure they were the ones who swiped the body of their cohort from the morgue."

"True, but they don't know that Violet isn't still in town. As long as they keep searching for her, you can keep searching for them." Connie's eyes blinked and damn if she didn't look human.

"So Violet was drawing them out by making herself visible." Sara didn't think that was a very smart idea. "Can't you just send someone to take her place?"

"We are a small group. We can't spare anyone else. She will be more useful to us at another location."

"What about the guy who drove the van?" Dagger asked. "You can't have that small of a splinter group." Better question, Dagger thought, was where did the driver come from? Did he drive cross-country? Fly into O'Hare Airport night before last?

"Most of those suspected of being loyal to our cause were eliminated. Our small group disbanded and went underground to throw off any suspicion that we were still alive."

Sara turned toward the bookcase. What was that noise? Was it a hum coming from the refrigerator? Did the monitor create the slight vibration she felt? She stepped closer and browsed the bookshelves, looking for dust that was disturbed, a book removed or added, signs that someone might have planted something in the apartment. The vents in the floor were for the heat and air conditioning, but Sara didn't think the sound was coming from that direction. It was more than just a hum. Something was pulsating, not so much sound as it was a slight shifting of the air. When photos appeared on the monitor, Sara gave them a passing glance and returned her attention to the bookcase.

The photos were of men and women, all young, all seemingly ordinary. Nothing that could make them memorable or easy to identify, like being Asian or African American, or runway model looks. Each of them was unremarkable. Hair worn short and straight and in different shades of brown. All in an effort to blend in.

"Let me guess," Dagger said. "They are all masters of disguises."

"Exactly. These are just a handful of the Director's latest recruits, but not one will look the way they do in these photographs. I would guess he would use seasoned veterans, as was your John Doe. But you have always had the ability to identify agents, Six-One-Seven. That was one

of the enhancements in your chip we made before we let you escape. For some reason, that ability has been blocked."

"It was probably destroyed when BettaTec blew up the plane." When an outer case of the chip was removed from Dagger's neck, Doc Akins planned to take it to an associate in California for analysis. The BettaTec satellite tracked the location, thinking it was Dagger on the plane. The plane exploded over Pyramid Lake in Nevada, the wreckage and passengers were never recovered. As far as the Director was concerned, Dagger was dead.

"What are those enhancements?" Dagger refrained from touching the black cord necklace Sara's grandmother left him. The silver wolf head pendant had eyes the color of Sara's, and the cord was wrapped around several strands of copper wire, which blocked electronic detection.

"My operative on the inside needed to gain access to the Director's laptop to activate it. By the time he was able to do that, something happened to your chip. We were unable to sync our computer with you. Those enhancements weren't part of the outer casing. It should still be functioning. We should check it out."

Images of a black van skidding to the curb, a bag thrown over his head, and him carted off to God knows where, flitted across his brain. He decided it best to ignore her comment even though she never really answered his question. "What about those nanobots? Do I have one?"

"After the situation with the Demko clones, we understand the Director has disabled the capability for explosives to be released. It drew too much attention when the bodies were destroyed.

Mother removed the one in your body before you left. "

"Has the Director ever jeopardized a mission by sending operatives back into a target site?"

"No, which is why we feel there was something more serious at work. You wouldn't know anything about that, Six-One-Seven. Would you? "

Sara turned from the bookcase and locked eyes with Dagger. How could Mother know? Or had Dagger reacted in the way he was trained? "I might." His response was met with silence which dragged on for almost a minute.

"You didn't destroy the weapon. "

How robotic eyes could look like cold steel was puzzling to Dagger. Or was it displaying Mother's reaction and distorting her image by using Connie?

"It's in about twenty-five pieces scattered on the floor of Lake Michigan. It was stripped down after I used it on Director Keyes. I know now it was the wrong thing to do. All I did was heat up his morning coffee, let him know that he didn't win." Dagger could swear he heard a snicker in the background. Obviously someone was amused. "I hoped Keyes believed whoever was responsible left town. What I ended up doing was putting Violet in danger."

There was a slight movement in the bookcase. Sara stepped back and watched as four of the shelves receded into the wall and a thin monitor slid down and filled the space. It was similar to the one in Dagger's vault that tracked the two satellites. However, this one was bigger, the images brighter. Dagger could swear he was looking at high definition. He pushed away from the desk and stood.

"How did you get that in here?" Silly question, Dagger thought. After all, someone did all the renovations.

"We felt you needed an updated monitor. The one you took from the facility is a couple of generations old. It was clever but stupid of you to place a tracker on the Director's assistant in the shape of a drone insect. Of course someone found it, which made Director Keyes suspicious about what enemies he might have in Cedar Point. You really need to stop using metal. There are better ways to make them. Oh, and you probably have been too busy to notice that one of the satellites is now stationary."

"Shit!" Dagger thought laying low would remove any concerns BettaTec might have. He couldn't have been more wrong. Now that he saw the blinking light, it definitely wasn't moving.

"Our sentiments exactly, which is why we need to remove any further suspicions. We will take care of extracting Violet. You need to take care of the three remaining operatives."

Dagger eyed the satellite monitor embedded in the wall. It was definitely better than the one in his vault. "I really don't like the computer and that monitor being here, above a bar. It's too vulnerable. What if there's a fire? A break-in? What if Casey sells the place? What if the city condemns it? It's a wonder the damn place hasn't fallen around Casey's ears."

"We own the property and the building."

Dagger wasn't sure whether to be angry or amazed. It was

obvious his every movement since escaping the facility in Nebraska had been under Mother's watchful eye.

"There is nothing to be concerned about. We needed to keep you safe, and the only way to do that was to keep close tabs."

"And how do you keep close tabs on the Director?"

"That was also part of your abilities. It was the one thing we had been counting on."

8 "Hey, my little taco. How's it hanging?" Sheila propped one firm cheek on the corner of Padre's desk and gave a passing glance at the family photos crowding the side credenza.

"Where's the visitor badge? No one called to announce your royal presence."

"I'm practically a fixture here. Everyone likes to cooperate with the press."

"Not everyone." Padre gave a shooing motion, trying to ignore the short leather skirt that exposed a lot of skin. "Sit like a lady."

"Fuck that lady shit."

"Such a mouth. Thought your parents sent you to finishing school." He watched her move reluctantly to the chair in front of his desk. One reason why Padre liked advance notice of Sheila's arrival was so he could hide any files or reports scattered on his desk. He casually gathered his notes on John Doe and shoved them into a folder. "What's on your mind? I have work to do."

"John Doe. My sources tell me that van targeted the kid. It wasn't just an accident."

"Great. That closes my case."

"Come on, Taco. Give. Maybe you can take me to dinner and let me get you drunk."

"Not a chance and nothing to give. No one saw the face of the driver, no markings on the van, no identity on the victim, no eyewitness with worthwhile information. Do you have anything to offer?"

"He didn't have a cell phone on him. What teen doesn't have a cell phone?"

"Who said he was a teen?" Sheila smiled slowly. *Oh shit. Fuck me.* Padre needed to backpedal out of this one. She tricked him again. He was confident neither Luther nor his staff would talk to the press, and Luther always typed up his own reports. As usual, Sheila was fishing. So far it didn't appear that the reporter knew about the stolen body. "Who said he didn't have anything else on him, like a store receipt, stolen merchandise, drugs?"

"Did he?" She was sitting on the edge of her seat now, watching his face so closely it felt like a staring contest.

He pointed his finger toward the door. "You know the procedure. The chief's press liaison handles all inquiries."

"I'll find out eventually. You know I will, so why don't you just tell me now."

"Nothing to tell. And if anything breaks on the case, I'll make sure the liaison gets in touch with you." He watched her pout and sway her cute ass out of his office. Then he remembered Dagger and Sara and how his cop nose detected a closer relationship than just business partners. Did Sheila know? And what would her reaction be if his suspicions were right? Dagger's only reaction to how his business card ended up on John Doe's body was that Casey kept a supply of the cards on his back bar. Even Simon and the squirrely guy, Skizzy, carried Dagger's cards. Now all Padre had to figure out was why John Doe needed Dagger's assistance.

9 There was something electrifying about Chicago. Maybe it was the hustle and bustle. Maybe the threat of crime around every corner or the fact that it was so crowded, so much going on that he could easily get lost in a crowd. The small towns practically rolled up the sidewalks at night, and that was when he liked to be on the prowl. Daytime was too bright, he felt too vulnerable. And besides, he did his best work at night.

He checked his reflection in the rearview mirror, added dark framed glasses, loosened his tie. The sweater vest gave him a collegiate air while the sport coat with suede patches on the elbows made him cringe. Did college professors still wear this shit? He would have to deal with it because this was the type of man his next victim liked.

There was a Starbucks next to the college library. That was where she spent three nights every week studying. Male students would stop by her table trying to strike up conversations, but she always blew them off with a brief smile and a shake of her head. At first she appeared shy, but after watching—okay, stalking her—he realized those boys didn't fit the age profile.

It was so easy to find victims on the Internet, especially Facebook. It displayed pictures of the women, their ages, and where they lived. And even if they didn't give a street address, they gave just enough information. Which stores were just blocks from their houses, where they went to high school or college, where they worked, the great view from their third floor apartment, how they were playing in a tennis tournament on such and such date. Women thought they were so safe, their information hidden. He knew to avoid married women and women with children because HE told him she was single and childless.

He followed her, knew she was attracted to professors. She'd lost her father when she was in high school, a fact mentioned multiple times on her Facebook page. She liked older men and self-analyzed herself as having a daddy complex. Guess it helped for her to take a psychology course.

He entered the coffee shop and avoided looking around. There was an open table next to hers, so he walked over, set his psychology books down, and approached the counter. He quietly ordered two coffees, paid for them, and carried them to the table. Feigning confusion, he swore under his breath, looked around the room at the idiots texting and bopping to some tune blaring from their earbuds, and with an embarrassed shrug, slowly turned his attention to her. "I'm sorry, but I'm in a bit of a snag," he said in his best British accent. He practiced it for a month. "They accidentally made two coffees and I don't want one of them to get cold." He held it out to her. "Would you please take one off my hands with my compliments?"

She hesitated as though sizing him up, then smiled. White teeth, gorgeous hair, looking absolutely beautiful even in the college hoodie she wore. "You sure you don't want money?"

"No, no. Please. You would be doing me a favor." He didn't wait for a reply, just set the cup on her table and took a seat at his own. It took five minutes before she asked him about the psychology books, another two minutes for her to join him at his table. Ten minutes later they were in his car headed to a restaurant southwest of Chicago, someplace near her apartment since he knew she lived in a town called Frankfort. The small pill he placed in her coffee cup was just enough to get her in the mood.

They made idle chit chat. Her name was Sarah Eastman. Details of her wonderful family life in small town Galena were quickly ignored. He knew all he needed to know about her. She was curious about England and he was glad he researched London so he could pepper his responses with vague details. He would only be in the U.S. for another week before returning to Oxford where he claimed to have majored in medieval history. This piqued her curiosity.

"You know, we are driving right past my hotel. Would you mind if I changed into something more comfortable? I've been in these clothes all day. You can wait in the lobby, of course." Such a gentleman, but he made her feel at ease so he knew she would gladly follow him to his room.

"Is the college paying for your hotel stay?"

"God, no. I'd be in, what do you call it? Motel Hell?"

She laughed. Her eyes lit up and he silently screamed for HIM to shut up.

"I paid for a suite for six months. A research grant is covering the costs."

"A suite, huh? I'd like to see what a suite looks like."

Course you would, you slut.

He avoided the main lobby, choosing a side entrance where they passed the hotel bar. Patrons were too busy making their own moves to notice him. Besides, he didn't look anything like the man who checked in under another name and was staying in a different room.

Although she refrained from gawking at the hotel's décor, he could tell she was impressed by the way her eyes lingered over every detail. When she stepped into the suite, she couldn't keep from blurting out, "Wow!"

"While I change, I'll let you make us a drink before we go to dinner." He used a wash cloth to turn on the faucets, careful not to leave any prints. Although the room was under one of his fictitious names, he hadn't stepped foot in it until today.

"What would you like to drink?" she called out.

"Jack Daniels for me." The bottles were all airline size and few women liked Jack. "Would you rather have wine? I can have some brought up."

"No. Vodka is fine."

The vodka was already spiked, and he hoped she didn't notice that the seal was broken on the cap. The refrigerator was stocked with tonic and soda, whichever she preferred. He had placed the pill in her coffee just in case she was a teetotaler.

He washed his hands, ran a wet wash cloth across his face, stripped out of his sport coat and sweater, removed the tie, carried everything to the walk in closet and dumped it into the opened suitcase on the stand. He closed the closet door and exited the bedroom.

She was admiring the view of Chicago and sipping her drink when he returned. Although it was thirty miles away, the city looked like miniature buildings against the horizon. Her brown hair hung down her back. He couldn't wait to run his hands through it, stare into her eyes, let HIM say if she was the one. He grabbed his drink off the bar and sidled next to her.

"How is your drink?"

"Ummm. Just what I needed after studying," she said, taking a long swallow.

A dark cloud shifted as though shoved aside by a bright ball of light. The moon, not quite full, was mesmerizing. He felt something stirring. It always did when the moon neared full. For six days, three days before and three days after a full moon, he felt like a different person. Sometimes it felt as though HE took over during that period. Now that he was beginning to enjoy these changes, he resented HIS intrusion into his life. He breathed deeply, inhaling her scent, close enough to feel the heat radiating from her body, hear the blood coursing through her veins.

"Have you thought of where you would like to go to dinner?"

She turned from the window, and he caught her as she swayed. "I thought maybe we could order in."

He grabbed her drink and set both of them on the side table. Her mouth was open, inviting. The drug produced an erotic effect. Now he could peer deeply into her eyes. NO, the voice in his head said. She wasn't the right one, again. A moan escaped as he covered her mouth with his. She couldn't get her clothes off fast enough. His eyes never closed as he tried to ignore the voice in his head. Not yet. He wouldn't kill her just yet. First, he wanted to have some fun.

10

Sara wasn't sure what woke her. Something felt out of place. She rolled over to an empty bed. Dagger was gone. Strange sounds cut through the silence, sounds she couldn't distinguish. She parted the blinds and looked out into the yard. A soft clinking could be heard, like bells tapping against metal. Sara had hung thimbles and bells at her grandmother's gravesite. Her grandmother had loved to quilt. It was believed if a spirit roamed at night, the sounds would lead them back to their resting place. If her grandmother's spirit was wandering, was she trying to contact her? Was she attempting to warn Sara of a danger? The clock on the dresser said it was almost three in the morning.

Sara slipped into a robe as she hurried through the darkened living room and into the kitchen. Dagger wasn't there. He wouldn't have driven somewhere without telling her. The feeling of dread deepened. Dagger barely spoke since his conversation with Connie. She ran up the stairs to the crosswalk and stood at the tall windows. Calling on the eyesight of the hawk, she searched the darkened yard. Movement on the right side of the yard proved to be deer. She scanned the doors to the garage. They were closed and the lights were off.

She peered deeper into the three hundred acres, and focused on the area where her grandmother was buried. And there he was, sitting on a bench that overlooked the stream.

Now her feeling of dread was overwhelming. Sara tried to think back to their conversation as she shrugged into jeans and a sweatshirt. Was she being over-cautious? Was it all in her imagination? If so, why was Dagger sitting on a bench in the back acres in the middle of the night?

The grass was damp as she raced barefoot to the stream. With the aid of the hawk's vision, Sara could see clearly in the dark, enabling her to weave through prairie grass and tall feather reed grass, dodge the pond, and leap over scurrying raccoons and other four-legged creatures. She slowed to a walk as she approached.

"Dagger."

"Go back, Sara."

"What are you doing out here?" The cold finally settled into her bones once she stopped running. Sara noticed a pair of wire cutters on the bench. That was it! That was the comment Connie made about the enhanced abilities the chip in his head provided, abilities which, for some reason, were blocked.

"I don't know what will happen when I cut it off." Dagger wasn't certain if the BettaTec satellite would target its laser beam once they located him.

"Connie said the section Doc Akins retrieved held the transponder. I believe her." Sara took a seat next to him.

"Your grandmother is buried right behind us, Sara. I promised her I would protect you. Please, if you love me, go back to the house."

She shook her head. "No."

"Sara…" He turned to face her and cupped her face in his hands. "You are the only beautiful thing that has ever happened to me. I won't let you sacrifice yourself." He pulled her close. The kiss was one of desperation, a farewell to a love started too late. But who was he kidding? Like images of the past that flashed in one's mind before he died, Dagger's flashed to the day Sara walked into his office. He felt something from the first nervous smile, the first glimpse of those mesmerizing eyes. Love? That was a word that was foreign to Dagger's lips. It was better to remain distant, to be able to flee at a moment's notice. He was engaged to Sheila at the time. He didn't believe in love at first sight. After all, Sara had been a child, a mere teenager, but far more knowledgeable and perceptive than a normal eighteen-year-old. He could have married one of Cedar Point's richest socialites. Instead, he had been enamored by a young woman wearing a handmade sack dress, with skin the color of an island native and dark waist-length hair that was streaked with too many shades to decipher. It was Sara's grandmother, Ada Kills Bull, who encouraged her granddaughter to go out into the world beyond their three hundred acres. Sara would walk the mall early in the morning before the crowds. She would attend the matinee movies and sit at sidewalk cafes to observe people, to learn how people acted, how women dressed. And it was Ada who encouraged Sara to use her talent to help people. And so she had. After witnessing the murder of an undercover cop, she needed the help of a private detective to prove what she had seen. Sara had been nervous approaching Dagger at the time. She sensed something strange in his eyes.

It was Ada Kills Bull who'd helped Dagger understand what Sara was after he brought her damaged body back to the elderly woman. He'd witnessed a wolf being shot, its leg severed. But the wolf suddenly changed and Sara appeared. Ada explained her granddaughter's gift and how Sara's secret needed to be protected. Watching Sara's leg grow back had been the most shocking thing he'd ever witnessed in his life, and he'd seen a lot.

Dagger was too engrossed in remembering that moment

and all the days that followed to have felt the slight shifting in Sara's fingers to talons, or to hear the talon slicing through the leather cord and strands of copper. Nor did he feel the leather cord and pendant slip from his neck.

He wrapped his arms around her in what he thought would be a final embrace. Sara held on tight, tears stinging her eyes. Her heart raced, and she could feel Dagger's pulse through her touch. He held her so tight she wasn't sure she could take a deep breath.

Dagger broke away first, beads of sweat forming on his forehead even though the night air was crisp. "You have your whole life ahead of you, Sara. Now please. Return to the house and turn your back to the windows. Don't watch."

"We made a pact, Dagger. Live together or die together."

Anger flashed in his dark eyes. And were those tears? "Dammit, Sara."

"You're too late." She held up the necklace. "I sliced it off ten minutes ago and nothing has happened."

"Why did…?" But he didn't finish. Slowly they sat back, hands clasped, and waited. Five minutes, ten, fifteen minutes more. Moonlight pierced through the trees, its brightness blocked by dark clouds drifting across the sky.

"That was a stupid thing to do, Sara. Maybe the guy with his finger on the switch is biding his time." He washed his hand over his face. "Maybe Mother is being coy. Maybe she still works with the Director and wanted me to trust her. Now she has me in a position to be eliminated."

"I don't think so. Why go through the trouble of furnishing your office with high tech equipment? She could have just wired it to explode and killed us both." Sara held up the necklace. "I can restring it on a plain black cord this time, if you still want to wear it."

He ran his fingers over the wolf's head as though reading

Braille. The clouds must have passed because the moon was so bright he could see every detail of the pendant. "Of course I still want to wear it." He could feel Sara shiver next to him. "We should get back. It's freezing out here."

He grabbed the penlight from the ground and shoved it in his shirt pocket. "Have I told you lately that it really grates on my nerves when you don't do what I ask?"

"Maybe you should stop asking me to do things I don't want to do." It was a two block walk down a path that snaked around clusters of pine trees and underbrush.

Dagger looked down at her feet. "Christ, Sara. You're barefoot." He swooped her up in his arms.

"You are going to trip. You need my hawk vision to make our way back."

"Why? The moon is so bright it almost looks like daylight out here."

"No, it isn't. I can hardly see my feet. It's pitch black."

Dagger stopped and took in his surroundings. He could see their house in the distance, her grandparents' gravesites, and airplanes overhead. If he were using night vision goggles everything would be cast in a green glow. But this was different. Details were crisp, colors were bright, images were distinct.

Slowly he put Sara down, a cold chill spreading over his body. "Oh, shit!"

"Does your head still hurt?" Sara rubbed her damp hair with a towel. The hot shower felt good after walking in the damp grass. Dagger hadn't needed any excuse to climb into the shower with her. He sat on the window seat in his bedroom, knees pulled up, a fist pressed to his forehead, his other hand wrapped around a glass. The moment he walked into the house the outdoors faded into its normal nighttime darkness.

"Like it's going to explode. Feels like someone crammed it with more than my skull can hold. And there are weird images. Can't turn them off."

She took a seat across from him, grabbed the glass from his hand, sniffed it, and took a swallow. "That is nasty." She handed the glass back to him. "I don't think it's going to help any. Has to be the computer chip. Connie said it was being blocked, which we now know was caused by the copper wires. Night vision may not be your only ability. Remember when we were in Nebraska and we needed a vehicle to get around? All we did was mention the word and a door opened revealing mopeds. The facility's computer heard us. Maybe now your chip is anticipating your commands. That was what Mother was talking about when she mentioned the abilities in your altered chip."

"This is going to take some getting used to. I doubt Mother would give me any abilities she couldn't use to her advantage. Whatever's happening in my head, it isn't anything I can see or appear to retain." He turned his attention to the sky, to the burst of stars that erupted. And directly overhead one of those stars wasn't a star at all but a BettaTec satellite. At any given moment there were over three thousand GPS and telecommunication satellites orbiting the earth. Some could orbit twice in twenty-four hours.

"Don't think about it."

Now she was a mind reader. "It's hard not to." He set the glass down and pressed both hands to the sides of his head. "Damn. I think I'd rather suffer a concussion than this."

Sara grabbed the glass and spilled the contents into the bathroom sink. "Do you want to put the pendant back on and see if the pain stops?"

"No. I want to find out what all this means and what other surprises Mother has in store for me. I just hope this headache isn't an everyday presence." Dagger let out an agonizing moan as he leaned back against the window frame.

Sara forced her hands under his. Her skin was cool to the touch and felt good. Her fingers gently kneaded his scalp as she bent down and kissed the side of his neck, ran her lips across his jaw and to the tip of his ear. "I think I can find something to take your mind off the pain," she whispered.

11

"Are you sure you want these displayed, Mister Logan? They are quite…different…from anything else in the gallery." Who was Carlton to protest? After all, Mister Logan paid him a substantial salary to run the Galleria. But this. He was in the store room where the shipment of Nightfall arrived promptly at nine in the morning. Cardboard and brown paper wrappings were scattered on the floor. Twenty paintings were leaning against the walls as well as four easels.

Mark's voice blared from the speaker phone. "I find them fascinating, Carlton. It brings out certain emotions and satisfies the deep dark thoughts we all have."

Not me, Carlton thought. He stopped at the paintings of the woman. There were three in all and in each she was faceless. "Perhaps I can talk to the artist to ask some questions. I would like to be able to explain the paintings should clients ask. For example, why is the woman faceless? It's obviously the same woman but in different poses."

"That's the beauty of it, don't you think?"

No. "Now, the paintings of the forest at night, the animals are breathtaking." He leaned closer to study the intricate details. Every hair, the various hues. He could practically feel the wind ruffling the feathers of the hawk. Every vein in the leaves, the bark of the tree. "Such beauty though is spoiled by the moon. It is so large and ominous." And wasn't that blood dripping from the moon?

"Of course, not everyone will see the beauty in his work, which is why the viewings should be by appointment only."

Right, only serial killers allowed. Carlton stopped in front of a painting of a woman hanging from a tree, her throat cut, blood staining the front of her shirt. Another painting of a wrecked motorcycle, a helmet lying on the ground several feet away. And was that a head…? Carlton leaned closer, then gasped and took a step back. Yes, it was a head staked on a tree limb. "My God."

"There is beauty in death," Mark said, unaffected by his assistant's gasp. If Mark were there to see the manager's face, he would notice his pale skin was now tinged with green.

"And the young man holding his…my God, are those his intestines?" Carlton felt sick. He was sure he was about to hurl his breakfast all over the paintings. "Pardon my asking, but what beauty is there in showing graphic horror?"

"It's for the younger crowd, Carlton. The trust fund selfies who can't wait to own the latest tech toy before their friends, the ones who run to the summer slash movies, who play those video games where more body parts fly than any you see in those paintings. As macabre as it may seem, there are those who enjoy the pain and suffering of others."

"Yes, but with all due respect, do we want those people as customers?"

"Trust me, Carlton. Have I been wrong yet? I'll be in town in a couple days to check things out before the grand opening. Oh, and Carlton, be sure to mention that the private showing of Nightfall during the grand opening will cost each person one thousand dollars. That should assure us of only serious buyers. Take care."

Serious buyers or the truly sick. Carlton listened as the dial tone reverberated in the room. He slipped the phone into his pocket, bent down and studied the initials in the lower right hand corner. C.A. Who on earth was C.A.? Would a Google search produce any viable names? "Probably stands for Creepy Ass," he said to the room.

12

"What you have is access to the Director's personal computer. This will tell us what projects he is working on, who his targets are, what agents are working the cases and other helpful information."

Although Connie's voice was more robot than human, Dagger believed it was a voice sensitizer vocalizing Mother's words because there was an underlying hint of excitement in the robotic responses.

Dagger pressed fingertips to his eyes. He was afraid when he opened them, data in bits and bytes would come spilling out. "How do I control it? How do I make sense out of this overload of information? I feel like I need a heroin drip."

"Patience and practice. Information is still being downloaded. Once that is complete, everything should be compartmentalized."

Call it innate suspicion or intuition, but Dagger's bullshit meter just banged like a mariachi band. "So, what's in it for you? I just report back on everything I see?"

"Not exactly." A pink tinge appeared on Connie's cheeks. *"You aren't the only one who ends up with access to the Director's laptop."*

"Ahhhhh. Of course you would do something for your benefit." Was that a tsk Dagger heard in the background? "What if he changes his password or changes laptops? And won't his I.T. guys know when someone is hacking their system?" Dagger wondered if he was becoming less human and more like Connie.

"It doesn't matter if he changes his password. Everything he does will be reflected in your chip. And, no. On their end it won't resemble hacking."

"How long will this downloading take?" Sara didn't like seeing Dagger not in control. Matter of fact, she didn't much care for Dagger being used as a guinea pig.

"No more than twenty-four hours, would be our best guess."

Sara continued to pace while nibbling on one knuckle, a nervous habit she hadn't been able to control. "If anyone can track an IP address, how can you be sure they aren't tracking the information back to Dagger?"

"Once the information is downloaded, Dagger will be out of his system. The Director always backs up his computer daily and always in the evening. That's when Dagger's chip will receive any new data. The new data is our main concern since we no longer have a mole inside."

"What happened to him?"

"Once he suspected his position was compromised, he went off grid."

"He's dead?"

The android blinked, but there wasn't a response. Connie changed the subject. *"At least we know this phase of the chip is operational."*

"So access to the Director's laptop and night vision are Dagger's new capabilities?"

"At present."

Sara looked at Dagger. What did that mean? She never had a chance to ask.

Connie said, *"Check back tomorrow."* The screen went dark.

"I don't like this." Sara continued her pacing.
Dagger pressed his hands against his head as though the pressure could keep his skull from exploding. He still didn't feel comfortable talking in his office, not trusting Mother to have bugged the place. At this point, he was beyond caring anymore. For all he knew, Mother could be monitoring all of his thoughts. "I need some coffee."

13 Sara pressed the buzzer firmly, hearing it echo from inside the building. She stamped her feet to help warm them, still feeling the cold from her barefoot run last night.

Dagger made a fist and pounded on the door. He heard expletives from the other side and the sound of numerous locks being slammed open. Finally, the door opened a scant two inches.

"Who goes there?"

"You know who it is, Skizzy. Let us in. It's freezing out here."

The door was pulled open farther and a face with two bulging eyes that moved in different directions jutted out forcing Sara and Dagger to step back. The head moved on a scrawny neck, searching both sides of the sidewalk for God knew what. To Skizzy Borden, either Big Brother was always watching or aliens were waiting to take him up in their spaceship.

"Are you alone?"

Dagger shoved the door open sending the skinny guy skidding against the side wall. "Do you want fresh coffee and donuts or not?"

Sara dutifully locked all seven deadbolts while Skizzy cricked his neck to confirm that all of the bones were still in place. "Well, goldarnit, you didn't have to be so rough." Several strands of gray hair wrestled free from his ponytail while camo pants hung loose on his thin frame. He walked around to the back showcase and stuck his face in the opened bag Dagger set on the counter. "Ahhhhh, fresh donuts." He pulled a cup of coffee from the cardboard carrier, opened the flip lid, and sniffed. "Thank you, boys and girls. Now, where have you all been hiding yourselves?"

Sara disappeared through the drape behind the counter and retrieved paper plates and napkins from the galley kitchen.

"Simon says you two been doing the nasty."

"Simon has an active imagination." Dagger took a plate from the stack and grabbed a donut.

"Simon says you two haven't gotten outta bed in months."

"Simon has a dirty mind. We've been working a case."

"Working a case or working out the kinks?" Skizzy's eyebrows appeared to jerk in opposite directions.

"How about I work a few kinks out on you." Dagger glared at the skinny guy.

Sara studied the items in the glass showcases. Sometimes it looked as though Skizzy never sold anything from his pawn shop. Then again, how could anyone tell? He was constantly getting in new items. To her it looked like junk people hoarded for decades, not wanting to part with a family treasure. There were old knives, watches, jewelry, bayonets, tools, cameras, cell phones, an old time pay phone in the corner and, of all things, a suit of armor. Items glistened as though Skizzy sanitized everything that came into the store. Antiques that looked too old to gleam had been slipped into a zip lock bag to keep any germs from daring to escape.

"An old lady brought in the strangest thing last week. Said her husband passed away and she had no use for it." Skizzy disappeared into the backroom and returned with what looked like a modified copier with a green shield shaped like a hood.

Dagger moved the plates and cups aside to make room for the contraption which, on closer inspection, was not much larger than a bread machine. Skizzy opened the lid and Dagger knew what it was.

"A mini 3-D imager," Skizzy said proudly. "Do you have any idea what I can do with this? And look what came with it." He opened a side panel, grabbed a pair of tweezers, and held up what looked like a mosquito. "A drone. These would be completely undetectable. I've never seen a machine this advanced before. I've got all different colored spools of ABS filaments in a box she gave me, along with power supplies and maintenance tools, too. Bet that woman's husband was a scientist of some sort. Should have asked her where he'd worked before he retired." He watched Dagger's eyes which suddenly shifted to Sara. Skizzy studied the two as though he were watching a tennis match. "What's wrong? What aren't you telling me?"

"What did she look like?" Sara asked.

"I don't know. A bag lady. She wore a long dress and a stupid hat with all kinds of flowers on it."

Dagger was sure this was going to put Skizzy right over the top. "It's from BettaTec."

Skizzy's mouth fell open and he stumbled back against the side cabinet. "Oh shit shit shit. They know where I work? Where I live? And you led them here?"

"Relax. It was probably the flower lady, someone we call Violet."

"She works with Mother, not the Director," Sara clarified.

Dagger explained how the Director found the tracker drone Skizzy planted on his assistant. Mother said Skizzy's were archaic. If he wanted to stay one step ahead of BettaTec, he needed to use something that couldn't be detected.

"Should have been suspicious when I saw it's hardly been used. Just thought the old lady was more of a clean freak than me. She actually spent a half hour showing me how to use it. I was even thinking of asking her out for coffee." This brought raised eyebrows from both Dagger and Sara.

Standing in front of Skizzy's prying eyes made them feel as though he were a human MRI machine. He cocked his head to one side and squinted. "What else aren't you telling me?"

Dagger took a sip of the hot coffee and weighed just how much he should share with his psychotic friend. He shrugged and spilled the beans. Told him about taking off the copper strand necklace, what Mother said about the chip, and how he had been able to see in the dark.

"No…fucking…way." Skizzy leaned over the showcase and fingered the black cord. It wasn't as thick as when it was wrapped around strands of copper. He tensed as he straightened. "Let me get this straight. You are no longer protected by the copper wire and can be zapped out of existence at any moment by that hovering satellite, and you are standing one fucking foot away from me?" His voice rose to a screech.

Dagger shrugged. "That about covers it."

Skizzy looked at Sara. "Why are you so calm?"

"It's been eight hours and, besides, Mother said the transponder was in the portion Doc Akins carried on the plane."

He swung his eyes back to Dagger. "And how do you feel?"

"Like someone opened up my head and stuffed it with cotton."

"And you believe the android that this is all safe? That you aren't going to be incinerated in your sleep?"

Dagger thought about how much planning Mother must

have gone through, how dangerous the Director was, and wondered what other psychotic projects the Director planned for the future. He was too curious and too focused on being a thorn in his side to worry about being discovered. "I have no choice."

"Bullshit. Everyone has a choice."

Dagger settled his gaze on Sara. He didn't doubt for one second that the videotape of Sara's shapeshifting would fall into the wrong hands. Both Mother and the Director lived by—"the ends justify the means."

"No. This is how it has to be."

"Well, okay then. But if you ask me this still sounds like some kinda Bermuda Triangle shit. Wouldn't be surprised if this cyborg and Mother Hen aren't sitting in some alien ship up there." He point toward the ceiling. Skizzy picked up his new toy and disappeared behind the drape. "Don't leave," he yelled from the back. "Need you to help me with something."

Sara fingered the pendant hanging from Dagger's neck. It hadn't taken her long to place it on another cord. "Looks perfect." She brushed her hand across his five o'clock shadow, even though he shaved an hour ago. His eyes were the darkest brown, a sharp contrast to her turquoise eyes. "Thought your eyes would look different after last night but they don't. Have you learned anything new?"

He leaned in for a kiss. "Tried X-ray vision on you just now, but it didn't work."

Sara laughed and wrapped her arms around him. "I can't wait to see what other talents you have."

Skizzy emerged wearing a dark suit. "How do I look?" He ran a hand down the lapels of the suit jacket. Stray hairs had been smoothed back into a neat ponytail.

"Like an undertaker or a Wild West elixir salesman."

"You look very nice, Skizzy. Don't listen to him." Sara

straightened the tie, and brushed the dust off the collar. The suit obviously hadn't been worn in quite sometime. "Where are you going?"

"I am a legally ordained minister of the Universal Life Church. Got my license online," Skizzy beamed.

Dagger barked out a laugh. "Who are you kidding?"

"I did, fur-real. Gonna marry Simon and Eunie."

"Thought they hired a minister," Sara said.

"What happens if he gets a flat tire or comes down with some virus? They will be stuck with all them guests and nobody to marry them." He waived a sheet of paper in front of them. "Been practicing. Trying to memorize this before the big day." He placed the paper down and moved around to the front of the counter. He positioned Dagger and Sara side by side. "Now you be Simon and Eunie."

Dagger emitted a long sigh. "Really? You can't practice on someone else?"

"Dagger, play nice. Go ahead, Skizzy."

Skizzy cleared his throat. "Dearly beloved, we are gathered here today to join this man and this woman in holy matrimony."

"You should probably rewrite that part, Skizzy. Maybe say that we are gathered to witness the renewing of vows between Simon and Eunie Robinson."

"Yeah, okay. Thanks, Sara." Skizzy picked up the pencil and scribbled notes.

"Aren't you supposed to hold a Bible or something?" Dagger tried not to laugh, but this was so not going to happen. Skizzy was too high strung to give a speech, albeit a short one, in front of a group of people.

"Yeah, I've got one somewhere." He scribbled another note, cleared his throat, and started again. "Okay, renewing of vows, blah blah. If there is anyone here who has reason to believe this renewing of vows should not take place, let him speak now or forever hold his peace."

"May have to change that one, too." Dagger wondered if Skizzy would pass out when the big day came. "Doesn't matter if anyone objects. Simon and Eunie are already married, so short of someone stepping forward and claiming to have been married to one of them before and the divorce never was finalized…"

"Okay okay. A minor blip. Now, where was I? Yes, okay. Do you Chase Dagger take Sara Morningsky to be your lawfully wedded wife, to love and to obey?"

"Simon and Eunice," Dagger corrected him.

Skizzy checked his notes. "That's not right."

"He doesn't do obey," Sara said, trying not to laugh at Skizzy's nervousness.

Skizzy cleared his throat, whispered the previous phrase to himself to try to remember where he left off. "Okay, to love and to cherish in sickness and in health, for richer or poorer, for all the days of your life?" Skizzy waited. "Well?"

Sara elbowed Dagger. "Pay attention."

"Yes," Dagger said.

"And do you Sara Morningsky, take Chase Dagger, to be your lawfully wedded husband, to love and to cherish etcetera, etcetera?"

Sara stifled a laugh. "I do."

"The rings." Skizzy looked up from his notes. "Well, pretend."

Dagger sighed. "Just get to the final part."

"Who goes first?" Skizzy checked his notes. "The man or the woman?"

"I think Simon puts the ring on Eunie's finger first." Sara saw perspiration forming on Skizzy's forehead. She would have to remind him to take a handkerchief.

"This is probably the part where the couple will say something they each wrote. I'll have to ask Simon if they wrote something." Skizzy made another note.

Having Skizzy as minister would absolutely ruin the event for Eunie, Dagger thought. He would have to forewarn Simon.

"Okay, join hands." Skizzy grabbed Sara's Dagger's left hands and held them. "By the powers invested in me by the state of Indiana..."

"More like by Cyberspace," Dagger whispered.

"...I now pronounce you husband and wife." Skizzy breathed a sigh of relief. "You may kiss the bride." When the two didn't move he barked, "Well, kiss already."

The two obliged, a little too long and a little too passionately. They broke away when Skizzy said, "Sign this."

"What?!" they said in unison.

But Skizzy didn't hear. He scooted off to the back room. "Just gotta make you a copy of your license," he called out.

Sara sighed. "Should we tell him his online license isn't legal and all marriages he performs also won't be legal?"

"Nah. We'll humor him."

Skizzy returned and handed them a gold embossed certificate in a frame. "Perfect for hanging."

14 Carlton checked his handiwork. The paintings were spaced appropriately. He tried to keep the more shocking pieces on the side walls. Why have a full frontal assault on the senses of rich clients the moment they stepped into the room? Some of the more palatable ones were on easels in the corners of the room. But there wasn't much he could do about the frightening ones other than hide them in the back until Mister Logan arrived. As his boss requested, the wall directly across from the entrance was empty. It was reserved for some new painting the artist was working on. Carlton just hoped it was on the tasteful side.

"Sick, sick, I tell you." When he took art appreciation at Northwestern, his professor would have kicked a student out of class if he caught him painting such rubbish. He tried to ease his mind by remembering some of the drawings by Andy Warhol. And what about Picasso? Really? A woman with three breasts or half a face? How bizarre was that? But look where they were today. Well, actually, they were dead, but their work lived on.

Carlton gave a long sigh. His name would be mud. He'd never get another job in this industry again. He could hear the critics laughing already. And what about opening night? Logan would definitely be here for the official ribbon cutting. Maybe, with any luck, the critics' barbs would be pointed in Logan's direction. After all, it was his gallery. And maybe, with a thousand dollar entrance fee, the critics wouldn't even stick around.

He turned a slow circle, eyeing each painting carefully, trying to put his finger on something that had been bothering him since he unwrapped the first painting. The forest scenes were beautiful. The painter definitely was talented. Not everyone could draw scenery in such detail and with such clarity as C.A. No, what struck him were the killings, the victims. A shiver ran down his spine as a thought came to him. If he didn't know better, he'd swear the artist was painting these from memory.

"Hello. Anybody here?" Sheila closed the door behind her. She was surprised Carlton didn't keep the doors locked until the grand opening. Most of her circle of friends wouldn't think of going to a shop or museum until the day of the ribbon cutting. That was when the press would be there. That was when the pictures for the society pages were taken.

She heard rustling in a back room and figured Igor was back there. He didn't exactly look like Igor. It wasn't like he had a hump on his back; but the pasty skin and funereal appearance did make her wonder if there was a coffin filled with dirt from the homeland somewhere in the basement.

Her attention was drawn to the closed doors, the one where the paintings for special viewing were to be hung. She gave the shop one last look, then tiptoed over to the French doors and turned the handle. It was unlocked.

Sheila pulled the door open partway and peered inside. "Oh. That's different." She saw the nighttime forest pictures first, not exactly something she would hang on her walls. The attention to detail was exceptional. She actually felt as though she were in the forest, that she could feel the dew on her lips, the wet leaves under her feet. The artist definitely showed talent.

She continued past the painting of the wolf with its unusual eyes, the bright moon shining through the trees. Matter of fact, in every painting there was a full moon. She took a step back when she saw the painting of the woman without a face. She was barefoot and dressed in a long flowing red gown, blood red. In another portrait she was wearing white and camouflaged among the tree branches. Again, she didn't have a face.

Sheila was puzzled. Was this a woman he hadn't met yet, or did he just not know how to finish it? She turned to the side wall and gasped, took a step back. Where the other paintings might have been dark and mysterious, these were downright sinister. Somehow her feet moved on their own, propelling her from one painting to the next. A body gutted, sitting against a tree in the forest. A woman wedged high up in a tree, her throat cut and blood staining her shirt. A helmet lying near a crushed Harley and nearby a head impaled on a tree limb. There was something eerily familiar about these. Had she seen the portraits before? And why was there a body of a woman in a tree not far from the Harley? Sheila wasn't sure but could swear the woman had been disemboweled. She saw the initials C.A. in the lower right corner of each portrait.

"Unsettling, aren't they?"

Sheila screamed at the sound of the voice and clutched a hand to her chest. "You scared me."

"I guess that's the reaction the artist wanted."

Sheila dragged her attention back to the decapitated head. "How can the artist believe anyone would want these hanging on the walls of a house?"

"I was thinking more of a biker bar," Carlton deadpanned,

his fingers grappling with another painting.

Sheila nodded toward the blank wall. "What are you going to hang there?"

"Don't know. Guess it's a surprise. Either the artist hasn't shipped it to us yet or Mister Logan is going to bring it when he comes into town. It's supposed to be the focal point of the display. I'm afraid to even think what this one will be like. Perhaps an inside view of an autopsy."

Sheila liked his dry sense of humor. "I guess like the hangings in the Wild West days, people will be lined up to see it on opening night."

"Oh, they would have to be very curious. The entrance fee is a thousand dollars."

"Really? You are charging? That will certainly put a damper on curiosity." Her eyes were drawn to a side wall, as blank as a new canvas. "What's going there?"

Carlton lifted the wrapped painting. "Just came. I can't wait to see what shock value this one has." He held it with both hands. "Want to do the honors?"

"Sure." Sheila tore at the brown wrapping like a kid on Christmas morning. She heard Carlton gasp. "What is it?"

"I should just hide this one in a closet." Carlton walked over to the wall, hung the painting, and stepped back, but Sheila wasn't following him.

Her hand slapped against her mouth as though forcing back a scream. The painting was of the interior of Sheila's old condo where the body of her former assistant had been mutilated, the blood decorating just about every square inch of Sheila's pristine white décor.

15 "Padre, my little jalapeno. Just the brain I was looking to pick." Sheila placed one well-rounded hip on the bar stool and fingered his suit jacket.

"All dressed up, too. Please tell me you aren't in the bar of the Embassy Suites looking to pick up chicks."

"Anniversary party."

"Yours? You mean I get to meet the lucky lady?"

"No, not mine. Simon and Eunie's." He nodded his thanks as the bartender set the scotch and water in front of him.

"Dagger's mailman." She said it as though Dagger were Simon's only customer.

"What part of my brain did you want to pick? I'm on my third drink so there may not be too many memory cells left."

The door to a side room opened as a waiter exited with a tray of empty glasses. The door remained open, and Sheila glimpsed a sea of black and white. "Everyone wearing tuxedos?"

"Some. Eunie wanted a black and white affair so some are in black suits, most in tuxes, and the ladies in black, white, or whatever."

Sheila bristled when she saw Sara. Her black dress clung like a second skin, and her olive complexion contrasted sharply with Sheila's natural pallor. She made a mental note to hit the spray tan salon tomorrow. A man's arm was around Sara's waist, her fingers laced through his. The mystery man was out of Sheila's view, but it was evident the way Sara leaned into him that they were more than just friends. "I didn't know Nick Tyler was back in town. Looks like he and Sara have gotten cozy since she refused his marriage proposal. I'll have to go say hi."

"I wouldn't…" But it was too late. Sheila was off to crash the party, but there was only one person who would crash tonight. "Don't say I didn't warn you." Padre weakened and lit up a cigarette. "And here I thought the bar would be a safe place." Nick Tyler was one of the heirs to the Tyler fortune and seen frequently with Sara whenever he was in town. The family owned a string of resorts and Nick currently managed one of the island locations. Although he once proposed to Sara, she'd only wanted to be friends.

Padre waved at the bartender who didn't look old enough to drink. Was everyone getting younger or was Padre getting older? "Dirty martini, shaken not stirred." He watched as Dagger appeared in view, his hand running up Sara's back and pulling her closer. If he pulled any tighter, Sara's body would leave an imprint. He watched as Sheila caught sight of Dagger. She did a quick one-eighty, almost falling off of her Jimmy Choo stilettos. She staggered back to the bar, her face a bright crimson.

The bartender set the martini in front of Padre who shoved it in front of Sheila. "I told you not to go there."

"Oh my God." Sheila was gasping for air. "How did…when did…? That lying sack of shit." She gulped down the martini in three swallows and pushed the glass toward the edge. "Fill it," she ordered. "We're just business partners, there's nothing going on between us," Sheila mocked.

"Come on. You saw this coming from the first day they met." The bartender placed the martini in front of Sheila. "Take it out of here." Padre shoved a twenty toward him. "Drink slowly. I don't want to have to arrest you on a DUI."

"Oh my God," she repeated. Tears dared to stream down her perfectly made face. It should have been her. She was supposed to marry Dagger. "He said he needed time," Sheila sobbed. "I was giving him time. That was a good thing, right? How could he do this to me? We're engaged."

"Were," Padre corrected her, but Sheila wasn't listening.

She pulled her compact from her purse and checked her face. "Now look what he's done. I look a mess."

"Thought you and Spagnola were tight." Joe Spagnola was a detective Sheila met the day the body of her assistant was found in her condominium. They dated off and on since.

"Oh, please. We have fun, nothing more."

"That guy loves you."

"Everyone loves me."

Padre tried not to laugh out loud. She really believed it. "Not everyone." He nodded toward the opened doorway where music from a three piece blues band could be heard. On the dance floor couples were interlocked in a slow dance, including Sara and Dagger.

Dagger never displayed affection in public when he and Sheila dated. She was always the one to grab his hand, to put her arm around him. And he never had eyes just for her. They were always roaming, as though looking for some assassin lurking behind a tree. He was always secretive, but with Sara he was completely different. "She's just a distraction. You'll see." Sheila sniffed as she finished her drink. "He'll tire of her soon enough."

"Where are you off to now? I trust you aren't going to go drown your sorrows in a bar and try to drive home."

"I'm going to go home, sit in the dark with just the fireplace on, make myself another drink, put in an Adele CD, and cry myself to sleep." She placed a kiss on Padre's cheek. "Want to join me?"

"If I might offer a word of advice."

"Please. No theological counseling. You are no longer a priest. Have a good night, Padre. And thanks for the drinks." She sashayed out of the bar, forgetting to tell Martinez about the paintings she'd seen at the gallery.

Padre crushed his cigarette in the ashtray and wondered just how far Sheila would go to break up Dagger and Sara. The affairs of the heart couldn't even be purchased for the right price.

Simon shuffled over to the bar and stood next to Padre. He waved a hand down his white tuxedo. "I look like a goddamn ice cream truck driver."

"Hey, gotta please the wife."

"Was that Sheila I just saw?"

"Oh, yeah. And she got an eyeful, drank two martinis, and left."

"Nothing worse than a woman scorned." Simon shook his head.

"How's Skizzy doing?"

"Actually better, now that he didn't have to do the officiating. He was pacing back and forth trying to memorize the lines, getting more paranoid by the minute. Thought he'd be upset if he couldn't do the ceremony, but once our minister showed up, he seemed to breathe a big sigh of relief."

"Did he finally eat?"

"Of course he doesn't trust that someone wouldn't try to poison him, so Dagger cut his filet in half to share with Skizzy, which he refused. Skizzy said there were more people out to poison Dagger. So Sara took a rare bite of the steak, and a sip of his drink to prove there was nothing in it. He knows she doesn't like red meat, so her sacrifice was enough to convince him the food was safe."

"But he's enjoying himself?"

Simon sighed. "Not sure. He's lurking in a corner watching everyone."

"When do you leave on your cruise?"

"Next week. Would you believe Dagger and Sara upgraded us to a suite on our cruise ship as an anniversary gift?"

"How much private detecting does one man have to do to make so much money? Ever wonder about that, Simon?"

Dagger paid Simon and Skizzy quite well for any assistance he needed. He already invested a sizeable sum for Padre when he retired. A fictitious uncle would name the cop in his will. Padre would never take money outright, especially since he was never sure what legal boundaries Dagger had crossed. The P.I. had relieved more than one corrupt person of wealth obtained in unscrupulous ways.

Simon rubbed a beefy hand across his face to hide the smile. "He's pretty expensive, I guess."

16 He ran a finger down her nude body. So beautiful in the glow of the moon. Her hair haloed around her head. Although it was chilly, he didn't feel the cold. Maybe it was because her blood was warm, still pumping from the opening in her neck. The moon hung like a giant globe in the sky. It struck like death rays between the trees, scaring four-legged creatures farther into the underbrush. Or was it him they feared? He stood and surveyed his surroundings. Was that a whisper he heard? Someone talking? Someone still breathing? He looked down at her body to make sure her chest wasn't rising and falling. Earlier he realized he could actually hear her heart beating, the blood pulsing. The heartbeats he heard now belonged to the animals in hiding. Soft, quick patters of fright. Yellow eyes glowed near a tree. Coyote maybe? He made a slight turn in that direction and the coyote cowered before bolting off.

This was puzzling. He looked back at the body, her dead eyes staring vacantly. The wrong eyes, again. This time he hadn't strangled her and didn't remember using a knife. His hands felt heavy. He raised them up to the light and saw long talons covered with pieces of bloody flesh.

He jerked to a sitting position gasping for air, his heart pounding in his chest. Another dream, this time more vivid, so lifelike. And the blood. He held up his hands to assure himself it was just a dream. Normal hands, all ten fingers. He swung his legs over the side of the bed and gave himself a few minutes before stumbling to the bathroom. The water was ice cold as he splashed it over his face and neck. He let the water drip for several seconds, grabbed a towel, and buried his face in it, rubbed the towel through his hair.

When he finally straightened and looked in the mirror, the front of his shirt was covered in blood.

17 Their bodies were drenched in sweat. When Sara first awakened, her leg brushed against Dagger's thigh, alerting every cell in their bodies. That's all it took, no matter how battered their bodies felt, somehow they found the energy, or it found them. The floor was littered with the clothes they wore the night before. Sara's heels rested against the dresser. Her dress draped the exercise bike. The tuxedo pants and jacket lay haphazardly on a chair in the corner of the room while the white shirt clung to the knob of a dresser drawer.

"I think this is how Samson felt after Delilah cut his hair." Dagger barely had the strength to push himself off of her.

"Ummmm, don't move," Sara whispered. "Not yet."

He inhaled the scent of her hair, tasted the salt of perspiration on her skin. The phone in the living room started ringing. They could hear Einstein squawk. "DAGGER INVESTIGATIONS. SHOOT TO KILL." The macaw was known on more than one occasion to fly over and knock the phone off its cradle. They learned to keep the grated door shut and locked. Although they both owned cell phones, Dagger kept a land line with an 800 number for business purposes. Few people knew his cell number.

"Let them leave a message. I don't think I have the strength to walk into the other room." He propped his head up with one elbow and studied the beauty beneath him. Her hair fanned out across the pillow. Bronzed cheekbones high, lips deliciously full, eyes framed in long lashes. How he had restrained himself for this long, even with Simon's constant prodding, should have won him a medal. "You are wearing me out. You know that?"

Sara sighed and ran a hand up his arm. Roped muscles were firm from years of training. Her fingers traced an old scar on his right shoulder. He no longer worried about scars. Although her olive complexion was from her Assiniboine ancestry, Dagger's looked more Mediterranean. The subtle residue from his woodsy aftershave was intoxicating.

"You're getting that look in your eyes."

Sara inhaled long and deep. "What look is that?"

The answer machine beeped. "Hey, Dagger. I know you're there. You gotta be somewhere because you ain't looking at your cell calls," Padre said.

"Maybe you should take that." The sunlight sliced through the edges of the window shades illuminating eyes that were the color of turquoise gems.

"I'm too comfortable to move."

"Marty Flynn called. Seems he hasn't been sitting on his laurels since retiring."

Just as Dagger bent closer to touch those luscious lips, the name Flynn made him stop. His lips hovered. He could feel Sara's breath on his face.

"He's been looking at homicide reports across the country and something strange popped out at him."

How serious could this be, Dagger wondered. He was lying next to the most beautiful woman in the world, feeling his junior P.I. coming to life again; and it would have to be a monumental catastrophe to get him to stop what was beginning to be round two of his morning serving of Sara's Delight.

"There have been seven women killed in the past seven

months from the state of Arizona to the Iowa border." Padre's voice echoed off the high ceilings in the living room. They could hear Einstein screeching in the aviary.

"Not even our territory. When it gets within our borders, let me know, Padre," he whispered into the hollow of Sara's neck.

"The curious thing is, Dagger, all the victims are named Sara."

They froze, their bodies in some type of suspended animation. Slowly Dagger rolled onto his back. His pulse started pounding like a jackhammer. They lay there, eyes cast to the ceiling, thoughts spinning, trying to decipher if they heard Padre correctly. He heard the scratching of fabric as Sara's fingers grappled across the sheet toward his hand.

Sara slowly turned her head toward Dagger, the uneasiness evident in her voice. "Do you think this is what Simon meant by a bucket of ice water moment?"

18 Sheila arrived at work late, her head pounding, her stomach queasy, and every slice of sunlight feeling like a knife through her eyes. She kept her sunglasses on and took a seat behind the desk. Her father had given her free reign over the checkbook when she redecorated the office. Sheila felt white was more elegant. However, after the white furniture in her former condo had been redecorated with her assistant's blood, she could no longer look at white furniture. Now her office was comprised of a custom made solid oak desk and a bookcase cabinet which covered one wall. A fireplace was on the opposite side of the room with a comfortable sitting area in front of it. She still missed the white furniture. It had added a touch of femininity to the room. Now she felt like she was sitting in a man cave. All she needed were NFL posters on the walls. When her door slammed shut, she thought a bomb had gone off in her head.

"'Bout time. Do you think I run a country club here?" Leyton Monroe wedged his bulk into the barrel chair in front of Sheila's desk. Billows of cigar smoke circled his helmet of white hair.

"Oh, God, Daddy. Not today. I can't take the cigar smell. I'm about ready to hurl."

"Something you drank, I presume." He pressed the buzzer on Sheila's phone and a mousy brunette came running in. Leyton handed the ashtray with his cigar in it to the timid soul. "Put this on my desk." The mouse practically bowed on her way out. Dealing with one Monroe was enough, but two made her quiver. It was a wonder she didn't drop the ashtray. Once the door closed behind her, Leyton turned on his daughter. "You are supposed to set an example here. I trust you didn't get drunk at the country club where I'd have to hear about it from every member."

Sheila lowered her glasses and glared at her father. "God forbid I should embarrass you, like marrying someone you despise." She didn't bother to stifle her sobs. May as well make an absolute fool of herself.

Her sobbing brought out the Papa Bear in her father. He popped to his feet and went over to his daughter, wrapping an arm around her and stroking her hair. "There, there. Tell Poppo what's wrong."

Sheila couldn't stop crying and was certain mascara was streaming down her face. "You'll be angry with me."

"No, no." He continued stroking her hair. "I could never be mad at you. You are my pride and joy, the apple of my eye, the pudding in my pie." That was the same refrain he'd used on her since she was five.

"It's Dagger," she wailed.

"WHAT?!" Poppo wasn't so gentle any more. He let loose of her head so fast it almost banged on the desk. "You're crying over that punk? Are you outta your mind?" Leyton glanced at the door to make sure it was closed. "Keep it down," he snapped. "People will think I'm beating you to death. And maybe that's what I should have done years ago. But you were too bullheaded then and you are still bullheaded." Leyton poured his daughter a glass of water and set it in front of her. "Dilute that alcohol you drowned yourself in last night." He returned to the chair in front of Sheila's desk. "Now what did that ass do this time?"

Sheila waved a damp hankie like a surrender flag. "He thinks he's in love."

"He doesn't think it. That idiot doesn't do anything halfway. If he's in love, he's in love. Who this time?"

"His—" Sheila made quote marks with her fingers, '—business associate.' The one he claimed was like a little sister to him."

"I saw that one coming a mile away. You never saw those killer eyes he directed at Nick Tyler every time young Nick touched Sara's shoulder or hand? You never saw the puppy dog eyes whenever she looked at him? How blind are you? Good thing he isn't a mass murderer or you'd be blind to that, too."

She clutched a fist to her chest. "It hurts so much. How could he do this to me?"

"Do what? It was over when he left you at the altar. That should have been your first clue." Leyton knew he was rough on her, but he needed to toughen her up. When it came to affairs of the heart, he was ill lacking in advice. "Call your mother and go have lunch with her. And for godsake, don't have anything to drink."

After three cups of coffee and a handful of crackers, Sheila finally turned on her computer and checked headlines across the world. More bombings in Iraq, a shooting at a North Carolina university, a head-on collision between a semi and a motorcycle in Chicago. The driver wasn't wearing a helmet. Sheila saw two tarps on the ground near the wreckage. One she assumed was the torso and the other the head.

Images of the paintings in Logan's Galleria came back to her in full color, reminding her that she never told Padre about them. The painting of her former condominium was more than graphic. It was frighteningly accurate. She Googled motorcycle accidents and found far too many. She tried motorcycle and decapitation. The sixth one down caught her eye. It occurred right here in Cedar Point, Indiana. Sheila printed out the information. She drummed her sculptured nails on the desktop trying to spark her drunken brain cells.

The woman wedged in the tree. She didn't have to enter it. These cases were only a few years old. The teens in the forest. The cop murdered and her body in the tree. The motorcycle rider whose collision with a semi separated him from his body. But she didn't recall anything about his head being impaled in a tree. Did the police leave that out of the news? Or was the artist stretching artistic freedom to the limit? And how could she forget the body in the condo, her condo.

It didn't take her long to find the cases in the archives. Lisa Cambridge was the first. An officer with CPPD, her body was found near a walking trail by the lake, wedged in a branch so tightly the techs had to cut the branch from the tree. Lisa's gun still had the safety on. Her one protector, her Doberman, was so scared he'd hidden for several days. Although her boyfriend, J.D. Draper, a fellow cop, was the number one suspect, he'd been cleared.

Although not connected, Sheila found the report on Tex Miller, whose decapitated body was found near his Harley. However, the police report said nothing about the head being impaled in a tree. There were very few details on the condition of Tex's body, and it wasn't until the next day that the wife's body was found. Again, very few details on the where and how. If it was strictly the force of the impact that caused the wife's body to end up in a tree, why did the painting show the body disemboweled, and why was there no mention of it in the police reports?

The next case proved difficult for Sheila to read. Caroline

Kirby had been her assistant. Sheila's plan to help Caroline with a project was sidetracked by dinner at her parents' house. Sheila gave her assistant a key to her condo, unaware someone was waiting there. The years couldn't erase the guilt. Scant information was made available to the press, but Sheila'd had a front row seat to the carnage in her condo. Just about every wall was sprayed with blood. Besides her parents, Dagger was the only person with a key to her penthouse. Eventually it was believed Professor William Sherlock was the killer. He left a note confessing to the murders before committing suicide. Sheila took a sip of water and ate more crackers. All of the cases had been closed.

Steve and Chrissy, names so deserving of the prom king and queen, thought they'd found a quiet place to make out. Sheila remembered the painting at the Galleria of the teen sitting against a tree, his insides in his lap. Several feet away from him lay Chrissy, her neck torn open as though by some escaped zoo animal. And that was exactly how the police report read.

Who could know so much about the cases that he could capture the murders on canvas in such great detail? A cop? Maybe someone who worked in the medical examiner's office? That was why she needed to talk to Padre. He would know if the details were precise or merely an artist's perverted sense of artistic expression.

19

"So when do we get the details, and how do we know if these murders are related?" Dagger watched shoppers enter and exit the mall.

They were seated on benches in the outdoor courtyard, where several smokers braved the cool air. Sara was huddled in her sweater coat, the hood framing her face while her hands were wrapped around a cup of hot tea.

Padre took a long drag on his cigarette. So much for gum replacing his addiction. The last place Padre wanted to meet was the office where prying eyes and ears might be too curious. Who would ever believe the case of a cursed family whose male members went on a killing spree when a full moon fell on a Friday the thirteenth? Paul was the sixth in the Addison family tree going back to the early 1800s. A few years ago, Padre sent William Sherlock, a university professor, and Marty, who had been an Indianapolis cop at the time, to the doorstep of Dagger Investigations. If anyone could verify the validity of their claims, it was Dagger.

"Marty sent copies of the files to me yesterday. I should have them by courier this afternoon. Let me go over them first. I may want to talk to the various detectives on those seven cases to verify what Marty suspects."

"How do you explain all of the victims named Sara?" Although Dagger hoped for a reasonable explanation, Sara's instincts told her the case didn't die with Paul Addison.

Padre cut a glance toward the young woman. There

was wisdom behind those eyes and a strong resolve that contradicted her youth. "I'm hoping some guy went off the deep end and is striking out against every woman with the same name as his girlfriend, wife, mother, someone who betrayed him or broke his heart. After all, the names aren't all the same. I mean, they are, but they are spelled differently. Sara. Sarah, Sareh."

"But they all have long, dark hair."

"Well, they have dark hair, but I don't know if they all had long hair. Let's not jump to conclusions. What do you think, Dagger?"

Dagger's attention was riveted elsewhere. He felt eyes on him since they entered the courtyard. Families were shopping. Workers on their breaks focused on cell phones and iPads. Maintenance people riding golf carts passed through the courtyard picking up litter. It didn't appear anyone was paying attention to his little group and yet he could feel the heat from the intense stares. Was the activated chip making him more sensitive? His eyes scanned the benches and stragglers leaning against posts. There were a number of males turned in his direction, but their eyes were riveted on Sara. Were they stalking her, or was this the normal attention her beauty always attracted?

"Dagger?"

"Sorry. I was thinking. I agree. Let's wait to see what the detectives on those cases say. I don't want to jump to any conclusions. Sergeant Flynn doesn't plan on coming?"

"Nah. He's retired and says he's too old for this shit. My sentiments exactly."

Sara snapped her eyes to Dagger, and the intensity in that stare told him she knew something was bothering him. If anyone had more of a spider sense than he, it was Sara.

"Does Marty have any other suggestions?"

"For now, he's going to check on Paul Addison's wife and kid. We think they are in Arizona somewhere, or at least that is where they were headed last, according to the doctor who delivered the baby. 'Course, she could have moved several times since."

"If you remember, he was going by the name Brian Andrews when he was here, so his wife might still be using Andrews. If he needs any help, I can put Skizzy on it." Dagger stood and pried his attention from his surroundings.

"I just hope to God this is nothing." Out of habit, Padre made the sign of the cross. They watched him walk away, hands stuffed in the pockets of his coat.

Sara tossed her empty cup away and moved close to Dagger. "Want to tell me what held your interest for so long?"

Dagger grabbed the fabric of the sweater hood and pulled her close, his lips near her ear. "I think someone is watching us."

"I feel it, too."

"Let's get out of here." Dagger pulled away and steered her toward the stacked parking garage where they had left his Lincoln Navigator. "I don't want to lead them to the house or my office. Let's see if they make a move."

The elevator in the garage could have used a good scrubbing. It smelled of urine and sweat. Of all things there was a spent shell casing on the floor. Few shoppers found it safe to shop in the late evenings for a good reason. Sara tensed as the elevator moved.

"You okay?"

"I think I'm just picking up your anxiety."

As the elevator doors opened on the third floor, the first thing that registered was the man in dark clothing with a shaved head and killer eyes. Before they could react, Dagger and Sara were hit with a spray of noxious mist. Then everything went dark.

20 Padre smelled the perfume and opened his eyes to see Sheila standing in front of his desk, bright red nails tapping an envelope. So much for his afternoon nap.

"Are you free Saturday night?"

"Why, Miss Monroe. Are you asking me out?"

Sheila checked the chair before sitting down. Dry cleaning charges were eating up her budget. "Oh, please. I have my reputation to protect." She gave him a wink as she waved an envelope in the air. "I actually stole several extras because I figured when I tell you where I am going and why, you're going to want to check it out."

Padre was waiting on the files from Marty Flynn and didn't have time to play games with Cedar Point's ardent reporter. She pulled the invite from the envelope and set it in front of Padre as she told him about the grand opening of Logan's Galleria and the Nightfall exhibit. Padre's interest was piqued, especially since it came on the heels of his phone call with Marty yesterday.

"I looked into those old cases and you caught the serial killer. I believe his name was William Sherlock, right? Kind of a fitting name."

Sheila was studying Padre a little too closely, so he tried to hide any sign of interest. "Yep. His suicide saved the state a lot of money." All information regarding Paul Addison and the family curse had been kept out of the press and shared with only a few people. Unfortunately, Professor Sherlock had to be the fall guy. After Paul Addison killed the professor, he typed a suicide note from Sherlock confessing to the killings. It proved to be a convenient way for Padre to keep the public's attention away from information about the Addison family curse.

"I'm curious about the details in the paintings and if they are accurate. Of course, I'm sure you wouldn't have held anything back from the public, right?"

Padre displayed his best patronizing smile. "The homicides were public knowledge. Anyone with a paint brush and a few lines of coke could envision just about anything. Of course, we wouldn't share the condition of Tex Miller's body with the public. The impact with a semi doing sixty and a cycle doing eighty can cause extreme trauma."

"So you are saying those details are accurate?"

"Yes."

"And the teens? The official police report mentioned a wild animal attack."

Padre found it much easier to show an honest face when talking about a wild animal attack. That's exactly what they thought of Paul Addison—a wild, vicious animal. "What parent wants to read details about her son's body being clawed open." Sheila seemed to accept that explanation. "'Course, now you definitely have me interested in those paintings. What time is this little soiree?"

"Eight o'clock. Wine and cheese, other fancy hors d'oeuvres. The owner's name is Mark Logan. He moved his gallery from the Lincoln Park area in Chicago. The manager's name is Carlton Abrams. One look at him and I wanted to check the basement for a crypt."

"Is this artist going to show up for the grand opening?"

"No. According to Carlton, he is a recluse."

"I don't suppose in your snooping you caught a return address on these packages."

"Believe me, I tried. They come from a postal box number and from different states. I don't know what kind of recluse does so much traveling, unless he has someone do his shipping for him."

Padre picked up the gold embossed invitation written in calligraphy. The owner spared no expense. "A thousand dollars? What the hell?!"

"Oh, I forgot to mention. To make sure only serious buyers see the Nightfall exhibit, they're charging an entrance fee."

"Are you paying my way?"

Sheila smiled as she tapped a manicured nail on the invite. "It says to bring a guest. Is there anyone else you think might be interested and has a spare couple of grand lying around?"

Marty Flynn was already back to his retirement abode and didn't want anything more to do with the case. Padre couldn't blame him. But he was sure Sheila had Dagger in mind. "Maybe."

She stood and started for the door but turned back. "Oh, and one more thing." She nodded toward the card in his hand. "Check the last sentence on the invite. Formal attire, please."

21

His head felt as though it were under the tire of an eighteen wheeler. Dagger tried to lift his hand to no avail. His eyelids fluttered revealing pitch black darkness. What the hell? The mall, the parking garage, the cloud of mist sprayed by a hulk dressed in black. He scuffed his shoe against the floor. It was solid, maybe concrete.

"Are you all right?" Dagger whispered.

"What happened? What was that spray we were hit with?"

"I don't know, but I swear it's still coating my throat."

"Why is it so dark?"

Code words. They agreed under circumstances such as these that they would not use their names. No sense letting enemies know whom they were dealing with. And now with Dagger's new found talents, Sara sometimes needed to remind him to use them. He took a deep breath and blinked slowly. The warehouse was no longer dark. All he did was think it, and the chip took over. Sara could also see in the dark with her hawk vision so she knew what he was seeing. Zip ties were restraining his arms and legs to a chair. The wall behind him was only a foot away. Pools of water dotted the floor from leaks in the metal roof. Rotting wood was piled in one corner near a loading door where a black van was parked. Across from him, about twenty yards away, was Sara. She appeared unharmed and was also restrained with zip ties. His leather trench coat was missing, as was Sara's sweater coat. Their abductors must have been searching for some type of identification.

"Can you tell where we are?"

Of course they both knew it was a large warehouse, but couldn't let the two men and one woman standing by the van let them know. The woman wore cropped hair and was built compact and muscular. The men had shaved heads, were pumped full of steroids, and sported matching black jumpsuits. Who were they and what did they want?

Dagger imagined a navigation map and suddenly an area map appeared in his field of vision, as though a projector screen dropped from the ceiling. *Yes!* He would have done a fist pump if his hands hadn't been tied down. "There's a place near the water that used to store boats."

"I smell fuel and fish. So maybe a storage garage of some type?"

"No. The old Falstaff Brewery by the power plant. Far away from prying eyes. Only one way in and out." This revelation Dagger was sure would get their captors talking.

"I think you're right." Sara didn't need the wolf's sense of smell to detect the fish odor. It was strong.

Bruiser One reached inside the driver's side window and turned on the van's headlights. The area map snapped off as quickly as it had appeared. The abductors slowly made their way over. Now new stats showed up, but the stats hanging in his field of vision shocked him. It was like having his personal version of Google glasses. Another gift from his newly exposed chip? And how nice. They were BettaTec operatives. He read their identification numbers, vitals, and instructions to locate the person whose photo appeared. The photo was of Violet. More stats appeared—heart rate, body temperature, initiation date, prior assignments, future targets. Names and faces which meant nothing to Dagger. However, what he saw,

Connie was recording.

"Neither of you has a driver's license, no wallets, no credit cards." She had a slight accent, one of the Scandinavian countries, Dagger guessed. He figured if she did have a name it was probably Inga. She was not much taller than Sara, but there was something in the way she carried herself that told him she was lethal. Her blonde hair could be a wig. After all, Connie said BettaTec operatives were good at camouflaging their appearances.

"I did have a wallet. Obviously, you stole it." Dagger saw a slight nod of her head and before he could come out with another smartass remark, one of the bruisers stepped forward. Dagger never saw the fist fly until it was an inch from his head. If he hadn't moved with the fist, Dagger was sure his jaw would have been broken. Instead his chair tipped back and Bruiser Two just happened to be there to shove it upright again.

"No identification. No phones. Why not?"

Dagger's wallet and Sara's purse, as well as their phones, were tucked away in one of the hidden compartments in the Navigator. Force of habit sometimes. However, he didn't see his Kimber in its belt holster.

"I'm sorry. I didn't catch your names."

"You tell us yours. We'll tell you ours."

"Let's see. You look like an Inga. Well, Inga, I see our weapons are missing. I'm pretty attached to the Kimber, so whoever took it will be one sorry ass."

She ignored the comment and dangled a photo of Violet in front of him.

Dagger was certain Inga couldn't read his stats. If she could, she would know his name, or at least his number. "Never saw her before."

This time the attack came from behind, but it wasn't a blow

to the head. A mitt of a hand slapped against his forehead to keep him from moving. A flicker of blue light appeared over his left shoulder. It looked like a butane lighter one would use to ignite a fireplace or candle. Dagger stared at the flame held one inch above his cheek. "Really? This is the best you can do?"

A flick of her eyebrow and the lighter touched skin. Dagger screamed as the skin seared and bubbled. He strained against the vice grip as the demon stirred in his head. The mitt suddenly released its hold.

Dagger huffed out a long breath and focused on Sara in an effort to marginalize his pain receptors. "Why are you so interested in her?"

"I'm asking the questions. How do you know her?"

When Dagger didn't reply, he saw something appear in her hand a few seconds before the blade impaled his right hand to the chair. Dagger let out a howl. His only thought was that he was glad he was ambidextrous.

"STOP IT!" Sara screamed.

Violet's picture was waved in front of his eyes again. "I repeat. How do you know her?"

Dagger studied the knife with feigned amazement. "Wow. A Leo Damascus pocket knife. Did you know how it got its name? It was forged out of the barrel of the German battle tank, Leopard." If the air in the warehouse hadn't been so chilly, Dagger was sure perspiration would start trailing from his forehead. The five-inch blade could only be sold to the military. Dagger should know. He stored a few in his vault.

The photo was waved again. "I'm losing my patience."

"You must be deaf. I have never seen her before."

Inga obviously owned more than one knife herself because the second one appeared and impaled his left hand. So much for being ambidextrous.

"SONOFABITCH," Dagger yelled.

"STOP IT," Sara screamed again as she struggled against the zip ties. She could easily get away by shifting, but couldn't chance this many witnesses. "We bought flowers from her. Nothing else."

The woman glanced over her shoulder as though just realizing someone else was in the room. "Really? I didn't even show you the photo. How do you know whose picture I'm holding?" She returned her attention to Dagger. "We have seen you with her on more than one occasion and you weren't buying flowers. Now, if you don't give me the answers I want, we will start on her."

Dagger said nothing.

She nodded in Sara's direction. "The butane torch will scar her for life."

Not likely, Dagger thought with a chuckle.

"You find that funny?"

"Fuck you."

"Burn the other side," she ordered. Strong hands clamped under his chin and pulled his head back. The upside down image split into a broad smile.

"Look, his cheek," one bruiser said. "How can he do that?"

The strong hands released and Dagger saw Inga's attention was riveted on the burn which he was certain was quickly healing, thanks to Sara's blood running through his veins. Instead of being curious about the burn, it seemed to anger Inga as she leaned on both knives, twisting and pushing them deeper.

Dagger grimaced in pain as he felt the demon shriek. "Ohhh, you don't want to do that."

Sara recognized that tone and saw the change in Dagger's eyes. The visual acuity of her hawk sight was eight times more powerful than a human's. She saw his pupils enlarge and the blackness shift and move, swirling like fog in a dark pool as it slowly took over the whites of his eyes. She remembered what Mother once said—"Everyone is a moon and has a dark side which he never shows to anybody." A quote from Mark Twain. Mother said she counted on Sara to keep Dagger's dark side in check.

An explosion of adrenaline raced through Dagger's body as the demon grew in strength, close to the point where he wouldn't be able to control it. The same change happened the time Sara was kidnapped and her assailant tried to rape her. Nothing could control the demon as Dagger swiftly and methodically broke the assailant's neck.

Inga pulled both knives from Dagger's hands bringing another howl of pain. She tossed a nod in Sara's direction. "Let's see if she is as talented. Burn her." They moved as one unit toward Sara.

The demon could no longer be contained. Dagger leaned forward, the chair still attached, then rammed the wall behind him with a strength that surprised him. The wooden chair shattered into pieces. Inga turned her attention back to Dagger. When the strip ties ripped off, he grabbed a splintered piece of wood; and as Inga charged, Dagger shoved the stake into her chest. How fitting to be staked like a vampire. Her eyes widened in horror as Dagger used both hands to ram the wood deeper, lifting her body a foot off the ground. Dagger ignored the pain in his hands as blood spilled from the knife wounds. He cocked his head as he waited for her stats to read *deceased*. He released his grip and let her crash to the floor.

Inga's sidekicks appeared to weigh their options – help Inga or finish with Sara. With the men distracted, Sara partially shifted her hands to the talons of the gray hawk, slipped out of the ties and then cut the ties around her ankles. As she leaped from the chair, arms outstretched, the talons ripped through her captors' throats, almost decapitating them.

Dagger stumbled back and sank against the wall. Sara stood amid the carnage they created. The two men sprawled in a pool of blood on either side of her while Inga lay on her back, eyes open.

Sara could hear Dagger's heartbeat racing, saw the blacks of his eyes. He was panting as though he just finished running a marathon.

"Don't come any closer." His voice was husky as he tried to slow down his breathing.

Sara ignored him and approached. She knew his dark side would never harm her, just as her wolf would never harm him. Her hands shook as she studied pieces of blood and tissue embedded under her nails. "Oh my God," she whispered. "I didn't mean to…I just…" She fell to her knees in front of Dagger. He grabbed her hands and locked eyes. She could see the demon retreating, the smoky dark of the pupils receding until his eyes were back to normal. It wasn't that she scared the demon away. She was always somehow able to calm it down.

"It's okay." Dagger ripped a handkerchief from his pocket and used it to clean most of the debris from her hands. Sara was not one to randomly kill, not like Dagger. It wasn't the first time she had acted on instinct in order to protect him or for survival.

Dagger pressed a button on his watch as he walked to the van. Skizzy's little invention could not only tell time, but it was also a phone and a GPS.

"Yo, at your service," Skizzy said.

"We need a major cleanup. We're at the old Falstaff plant."

"Roger. I've got your location."

"You need to be creative on this one, Skizzy. Nothing left for identification."

"I love creativity. Over and out."

Dagger returned with a bottle of water he found in the van. He poured water over Sara's hands to wash off the debris.

"Do you think they had video capabilities?"

Dagger shook his head. "No way to know unless we crack their heads open."

"Skizzy will bring a scanner, right?"

"These days, he never leaves home without one." He used the rest of the water to rinse the blood from his hands and regretted not asking Skizzy to bring them a change of clothes.

"We aren't much different," Sara said. "There can be no witnesses to my shifting, so I have no control over killing people. And once your dark side emerges, you have no way of stopping yourself from killing."

Dagger paused and studied her face. He could see it in her eyes, the innocence, the complete faith that down deep he was a good person. Could anyone really be that trusting? "There is one major difference, Sara."

"What's that?"

"You feel remorse."

22 "So your chip is reading the chips in those other guys' heads. Kinda sympatico." Skizzy shoved a pickle into his mouth. "And you're sure they can't read yours."

"I think she would have said something."

When Skizzy scanned the bodies, he hadn't detected any video capabilities on the three operatives. More importantly, the scanner didn't detect any microchips that might have been implanted in Dagger and Sara while they were unconscious.

Dagger located their coats and weapons in the black van. They'd left Skizzy to destroy the warehouse while Dagger drove the black van back to the mall parking garage to retrieve the Navigator. After pulling over twice so Sara could run out of the vehicle and vomit from the chemicals used to knock them out, they stopped off at home to shower and change before hitting the drive-thru at Panera's.

"Where did you find all those chemicals to turn that warehouse into a meth lab?" Sara closed the lid on the empty soup container and opened a second one.

Skizzy inspected the chicken panini sandwich Dagger purchased for him. He was just about to sniff it when he noticed Dagger giving him one of his warning glares. For some reason, Skizzy trusted food purchased by someone else. He figured as long as he didn't show his face, Big Brother wouldn't know whom to poison.

"Months ago some woman came in with the stuff she

found in her greenhouse. Guess her son and his friends were making the shit. I kept it in the garage, not here, thinking it might come to good use. Set up a pretty good explosion in that warehouse. No way those bodies won't be burned beyond recognition." Skizzy pointed the panini at Dagger. "Shouldn't you let the Mother Ship know what's going on?"

"We're headed there next." Dagger balled up the wrapper and tossed it in the bag. "I'm curious what kind of drug they used on us and if there are any long term effects."

"Didn't seem to bother you any."

"I think the amount they needed to knock me out was too much for someone Sara's size, which is why she got sick." He would have to remember to ask Mother if she knew. He studied the tops of his hands. The external wounds already healed, but it was the internal damage that would take more time.

"I think we should let Skizzy in on Padre's phone call." Sara finished the second carton of soup and placed the empty carton in the bag.

Skizzy stopped in mid-chew and glared at them. One eye appeared to focus on Dagger, the other one on Sara. He slowly chewed while Dagger explained the list of victims that garnered the attention of Marty Flynn.

"That fucker is dead. I incinerated his ass and spread the ashes myself. Ain't no way he put himself together again." He tossed the rest of his meal into the bag and shook his head. "Gotta be another explanation."

"We'll find out more once Padre finishes with the paperwork from Marty."

Skizzy leveled one eye at his friend, his head cocked much the same way Einstein would stare. "There's something more. What ain't you tellin' me?"

Skizzy may seem a couple dimes short of a full roll, but he

had gut instincts. Or maybe it was Dagger's influence.

"All the victims are named Sara." Sara could see the wheels in Skizzy's head turning, perhaps thinking back to that night in the forest.

He rubbed bony fingers across the stubble on his chin. "Well, this certainly calls for more contemplation." The stubble sounded like sandpaper as he scratched in thought. "Pissed off husband or father. Maybe some guy with latent homicidal feelings about his mother who ignored him or abused him and her name was Sara. Yeah, that's gotta be it. Does Columbo have any other theories?"

Dagger chuckled at that. Padre's disheveled appearance always reminded people of the television show, *Columbo*. "For now, that's all he's going on." A sudden thought hit Dagger "Skizzy, is it possible for you to hack the Alpha computer in my office and record everything Connie is downloading from my chip?"

"Sure. Piece of cake."

"Really?"

"Fuck, no. Like BettaTec, the Mother Hen's computers are bouncing through every country in the world. Besides, we have no way of knowing if the Wicked Father might one day be able to see everything happening at the Mother Ship. I hack it and it would be traced right back to me. What part of laser beam annihilation don't you get?"

Skizzy was right. BettaTec possessed skills unheard of in the geek world. Dagger couldn't take the chance.

23 *"We are glad you are unharmed."* Connie's robotic eyes blinked and moved left to right as though examining the person she was speaking with. It was very unnerving.

"I wouldn't say that. They used some type of vapor that completely immobilized us. Do you have any idea what it might have been?"

"Describe the effects."

"Muscles were weak, could barely move. I think my eyes were open. There were two men and one woman and they weren't wearing gas masks."

"It wasn't just a small aerosol can they used," Sara offered.

"Was there an odor?"

"Sweet." Sara looked to Dagger for agreement.

"Not too sweet, though."

"Nitrous oxide smells sweet, but to knock you out that quickly it probably included zolpidem. Not sure. The Director's lab concocts all kinds of designer drugs, most not on the market much less approved by the FDA. Since his operatives were close by and they weren't wearing masks, I

doubt there would be any long-term effects he would expose his operatives to. Any idea how long you were out?"

Dagger tried to remember what time they left the mall and how far the mall was from the brewing company. "They had to drive to the lake, get us out of the van and tied to chairs. Not sure how long it took us to come around. From the time we left the mall to when I called Skizzy, it was no more than two hours, tops."

"They wanted to know about Violet. Naturally, we didn't tell them anything. Where is Violet now?"

"She is safe. Nice work on the warehouse. We gave Violet a cover while we extracted her. The police will find the body of a woman dressed in Violet's clothes and a basket of flowers nearby, a victim of a hit and run. And, no, before you ask, we did not kill anyone. It was a homeless woman whose body we found early this morning. We felt it advantageous if the Director assumed his operatives captured and killed Violet. Of course, he will now have to deal with why and how his three operatives died. My best guess is that he will assume Violet killed them before her untimely, fake, death."

"So you knew we were in danger and did nothing?" A slight irritation crept into Sara's voice.

"We knew you could take care of yourselves. We received the operatives' stats via your chip, something we weren't able to do before. What have you done to activate it?"

"I removed the copper from the leather cord."

"Ahhhh, of course. Have you experienced anything else?"

"If you mean night vision, yes. And I was able to retrieve a map of our location. Anything else I should know?"

"Perhaps." But Connie didn't elaborate.

"Other than the demon inside of him?" Sara asked.

There was an uncomfortable silence. Were they conferring again? It was a simple yes or no question, Dagger thought.

"That was the basis of the betta fish research. All assassins were given that ability. But yours is stronger. Much stronger."

Dagger waited for more. He looked across the desk at Sara who raised her eyebrows to prompt him. "And why is that?" he finally asked.

"Mother made it that way. Someone had to be stronger than Father's elite team. You are the only one with the altered chip."

"What about the clones?"

Connie turned one hundred eighty degrees until she faced Sara, who slowly inched away.

"What about the clones?"

"The Demko twins were able to record everything they saw when I shoved one of them out of the hotel window. Did the operatives today have that same capability? Was the Director watching everything that transpired?"

"Operatives don't have that capability, only the clones. As far as we know, you eliminated the remaining ones. Now that we have access to the Director's laptop, we will know if he has improved on the outdated test subjects. We are curious, though."

We. There was that word again, which gave Dagger the impression there was a panel seated at a conference table manipulating Connie's replies. Connie's head did a one-eighty again and now she returned her gaze to Dagger.

"How were you able to heal so quickly? We heard one of the operatives say your skin healed and we saw the stab wounds disappear almost instantly."

"Wait. I thought you said the BettaTec operatives weren't recording anything?"

"They weren't." There was an irritation in Connie's voice, as though a robot could display an emotion. *"The live feed was from when your dark side stirred."* There was a slight pause. Just when Dagger thought they were going to drop the subject, they brought it up. *"Again, Six-One-Seven. How were you able to heal so quickly? That isn't an ability we gave you."*

"I take a lot of vitamin E," Dagger replied. He looked through the image of Connie to Sara seated across from him. The silence dragged on.

"I gave him that ability," Sara offered.

Connie's eyes widened. How they enabled a robotic face to do that, Dagger didn't know. Why Sara admitted her role in the healing process puzzled him even more. The face on the monitor swiveled again.

"Explain."

"Sara," Dagger cautioned.

Ignoring him, Sara told them about Nebraska and how Dagger almost died until she forced a veterinarian, the only physician she could find out in the middle of the corn fields, to give him four pints of her blood. She admitted that she could regenerate. Dagger washed his hands over his face and let out a long sigh.

"Regenerate?"

"Injuries, arms, legs."

There was more murmuring in the background. Dagger tried to decipher how many people were in the War Room; if he had to guess, he would say no more than ten.

"And your blood?"

"Yes. It can also regenerate, which is why I told the vet to take as much as she needed, much to her protests. My blood isn't all human either, which is why I am hesitant to end up in a hospital and risk having my blood taken. Now your turn," Sara said. "Tell us why you set us up. You knew Violet was being targeted and didn't warn us. You say you wanted us to find the operatives looking for her, but I think it was because you wanted to see what Dagger and I were capable of. Were you impressed?"

Connie blinked through the silence. Dagger suppressed a smile at Sara's bold accusation.

The image of Connie was replaced with a recording in

slow motion of Sara shifting from the strip ties. Just like with the recording from the hotel, Dagger was able to see firsthand what Sara could do. The slow motion image of the talons ripping through the clones' necks was riveting. Dagger almost felt guilty that he found it so fascinating.

"We can download everything you see, Six-One-Seven, when your chip is activated. That includes when your dark side emerges. Needless to say, we were quite astonished at Sara's capabilities. We would like to know more, like when you were first aware of this gift and how you have used it."

"This might take awhile." Sara looked at Dagger and nodded toward the bar in the corner of the room. He heard the story before, details about how her parents died in a fire when she was six years old, a fire started by a nervous mob of people who thought her father was the shapeshifter. She would also have to educate Mother on Native American mythology. "Could you make me a drink?"

"I think I will make both of us one."

24 Padre dropped by early the next morning after finally speaking to all of the lead investigating officers involved in the seven homicides. He stopped by the aviary and poked a finger gun at the macaw. Einstein eyed him wearily from the top of a fifteen-foot high tree in the corner. The room was forty by thirty feet and humidity controlled. A floor of fake grass was under the tree while food dishes and perches were strategically placed. Einstein had a virtual wonderland to play in. He flashed his bright blue, red, and gold wings at the cop, then made a finger gun with his claws.

"That's my boy," Padre said with a laugh.

"Coffee, Padre?"

"If Dagger made it, I'd rather keep the lining of my kidneys." Padre followed Sara into the kitchen and tossed a satchel on the granite kitchen table. It looked as though it survived the Pony Express.

"Nothing wrong with my coffee. Besides, we also have one of those single cup Keurig's."

"In that case, yes." Padre stripped out of a jacket that looked as tattered as his briefcase. "Getting too damn old for this." He sank with a sigh into a chair.

"Sergeant Flynn didn't change his mind?" Sara removed the floral arrangement from the center of the table and placed it on the counter.

"No. We're on our own." He pulled a thick manila folder

from the satchel, and placed the satchel on the floor.

"Thought we bought you a new briefcase?" Sara studied the floor as though expecting carpet beetles to come crawling out.

"I use it. Just save my satchel for information I want to hide from snoopers. Damn thing looks like it once held body parts." He turned a page on a notepad containing scribbling a physician would be proud of. "Don't worry. You won't have to decipher this. It's just my notes condensing what's in those reports after I spoke with investigating officers yesterday."

Dagger lifted his eyes toward Sara. "Does Einstein have fresh fruit and vegetables?"

Sara paused a beat, pulled out a chair next to Dagger, and sat down. "You aren't getting rid of me that quickly. And yes, Einstein has all that he needs."

Dagger looked to Padre for help. "Hey, don't look at me to dig your grave," the cop said.

"Have you identified the bodies in that warehouse fire?" Dagger asked.

Padre leveled a suspicious glare at Dagger. "And you are interested because...?"

"Just nosy." Dagger gave a shrug. What he really wanted to know was if the police found anything to tie him and Sara to the warehouse.

"Nothing left to identify. Can't get prints or DNA. Night shift caught a hit and run. Some woman was crossing the street or walking on the side of the rode and got clipped. Luther figures it happened earlier in the day. Must have been a jacked up truck 'cause we have to get a forensics reconstruction artist to create a composite picture. Poor thing."

Dagger kept his attention on the reports in front of him and not on the stand-in for Violet. "Seven women you said?"

"Yes. In a nutshell, all different occupations, different

parts of the country, different sizes and shapes. Similarities are—" Padre ticked them off on his fingers, "—no husbands, no children, all with long brown hair, all named Sara or any variation in spelling. Didn't seem to matter to the killer."

Sara picked up a couple of the reports and quickly scanned them. "The first victim was strangled. He literally ripped the throat out of the last one. Murder weapon wasn't anything sharp, so it appears he is getting more violent."

"More pissed," Dagger added. "He isn't finding the right Sara." He snapped his gaze to his partner. If ever there was a time to pack her bag and shipped her off to a safe haven like the reservation, it was now.

Padre stood and grabbed his cup. "I'll make that, Padre," Sara reached for his cup.

"No, no. I need to learn how to use modern technology. We're getting one for the office." He carried the cup to the counter and flicked through the different flavored coffees, selecting a hazelnut. "I reviewed the investigating officers' reports. They checked into relatives and friends of the victims. Everyone was cleared. One woman, age twenty-six, a dental hygienist who left work around six and never made it home. She was the third vic found in a ditch off a side road in Tucson, Arizona. Third found but Marty and I believe she was the first one killed. The heat and decomposition made it hard to determine time of death until the police discovered the last time friends and family saw her. She was strangled, larynx crushed. From that point on, everything escalated. Throats ripped, multiple stab wounds by an unidentified weapon. Course, Marty believes they were made by talons. Although the medical examiners could not pinpoint a precise time of death, Marty believes they were all killed around the full moon."

"DNA under any of their fingernails?" Sara asked. Dagger

handed her the first crime scene photo as he sifted through the rest.

"Nada." Padre pulled the cup from the machine, gave the aroma a whiff, nodded his approval and returned to his chair.

"Autopsy results?" Sara asked.

"No drugs ingested, no needle marks. A couple of them had been drinking. It seems the killer gets to know his targets' movements, knows their hangouts, knows when to strike, how not to be seen. If he is using some type of drug, it is undetectable."

"Any victims who got away, ones who got suspicious?" Dagger continued sifting through the folder, hoping to find that the women were uniquely different from his partner. But they were all young, had long dark hair, and were named Sara.

Sara held up a map with a red line from Arizona to Iowa. "Marty faxed that to me," Padre said. "Shows the trail and the location of the murders. Marty thinks the killer is headed here." Denial, fear, disbelief. Padre could see it all on their faces.

Dagger shook his head. "Paul Addison is dead. We made sure of it. Skizzy made sure of it. We killed him in his human form, just like Sherlock suggested. The ashes were scattered, dammit."

"His son would still be too young," Sara countered.

"That's the bigger puzzle." Padre turned a page in his notepad. He was saving the best for last. "Remember, Josie Andrews took off after Paul's death, left the hospital after giving birth."

"Right. And the doctor gave her a few names of orthopedic experts in the country because the baby was born with a severe club foot." Dagger winced as he saw the position of one of the victim's in the photo. Her head had been violently twisted. He knew personally how much strength that took to almost decapitate a person.

"Well, Marty kept track of her, found the surgeon she used in Arizona."

"That's where the first body was found."

"Correct, Sara. And lo and behold Marty discovered that seven months ago there was a murder suicide in Phoenix. A woman believed she was exorcising the devil from her son. It was Josie, and she had kept the name Andrews."

There was silence in the kitchen as that news bit settled in. Muffled sounds from the aviary could be heard. Water hissed in the freezer where the ice cube trays were being filled. Dagger slowly shuffled the reports into a stack and shoved them into the folder.

Padre continued. "Josie killed her son and herself, and right after that the murders started."

"Fuck me," Dagger whispered. "Please tell me Sherlock's notes have some answers in them because I hope to hell there isn't another Addison running around."

"Nothing so far. Marty is still wading through the stack of notes he found. If he finds anything of interest, he will give me a call. What I can't figure out is how long it must take the killer to find these women. That's a hell of a lot of research to look for a specific name, see if she is a brunette, discover her patterns, and all the other details of her life."

"Facebook," Sara said. "If you have a Facebook account, you can search for anyone by a first name, narrow it down to a city, check their photo on their home page, read their profiles and their posts and learn just about anything about that person. Where they are going for dinner, who they are dating, which gym they use, where they are going on vacation."

"People scream about the government or law enforcement invading their privacy, not realizing how much information they are posting." Dagger carried his empty cup to the counter

"Damn, I think you're right." Padre scribbled notes on the notepad. "People post their doctor appointments, stores where they shop, if they are going to be out of town, where and when they are meeting friends for drinks. Idiots. Thanks Sara. Now, as I said, he's escalating. As you can tell by the pattern, he started in Arizona and is moving this way." Padre gave an involuntary shiver, spilling coffee on his notepad. Dagger tossed him several napkins and carried his cup back to the table.

"By the way, are you free Saturday night, Dagger? I need a date." He blotted the spill as he told them about Logan's Galleria and the Nightfall exhibit.

"Did you see these paintings?"

"No. Sheila told me, and naturally she is curious if we kept details from the press. We never mentioned the damage to Officer Cambridge's body or that Tex Miller's head was impaled, nor the condition of his wife's body in the tree. We kept all those gory details away from public consumption, including photos of Sheila's condo after her assistant was murdered. So either someone in the M.E.'s office has taken up painting, which I doubt, or is giving out details to some sick art student. Anyway, the Galleria is charging a thousand bucks a head, no pun intended, to gain access. The grand opening of the gallery itself is at eight with drinks and some canapé shit. Then at ten the place empties out and the fun begins for those with thick billfolds. Want to buy my way?"

"Sure. The curiosity is killing me." Sara opened her mouth to speak but Dagger raised a finger. "No. Until we find out who this artist is and if he's tied to these killings, you are staying out of harm's way."

One perfect eyebrow jerked like a violin bow. "You can't stop me. Besides, the killings aren't even close to Indiana."

"Sara." Dagger leveled one of his all business glares which she brushed away with a wave of her hand.

Padre's phone rang. They waited as he answered and noticed the cop's face turn ashen as he hung up. "Marty found another possible victim from three days ago. This one is near Chicago."

25 "It finally arrived?" Carlton's reaction wasn't excitement at seeing the main attraction to Nightfall. It was more fear of what this centerpiece of the collection would look like. How could the paintings get any more bizarre than they already were?

"Yes. I haven't even looked at it myself." Mark Logan's three-piece suit was as close to work clothes as Carlton ever saw his boss wear. Every shirt was embroidered with the initials *ML* on the cuffs. "I was afraid it wouldn't get here before the gala event." He set the package against the wall and turned to the manager. "Tell me about the caterers. Is everything set for Saturday?"

"Uh, yes." Carlton's attention was riveted on the contents of the brown paper. "Caviar, jumbo shrimp cocktail, canapés of all types, the best wine and enough champagne for the toast."

"And the hired help?"

He tried to see if the packing tape had been removed. Carlton found it hard to believe that Logan hadn't taken a peek. "Four wait staff."

"Make it eight."

"Eight it is." His attention kept drifting back to the wrapped painting, the corners protected with Styrofoam. The artist always packed his paintings in boxes with Styrofoam cushion. Payment was made to an account in the Cayman

Islands and handled by Logan. If Logan knew what the artist's initials stood for, he wasn't sharing.

Carlton couldn't wait any longer. "Oh, for heaven's sake, Mark. Just unwrap the damn thing already and let me hang it."

Logan laughed. "I knew your curiosity would get the best of you."

"Have you seen it?"

"No. I've been saving the revelation to share with you."

The package was larger than any of the other paintings in the collection. Mark was careful unwrapping the treasure. This would be the first painting clients would see when they entered the room. Carlton hoped it wasn't a painting of a large jar with a head or body parts inside. How would the guests at the grand opening receive such a grotesque display?

With an exaggerated flourish, Mark removed the final paper, stared wide-eyed at the artwork before him, and slowly smiled. "What do you think?" He turned the painting toward Carlton.

The gallery manager gasped.

26 The file folder from Padre lay on the coffee table. The photos, autopsy and police investigation reports on the seven murders were in separate piles. Sara was trying to coax information from her laptop. Her hair was plaited in one long braid to keep it out of her way. Two days worth of research was scattered on the loveseat.

"What are you looking for?" Dagger took a seat next to her on the couch.

"These women didn't fight back. There wasn't any DNA under the nails yet the tox screens came up empty. There has to be something the police have missed. If the killer is that clever, he had to have a backup plan if he couldn't get them drunk."

"Any needle marks?"

Sara shook her head. "And chloroform would have shown up." She typed a few keys and scrolled through a web site. "Did you know you can drip fingernail polish remover on a cigarette and with just a few puffs your victim would feel the effects?"

"Really?"

She nodded at the words on a website. "Any type of fluid that contains alcohol can produce a PCP or Angel Dust-type reaction. These cigarettes are called fry, drank, water-water, and wetdaddy."

"So that means formaldehyde or fingernail polish remover. Any victim would smell it if the damn cigarette didn't blow up first."

"All you need is one or two puffs to create disorientation and drowsiness. Too much and the victim can lose consciousness."

"I don't recall the police finding any laced cigarettes at the crime scene."

"Smart killer would remove all evidence. What about the murder in Frankfort, Illinois? Did Padre send you that report?"

Dagger found a note attached with a paperclip to a report from the Frankfort, Illinois police department. "Sarah Eastman was a psychology student. Her body was found in a room at the Homestead Suites and Inn. The room was registered to a Professor Gavin Jacoby. Police were unable to confirm his existence nor could they find anyone by that name teaching in any of the colleges in the Chicago area. Video from the hotel lobby doesn't show a clear image of the professor." Dagger flipped to the next page and skimmed the typed notes. "Doorknobs, fixtures, and glasses in the hotel room all seemed to have been wiped down."

"What did she die from?"

Dagger flicked his gaze to Sara and back to the report. The medical examiner's report was too clinical to decipher, but he got the gist of it. "Consensual sex before she died. Crushed hyoid bone. Sliced carotid by an undetermined instrument. Course, we both know what that was."

Sara drilled him with a glare. "There's more."

How like her to read him like a book. Dagger sighed and set the report down. "Next to her body were her eyeballs."

Sara nodded as though she expected no less from the killer. "What about Sherlock's notes? You've been buried in those research papers on the Addison family that you kept after Sherlock's death. Anything new jump out at you?"

Sergeant Flynn hadn't wanted to keep any of the papers on witchcraft or wiccan spells. "Nothing we don't already know." Dagger thought back to Sherlock's research. It was believed Nathan Addison had been a witch. He'd delved into spells to conjure up the devil, even resorting to conducting human sacrifices. Nathan was born in 1835, and every generation since then produced a male family member born on a Friday the 13th during a full moon. Each of those males possessed the shifting ability and craving for blood. The only thing that drove them, other than their lust to destroy, was the desire for power and to carry on the family name. The next generation Addison grew stronger with the death of the previous shapeshifter. Paul Addison knew of Sara's abilities. He had communicated with her telepathically, the way Dagger could. However, with Addison, Sara hadn't been in a shifted form. She heard the voice in her sleep. So far he hadn't tried to communicate. Perhaps he was unaware of that skill. Perhaps he was unaware how much more powerful he could be if he could absorb Sara's abilities.

"What?" Sara saw the veins in Dagger's temples throbbing.

"You haven't heard his voice, have you?"

"No."

"You would tell me if you did, right?"

"Of course."

Dagger tried to hide his relief. "I just hope these are copycat killings. Unless Sherlock missed something in his research, there isn't any other explanation."

"Did Padre talk to Luther?"

"Luther vouches for all of his employees. Gretchen is the only one who helped with the autopsies on the six victims here in Cedar Point that are allegedly so well documented in those paintings I will see tonight." He stressed "I" and hoped that, just this one time, she would not get involved.

27

The moment Sheila stepped into the gallery, she knew all eyes would be on her, from her Manolo Blahnik pink alligator shoes that set her back sixteen hundred dollars, to the black backless sequin dress hitting mid-thigh. She clutched a pink handbag trimmed in diamond sequins and hoped she didn't slip in the drool of envy coming from the other women in the room.

One chapter of her finishing school lessons she received in her teens taught her how to feel the strongest stare riveted in her direction, and she could feel this one with her eyes closed. She blinked demurely in the direction of the lasers and caught the eyes of a man in a tuxedo with a white satin jacket. His eyes were dark, hair black with strands of silver, features chiseled, physique slender but with an air of nobility. Could he be Mark Logan? She let her eyes linger long enough to reveal her interest before sweeping her gaze to the other tuxedo and satin-clad guests.

As she hoped, Padre brought Dagger. Damn, he always looked good in a tux. He was sporting black square framed glasses and wore his hair in a ponytail. Was he trying to pass himself off as an art critic? And thank God, he didn't have his little secretary in tow. Sheila moved toward a waiter carrying a tray, and gave a slight smile and nod to friends of her parents from the country club.

"Miss Monroe? I'm so glad you could make it." Carlton held out a glass of champagne. "For you." Although Igor looked dapper in a black tux, his skin looked even whiter against the white shirt collar.

"Thank you." She took a polite sip, then smiled appreciatively. "Moet and Chandon Dom Perignon 2003? Excellent taste, Carlton."

"Only thirty-eight vintages have been produced. Mister Logan wanted to make a good impression."

Finishing School Lesson Number Two. Never look interested. She avoided lingering in the direction of the white tuxedo, which wasn't hard to do. A thin man in a black Stetson, undertaker suit, and bolo tie stood next to a punk rocker with short red hair, a short black dress and black ankle boots. A pink boa snaked her shoulders. Both the man and the woman wore pink tinted glasses.

Carlton followed her gaze. "Mister Harlan Bonaparte. He owns three thousand acres of bison in South Dakota and a casino in South Lake Tahoe. The way that little lady is clinging to him, my guess is that is NOT his granddaughter. But you could say he certainly has an eye for great art."

"Really? A sugar daddy and his role-playing escort? How tacky."

The dark-haired aristocrat slithered up as silent as a cat. "Carlton, the catering manager has a question. He's in the kitchen."

"Of course. Sheila Monroe, may I present Mark Logan, the owner of Logan Galleria. I will leave you in good hands."

"Mister Logan." Sheila held out her hand. "I should warn you. I'm a reporter with the *Daily Herald.*"

Logan smiled. "Well, then. This is my lucky night." As they shook hands, Logan cast a glance at her left hand. "I thought there was a reporter here from the Entertainment section of your newspaper."

"One can never get too much publicity, right?" Sheila

laughed. Not too loudly, though. Her mother wouldn't approve. And where were her parents? Her father claimed it was poker night, and nothing Anna Monroe could do or say would get his porky body into a tux. "But I'm here tonight as an art enthusiast."

Gabby Goldstein, the Lifestyle editor for the Entertainment section of the *Daily Herald* bustled over and grabbed Logan's arm. A bright yellow knit dress was not a good choice for a plump body with thick piano legs. "I'm so sorry, Sheila, dahhhling, but I need to kidnap this hunk for the cameraman who is waiting in the Landscape Room. I'm sure you don't mind."

Sheila forced a smile. *The witch.* "Of course not. I'm here to see the artwork." She leaned close to Logan's ear. "But I would like to see your mystery exhibit Carlton has told me so much about." She turned and sashayed away, confident his eyes were on all of her enhanced qualities. What made her smile even more was that she caught Dagger watching when she was speaking with Mark Logan. Was there a hint of jealousy in his eyes?

"What do you think Sheila is up to?" Dagger took a sip of champagne and winced. "Shit tastes like stale pretzels."

"I have no idea. She's your ex." Padre caught a waiter with a tray and exchanged the half empty champagne glass for a glass of wine. "If these paintings are as graphic as she says, there's no way we can let her know they depict actual details. If she catches wind of it, she just might suspect Professor Sherlock wasn't the killer."

"She won't hear it from me. Where are these paintings she mentioned?"

Padre nodded toward the French doors across from them.

"Access for interested buyers only." He flagged a waiter down and asked for ice.

"Ice, sir?"

"Yeah, ice. Something to make this hot piss cold."

The waiter rolled his eyes and left.

"I don't think we're used to the finer things in life, Padre."

"Someone is." Padre nodded toward the cowboy and the punk girl in the short black dress. The old cowboy kept drifting his hand down to the young woman's firm, round ass. She pulled his hand up and squeezed. The old man muffled a yelp. "How does someone like him get a shapely creature like her?"

"Must be rich." Dagger found himself drawn to the shapely calves and the firm ass where the cowboy's hand was slowly drifting again. The young woman extricated herself from him and made her way to the hall that led to the restroom. The cowboy studied his hand, probably making sure his bones were still intact.

Dagger tapped the invite against his hand and slowly moved toward the cowboy. Curious, Padre followed.

"What's your secret?" Dagger whispered.

The cowboy looked up at him, and straightened his hat. "What? You don't think it's true love?" Even the cowboy couldn't keep the chuckle out of his throat.

"I'm sure it is. But a word of caution, Skizzy. If you touch Sara's ass one more time, you'll have two fingers left for typing."

"Just playing a role."

"Skizzy?"

"Roger that."

Dagger moved away just as Sara reappeared. She caught the look in Dagger's eyes and turned away. She nestled close to her Sugar Daddy and snaked her arm through his.

"That's Skizzy and Sara?" Padre whispered. "Thought you told her to stay home."

"Yeah, that worked out well." Dagger saw a tray floating by carried by a waiter. The two men quickly deposited their glasses. "You wouldn't happen to have a beer, would you?" Dagger could have been asking for a glass of blood. "Thought so."

Padre studied the invite in his hand. It was black with a glowing full moon in the background of a dense forest. At ten o'clock, at the close of the event, those who paid the hefty fee, would be shown into the Nightfall exhibit.

28 After an hour of people watching and attempting to show an interest in the landscape paintings, bowls of fruit, flower meadows, and medieval half-dressed women, Dagger couldn't think of a time when he had been more bored. Other attendees appeared to give him a wide berth. He wasn't sure if it was the killer eyes, the ponytail, or the Middle Eastern tan. He thought he presented the image of an art critic with the black square framed glasses he wore. No disguise, though, could hide the danger oozing from every pore of his body. There were few people he cared to be in the company of; and the last thing he wanted to do was small talk with a bunch of snooty country club elites. His eyes took in the skylight above the lobby and the transom windows near the entrance. How soon until some art thief found a way into this gallery?

"Well, well."

Dagger winced. He knew that voice.

"Seems it's rare these days to see you without that little secretary of yours." Sheila retrieved a glass of champagne from a waiter on the move and slipped her arm through Dagger's.

"How many is that, Sheila?" Dagger's gaze raced around the room looking for Padre, Skizzy, and Sara.

"Only my second, but thanks for caring." He leveled a glare that made her release the hold on his arm. "I haven't seen you since Simon's anniversary. How long have you been lying about your 'only business, we work together, there's nothing going on' little slut you are living with?"

There was so much Dagger wanted to say, but he knew how Sheila manipulated. She wanted him to start an argument, to make a scene, to play the bad guy so she would look like the one wronged.

"I'm surprised she let you out of her sight tonight with all these rich women around."

Dagger saw Padre head his way. The cop made a quick ninety degree turn into the Landscape Room. How like Padre not to rescue him from Sheila's clutches.

"I take it you're sticking around for the Nightfall exhibit."

"Ahhh, changing the subject. Something you're good at. That and lying. I'm actually sticking around for Mark. We're going to dinner afterwards."

He shifted his gaze to Sheila's face. She had taken extra care in preparing for tonight. The bling rattling around both wrists were probably gifts to herself. The makeup was flawless, as was the hair. The outfit was a one-of-a-kind. Sheila would never chance someone else showing up in an identical outfit. It was a pity she was so vindictive and self-centered. And then there was the engagement ring she refused to remove. At least now she wore it on her right hand.

"Good. Maybe you can get some information out of him."

Padre finally returned and caught the tail end of the conversation. "Yes. I'm sure Miss Monroe can use her feminine wiles on him. If anything, just get us the name of the artist. It would be interesting to pick the brain of a serial killer enthusiast."

"Are you two trying to pimp me out?" There was anything but humor in her remark. If anything, Sheila was downright seething.

Dagger knew for a fact there were few lines she wouldn't

cross to get a story. "You keep telling us you're an ace reporter, an expert at digging the truth out of the most challenging interviews. We aren't telling you to sleep with him."

Sheila stepped close and straightened the collar of Dagger's tux. "You would be jealous, wouldn't you? Admit it."

Dagger stepped back, gave her one of his patented death stares, and walked away, just as the lights dimmed.

Carlton appeared in the center of the room, standing on the mosaic Logan crest embedded in the floor. "Thank you all for coming. Our hours are on the pamphlet by the door. We hope you will come back soon."

"No one knows Dagger better than me, Padre. Soon he will tire of his young Barbie doll and come crawling back. I am the only woman for him."

Padre rolled his eyes.

The lights flickered again as the guests started filing out, leaving no fewer than four dozen attendees behind anxiously awaiting the presentation of the Nightfall exhibit.

29 Mark stood by the front entrance thanking the guests for coming. Once Carlton locked the doors, Mark moved to the French doors.

"Ladies and gentlemen, what you are about to see is a talent beyond your imagination. The artist captures the dark side of humanity. I received his first painting at my gallery in San Francisco. This was followed up with a phone call and an apology from the artist. He was a recluse and did not venture out much. When I expressed an interest in seeing all of his artwork, the paintings were delivered again at the San Francisco gallery, and then at the Chicago gallery. I have since closed those two and opened the gallery here in Cedar Point. I personally believe the artist's anonymity adds to the uniqueness of his paintings. To me, he is just a number." He gave a little laugh. "Actually, a bank account number in the Cayman Islands."

A trickle of laughter filtered through the room. Dagger saw Skizzy and Sara hanging back, as were he and Padre. Dagger wanted to wait until the crowd thinned.

"I do request," Mark continued, "that no photos be taken. So please turn off your phones and leave your cameras with Carlton if you have one." Mark turned, grabbed the door handles, and pulled open the French doors. "I give you… Nightfall."

Gasps and murmurs wove like a tsunami through the hall as guests were led into the private collection in groups of four. Tiki torches rested on top of tall pillars and cast eerie shadows onto the ceiling. Brass lights above each painting added to the glow from the torches to provide the only light in the room.

Dagger was able to see over the heads of the group in front. The focal point, the large painting that hit visitors the minute they stepped into the room, was of a woman in a see-through white gown standing in a moonlit forest. Half of her face was painted with features of a hawk, the other half, a wolf. It was clear, in Dagger's mind, that the painting depicted Sara's shapeshifting abilities. He looked for Sara and saw her near the door. She did a stutter-stop when she saw the large painting.

One woman pushed through the crowd mumbling, "Absolutely disgusting." She stopped in front of Logan and Carlton. "You should be ashamed of yourselves putting such filth amid all these other beautiful paintings."

"I gather that our use of the words 'the dark side of human nature' and 'not for the faint at heart,'" Carlton said, "were not grasped by your feeble mind, madam."

She straightened her jacket and glowered. "My friends at the country club will hear about this."

"I certainly hope so," Mark said under his breath as she stormed toward the exit. "Curiosity always brings in more customers."

Bringing up the end of the line, Dagger stopped in front of the portrait of the woman with two faces. He could even vouch that the artist caught the curves of Sara's body under the gauzy white fabric quite accurately.

"That's different," Padre said.

Mark sidled up to them. "Have you ever heard of—?"

"A shapeshifter." Dagger stepped closer, studying the detail, how it appeared that the wind was ruffling the feathers of the hawk. "Usually artists get the clearest view of their subject by seeing it up close and personal. Are we to assume the artist has seen a shapeshifter?"

"Hieronymus Bosch didn't have to visit Hell to paint *The Fall of the Rebel Angels*. William Blake may have been known for his romantic poetry, but his watercolor of the great red dragon from the *Book of Revelations* hardly means he witnessed the dragon up close and personal. And let's not forget how many artists were influenced by *Dante's Inferno*."

"Point taken." Although Dagger hated to say it, the guy knew his stuff. Still, he didn't trust him. Mark Logan had to have met the artist, probably knew where he lived and how to contact him. Why would he take a chance on a complete stranger? Dagger made his way to the next painting, trying not to pay too much attention to what was obviously a portrait of Sara.

Padre spent considerable amount of time studying each of the paintings that were replicas in color of the actual murders. His gaze drifted to the initials in the bottom right-hand corner. "So the artist never gave you his full name?"

"No."

The cowboy and his hooker girlfriend appeared, having viewed all of the collection. "My darling here is really fond of this painting. How much for the woman with two animal faces?" Skizzy pulled out his wallet as though he carried thousands of dollars on him at all times.

"He hasn't set a price yet on any of the paintings. We want to garner as much attention on the entire collection as possible."

"Really?" The cowboy rubbed a hand across the stubble on his chin. He looked like a short, skinny Colonel Sanders. "Even a million bucks wouldn't entice him?"

Mark laughed. "We haven't decided yet whether to sell the

entire collection or each piece separately. It's up to the artist."

Dagger and Padre drifted toward the rest of the collection. They wanted to be the last to view the paintings in order to study those in attendance. It was possible the artist wanted to see the reaction to his artwork. So far not one person looked suspicious.

The cowboy tried another approach. "What about portraits for hire? I'd like to have a large portrait of myself to pass on to my kin." He pulled Sara in close. If he squeezed her any tighter, her nipples would have left an imprint on his chest. She smiled adoringly, but Dagger could swear he read "step back you pervert" on her lips.

Padre nodded toward the wall that held several of the paintings. "By the looks of those, I'm not sure I would want to see how my portrait turned out."

30 "So, what did you think?" Mark waited until after dinner before asking Sheila's opinion of the exhibit. Up to now, their conversation had been peppered with insignificant questions about Cedar Point from Mark. Sheila tried unsuccessfully to get information on Mark's background. Other than the names of all the countries he visited to purchase artwork and how he had a two-month marriage after college, she'd learned very little.

"The paintings in the gallery are exquisite. If you're asking about the Nightfall exhibit, though, I have to admit there is something eerily familiar about some of the more—" she struggled for a word that wouldn't offend, "—graphic ones."

"How so?" He twirled his wine glass and waited.

"I admit to telling a small fib." Sheila held her fingers up just a scant distance apart. "I cover the crime scene for the *Daily Herald*. And I have to admit, those paintings are similar to murders that took place here in Cedar Point."

"Really." Mark coaxed a few drops of wine from his glass, then set the glass down. "I, myself, have painted a picture from something I read about in the paper. I once saw a photo of an iron worker on top of the world's tallest building in Dubai. I used a similar scene, placing an angel on the beam, wings extended, ready for flight. It gave me the idea and didn't necessitate a trip to Dubai to have an eyewitness view."

The waiter deposited the bill on the table and left.

"Are you sure the artist isn't local?"

Mark shrugged. "If he's local, why travel all the way to San Francisco just to have his paintings delivered to the gallery there?"

"These were local murders. One would assume he read about them while living here."

"You sell your newspaper short. I believe the *Daily Herald* is available even in California."

"True. One of our homicide detectives was at the gallery tonight. I wouldn't doubt that he rushed back to his office to dig out the files from the archives."

"Did they find the killer?" He pulled out a credit card, slipped it into the slot in the black folder, and set it near the edge of the table. The waiter swooped it up as he passed.

"Yes. A college professor who made a living out of studying the occult, I'm told. He committed suicide."

"Well, that certainly doesn't make me feel comfortable seeing that I have never met this artist. Now you have me wondering how he knows the details of these murders. My guess would be he has a friend in the police department, perhaps. However, if the murders garnered nationwide attention, he could be from anywhere."

"What do you suppose C.A. stands for? Please tell me it isn't Carlton."

Mark tipped his head back and laughed. His eyes shone with amusement. "Don't let Carlton hear you say that." The waiter returned, set the black folder on the table, and thanked them. Mark retrieved his credit card and slipped it into his wallet. "Unfortunately, I don't know of any artist with those initials, and they don't necessarily have to be initials. Some artists use an insignia or a flower. If you would like, I'll do a little sleuthing myself. I'm sure he will be in touch to find out how the exhibit went."

"Did any of the paintings sell?"

"They aren't for sale yet. We are determining interest first. The artist actually hasn't set a price. Mister Harlan Bonaparte expressed an interest in the focal point of the exhibit, the woman with two animal faces. He offered a million dollars."

"The skinny cowboy whose date was young enough to be his granddaughter." Sheila quickly returned her jaw to a dignified position. "I would have never guessed he was that wealthy. Never saw him before, and I know just about every rich person in town. Half of them were there tonight."

"According to Carlton, he owns a casino and lots of land in South Dakota. Unfortunately, I had to tell him the painting wasn't for sale. And to tell you the truth, I have taken quite a liking to it myself."

"I don't think I need another drink." Padre set his empty glass on the bar and glanced at the red wig lying on the bar stool. "Even Sheila didn't recognize Sara tonight, although I don't understand why she had to go incognito."

It was best that Padre think Sara disguised herself so Dagger wouldn't recognize her, rather than the artist, should he have been lurking among the attendees. They walked Padre to the door. It was after midnight and other than confirming that the paintings included many of the details not shared with the public, they weren't sure where to go from here. "I just hope your ex has better luck finding out the name of the artist."

"You didn't let her know all the details in the paintings were authentic, did you?"

Padre turned to Sara. "Do I look like someone who could be swayed by a beautiful woman?"

"Yes," Dagger said.

Padre tapped Sara's chin. "Only you, *precioso*." He waved a stack of photos in the air. "And thanks for taking pictures of everyone there, Sara. Would have never known your glasses could take pictures. Skizzy's cleverness belies his appearance."

They said their goodnights and watched as Padre drove his car down the drive and out of the gate.

"You did keep copies of all the pictures, right?"

"Absolutely." Dagger wrapped his arms around her and settled his chin on the top of her head. "We need to do more research into this artist."

"Because he knows too much about the murders?"

Dagger pulled away and studied Sara. There was no mistaking the concern on her face when she saw the paintings. Although Padre, Skizzy, and Simon knew about the Addison curse, Dagger was the only one who knew why Addison had been interested in Sara. "No. Because he knows too much about you."

The gray hawk circled slowly, its underwing coverts trapping the rising air currents. Below it could see one car in the parking lot of Logan's Galleria. It drifted lower, folded its forty-inch wingspan and settled on top of one of the Victorian street lights. The hawk listened for movements behind closed up shops, gazed through darkened windows for signs of shop owners working late. Not even one police car was monitoring the area.

Dagger preferred that Sara not shift until this entire puzzle was solved, but she was getting more hard-headed every day, in Dagger's opinion. Instead, they agreed on more ground rules. They were not to communicate telepathically when she shifted, except in emergencies. Should an emergency occur, under no circumstance should they use their names. That was how Paul Addison had learned about them in the past. If he somehow miraculously returned from the grave, Dagger didn't want Addison to be aware they were onto him.

A black Lexus barreled down the road and pulled into the parking lot next to the gallery. Through the darkened windows the hawk could see two people in the front seat. The woman leaned over and kissed the man on the cheek. Before she could pull away, the man drew her closer and kissed her on the mouth. She pressed her body against his. The hawk could hear their hearts beating, could hear her thanking him for dinner. He asked the woman if she would like to follow him to his hotel room for a nightcap. She said maybe another time.

The two emerged from the Lexus, and the man walked Sheila to her Jaguar parked next to the building. The lights flashed on the Jag, he opened her car door, and she slipped inside.

He watched as she pulled from the lot. Sheila wasted little time dialing someone. The hawk's excellent visual acuity could make out the number on the dashboard. Sheila was calling Dagger.

The hawk returned its attention to the man. Mark Logan unlocked the front door and entered. The hawk lifted from the light pole and flew to the top of an air conditioning unit hanging on the side of a jewelry store, which gave it a clear view through the transom windows. Mark went straight to the Nightfall exhibit. The lights above each painting were on, but even from this distance the hawk could see each brushstroke of the painting of the woman with two faces. Mark studied the artwork for several seconds, absorbing the intricate details.

The hawk noticed the light filtering from the roof. It lifted off and landed near one of the skylights above the exhibit.

It watched as the man brought out his cell phone and took several pictures, as though not trusting the details to memory. He slipped his phone into his pocket, turned off the lights, and exited the gallery. He sat in his car for several minutes staring into the dark before starting the engine and pulling away.

"So he didn't make any calls? Didn't meet anyone? Didn't have anyone staying with him?"

"Sheila went to dinner with him. I saw her when they returned and he dropped her off at her car." Sara dried her damp hair with a towel. It was almost two in the morning and all she wanted to do was sleep. "He didn't appear to have a laptop at the gallery. I followed him as far as the Suisse Hotel, but he didn't call anyone or receive any calls."

"Sheila didn't learn anything at dinner other than he was shocked that the paintings depicted actual murders. According to Mark, he doesn't contact the artist, the artist contacts him. Pretty strange not to know someone's full name. Even the off shore bank account has a fictitious company name of C.A. Holdings. The A could stand for Addison. Hard to say. Mark has Sheila's phone number so Sheila expects to see more of him." Dagger pulled down the covers and climbed into bed.

Sara returned the towel to the bathroom and then climbed in next to Dagger. "There has to be a way we can find out all the incoming calls on Mark's phone. Skizzy can do that, right? Padre would need a court order, but not Skizzy. He can walk past him and clone it, or however he does it."

Dagger pulled his phone from the nightstand and sent Skizzy a text message. "This artist could be using a burner phone. Might not be able to trace his calls. If anyone can dig into it, it's Skizzy." He set the phone down, and turned off the lights.

Sara settled in close as Dagger wrapped his arms around her. "By the way, remind me to break both of Skizzy's arms tomorrow. He was getting just a little too touchy feely." He could feel Sara smiling in the dark.

"He asked me to marry him."

Dagger laughed at that. "Did you tell Skizzy you're already taken?"

"He said he falsified a marriage license, so he can also falsify divorce papers."

Dagger laughed again. "Guess I'll have to break both of his arms so he can't do that." He threaded his fingers through her damp hair. It felt like silk as it brushed against his arm. Long, dark hair. Women named Sara. The body found in Frankfort was the most recent victim. How long did the killer research her routine? Did the killer have his next victim picked out?

By the way," he whispered, "we have a conference call with Marty at nine tomorrow morning. Padre will be here, too."

While he stared at the ceiling, nagging thoughts running through his head, Sara was already asleep.

31

They were seated at the kitchen table the next morning, clustered around Padre's cell phone which was propped up on a napkin holder.

Padre arrived early, hoping to eat whatever Sara was making for breakfast. Since this meeting had the makings of a long one, she made a full pot of coffee. With the plates cleared away and coffee cups filled, they waited for Marty's call.

The kitchen smelled of bacon and cinnamon with a hint of lilac as the breeze from the opened windows carried the odors from the front yard. Vases of fresh cut flowers were in the living room and each of the bathrooms. How she could split her attention between gardening and murder, Dagger failed to understand.

Marty's voice blared from the speaker phone. "Well, warm up your engines because this is going to knock your socks off. I found a few passages in the research Professor Sherlock was doing. This has never happened before, I mean the whole Addison family thing, so he delved deeper into the curse itself to see if it jumps generations."

"Curse?" Padre asked.

"For want of a better word. Let me start with what we do know. When Paul Addison was killed he left behind a wife and a baby boy who was born at the exact hour that a full moon and a Friday the thirteenth coincided. Now, she did move to Arizona to be close to that pediatric orthopedic surgeon so her infant could be treated for his club foot. I sent Padre a copy of the newspaper article. Neighbors reported she ranted about how her son was possessed. Josie drowned him in the tub before slitting her own wrists."

"With the death of the mother and boy last year, that should have been the end of the lineage," Dagger said.

"My thoughts, too. But when the murders of these young women started around the time of the murder-suicide, I thought it was too much of a coincidence, that all of the victims were named Sara." Marty coughed, apologized, then sniffed. "Damn allergies." They heard what sounded like a swipe of a hankie against skin. "Sorry about that. Anyway, I got curious. I may be retired, but the cop in me hadn't retired. Talked to some of the neighbors to find out Josie's state of mind. What would set her off? Why now, when she was living with Paul Addison without a hint that there was something strange about him?" Marty sneezed, then blew his nose.

Dagger wanted to tell him to speed it up, to get to the punch line. Unless Marty found proof that Paul Addison somehow reassembled his ashes and returned to his murderous ways, he was going to chalk this up to coincidence.

"Found out from a neighbor that a man visited Josie the day before she killed herself and her son. The neighbor told the police this at the time, but they thought nothing of it. Not much of a description of the man. Josie kept to herself so for all they knew it could have been a church member, insurance salesman, relative. Well, the word relative struck me for some reason."

They could hear Marty shuffling papers. Dagger's phone rang. He checked the screen. It was Casey.

"Make it quick," Dagger barked. He listened and nodded. "Yeah. I'll drop off the rent next time I'm in the area." Casey's voice increased in volume. "I know, cash. But can't you wait until tomorrow?" Dagger stole a glance at Sara. Casey obviously mentioned her name.

"I'll go." Sara rose from the table. "You can handle things here."

"All right," Dagger said with a sigh. "Yes, she'll bring enough cash for six months rent. Anything to shut you up." He pushed the off button and shook his head. "Sorry about that. I'm so used to paying in advance that I lose track of when the rent is due."

"I'll be back." Sara grabbed her jacket and keys.

"Take the cash from the safe," Dagger called out.

"Okay." Marty cleared his throat again. "According to Sherlock's notes, he started to check the hospital where Madeline Addison gave birth. 'Course, he died before he could finish. I know a cop in Sturgis, Michigan, so I asked Lenny to do me a favor and nose around. He got the name of the obstetrician. Doctor Pushing, save the jokes, died several years ago, but the nurse remembered the case quite well. Madeline gave birth to twins."

"Could it get any better than this?" Dagger couldn't help but laugh. "The evil twin brother scenario. Why is it both of them weren't working in tandem the last time Addison was in town or wreaking havoc in another part of the country where it would have garnered the attention of the police?"

"There can be only one," Padre said quietly. "Remember, the moment Paul Addison died, his son was born and he inherited the family curse. His uncle couldn't obtain his full power with the child still alive. I bet he filled Josie's head with all kinds of satanic shit and she went off the deep end. Hell, maybe the uncle made it look like murder-suicide."

"Wait, did this brother not know he was an Addison?"

Dagger asked.

"Paul didn't even know he had a brother," Marty replied. "The reason this nurse, Anna Connelly, recalled the case so clearly is that Madeline insisted her husband not be told. She immediately gave up one of the boys for adoption. Nurse Connelly said she never saw a woman so fearful before. So Doctor Pushing told the husband there was only one baby. He wrote on the adoption papers that the second baby was abandoned, parents unknown."

"Interesting." Dagger grabbed the carafe of coffee. "I take it Madeline knew about the curse and what was in store for one of her boys. Do we know who adopted him?" He set the carafe in the center of the table and sat down.

"Nurse Connelly said there was a Little Shepherd Adoption Agency working with the hospital, but it has since closed up."

Padre patted his pocket, pulled out his cigarette pack and tossed it on the table. "What about the adoption records?"

"All of the records were transferred to a storage room in the basement of the hospital."

"What state are we talking about?" Dagger thought if it wasn't too far that he would just take a little drive. "Michigan, right?" He picked up his cell phone and tapped out a search.

"Right. It would have been 1970," Marty replied.

"Got it. Damn. Michigan only has open adoption records prior to 1955 or after 1980." Dagger set his phone back on the table. "What city again?"

"Sturgis, Michigan." Marty coughed up another lung.

"That's about a two hour drive." Dagger didn't have anything pressing that couldn't wait. "Sara and I can drive over as soon as she gets back. What's the name of the hospital?"

They could hear the flipping of pages through the speaker phone. "Fayette Hospital." Marty waited a beat before asking, "How do you plan to get a look at those sealed records?"

"You forget who you're asking," Padre said.

"I'm still confused. Why was Paul interested in Sara, and how would a brother who knew nothing about Paul suddenly have a fascination about all women named Sara? Did he have an unrequited love for her?"

"You could say that," Dagger replied.

"I think he was trying to get back at Dagger by fixating on Sara. After all, Dagger was his major obstacle." Padre looked outside the kitchen window and down the drive to the front gate. "Shouldn't she be back by now?"

Dagger pressed the heels of his hands to his eyes. He felt like his head was going to explode. He was the only one who knew Paul's true interest in Sara, but he couldn't say anything. He typed out a quick text to Sara. It shouldn't have taken that long to toss money on the bar and leave.

"I think I remember seeing something else about that." They could hear more shuffling of papers in the background. "Now remember, this is just Sherlock's opinion. We already determined that only one person at a time could have the power. When one Addison dies, he not only passes on the power, but he also passes on his memories. Again, Sherlock's theory. Now my theory is, this new guy suspected he wasn't quite right. Maybe he killed neighborhood dogs in his youth, dreamed of ways to harm people. Maybe his adoptive parents took him to a shrink. Maybe whatever Paul was doing when he was alive, his twin could see in his dreams. Either way, the killings of the women named Sara started after Josie killed her son and herself. Now there was truly only one. Any questions?"

Marty's theory was met with shocked silence.

32 Dagger checked his phone again. It wasn't like Sara not to reply. He kept his eye on the flashing red light on the Lincoln Navigator's dashboard.

According to the map, Sara was in the office above Casey's bar. An earring Dagger gave her several years ago contained a tracking device. If she ever got into trouble when she shifted, he needed to be able to locate her. Now it came in handy even when she wasn't in one of her shifted forms.

Knowing Sara, she was probably cleaning, and the vacuum cleaner prevented her from hearing the phone. If only the sense of uneasiness hadn't crept into every fiber of his body, he wouldn't have given it a second thought.

He pulled to a stop in the alley behind the bar and climbed the wrought iron stairs. The door to the office was unlocked. "Sara?" There wasn't anyone seated at the desk. He was certain she wouldn't be sitting at the bar with Casey while leaving the office door unlocked. He flipped the light on in the bathroom. It was empty. He heard a soft moan from the bedroom. Out of habit he pulled the Kimber from its holster, stepped closer to the darkened room, and flipped on the light switch. Sara was lying on the bed, her jacket tossed on a chair in the corner.

"Sara." Dagger holstered the Kimber and sat on the bed. "Sara? What happened."

"Dagger?" She tried to raise up on one elbow, but fell back

against the pillow. "So tired."

"What happened to you?"

She struggled to open her eyes. "Can't remember. I came here to get money from the safe, I think."

"Was someone here? Did you see anyone? Hear anything?" His first thought was BettaTec. Were there other operatives prowling the streets? Had Sara been followed? Did they know where he and Sara lived?

Sara struggled again to sit up. Dagger helped her and propped pillows against the headboard. He checked her hairline for a bruise or bump. "I unlocked the door and was going to get the money from the safe." She raked a hand through her hair. Her fingers touched a sore spot on her neck. "Sting. I felt a sting."

"Let me see." If BettaTec was involved, he half expected to see a scar on the back of Sara's neck. He lifted her hair and saw a red dot that was slightly swollen. "Was someone here or did he follow you in?"

She fell back against the pillows, fighting the fatigue invading her body. "Lemons. I remember the smell of lemons."

Dagger slowly straightened. "Like lemon wax?" His gaze dropped to Sara's left arm. He would have missed it except the overhead lights made it glisten. It was a clear, round bandage in the crook of her elbow.

"Sonofabitch!" Dagger tore out of the office and launched himself down the wrought iron stairs, taking them two at a time. The back door to the Hideaway slammed against the wall as he barged in and down the hallway into the sitting area, his leather trench coat billowing behind like large, black wings. Two men seated at the end of the bar peered over their beer glasses. It didn't take long for the anger to build, and Dagger was sure the killer look in his eyes was the reason the two patrons were inching away from their seats.

Casey paused in mid-wipe. Every piece of wood in the place glistened from the endless layers of lemon wax. "Hey, Dagger, want a drink?"

Before the last consonant left Casey's mouth, Dagger reached across the bar and hauled Casey's two hundred and fifty pound carcass up and over the gleaming wood, then tossed him onto the pool table as though he were a twenty pound sack of mulch. He landed with a thud. "Holy, Christ. What the hell?"

Dagger heard the rush of footsteps and the slamming of the front door as the patrons left their drinks and high-tailed it out of there. "What did you do to her?"

"Who her?" Casey's eyes were wild with fear at the look in Dagger's eyes and the inhuman strength.

Dagger had been too enraged to notice it when he first walked in, but now that Casey was in front of him, he saw the stats next to his head like a cartoon text box. Now the demon was furious. Casey was BettaTec. How could Dagger not have known? Of course. Dagger hadn't been able to see the stats before. He grabbed fistfuls of fabric, hauled Casey's body off the pool table, and slammed him against a wall, the bar owner's feet barely touching the floor. "You know damn well who I'm talking about. You're with BettaTec, you sonofabitch."

Casey slowly broke out in a broad smile. "You think you ended up in Cedar Point by accident? You were programmed to come here, to rent a room from me." His brows furrowed as he studied Dagger's eyes, the pupils expanding until that was all anyone could see. The various shades of black moved and shifted, as though something stirred. "Holy shit." Casey's legs backpedaled, hitting the wall as he tried to distance himself, but the effort was futile. "I was told you were exceptional, but hell. Look at your eyes. It's like you ain't got any whites to them. Fuckin' A, man."

A bottom line on Casey's stats flashed red. *Deceased.* Dagger cocked his head as though it were a word the demon had never seen before. He ripped the Kimber from its holster and pressed it against Casey's neck. They programmed him to come to Cedar Point? Casey had to be lying. Dagger could have stopped at any city after leaving Nebraska. Casey was using a delay tactic. "What did you do to Sara? Tell me now or so help me…"

"RELEASE HIM."

The shout came from behind him. The shock at the familiarity made Dagger loosen his grip. Casey dropped with a thud and sat there catching his breath. The voice sounded like Connie's, and Dagger wouldn't have been surprised to turn and find the android face floating in the air. He slowly turned, arm outstretched, the Kimber pointed at a woman who looked nothing like Connie. She was no more than five and a half feet tall and dressed in a dark suit, white blouse, sensible shoes. He half expected her to click her heels releasing a knife from the toe of her shoe. Hair salt and pepper was cut short, but there was no mistaking that she was a striking woman. He guessed her to be anywhere between forty and one hundred in age. The eyes looked as though they carried a century of secrets. But if she was with BettaTec, where were the stats? The computer chip in his head started doing a facial recognition. It was then that her stats appeared with a red flashing word –*Deceased.* He was looking at Mother.

33 "Leave us." This time it wasn't a shout; and it was meant for Casey, who scrambled up and left through the front door. Mother gave the Kimber a passing glance and a shake of her head. "You always did like your toys." She motioned with her head. "Sit." She pulled out a chair and sat at one of the tables.

Dagger felt his pulse slowly return to normal and looked at the Kimber as though wondering how it got in his hand. He holstered it, kicked out a chair, and sat a safe distance away. "You did say you own this property. How stupid of me to not think Casey worked with you. What's confusing, though, is why yours and Casey's stats say you are deceased."

"As far as the Director knows, we are dead. There were tunnels under the facility in Nebraska which he blew up. The alliance I assembled took another route, set up a facility near here."

"So, what Casey said, that I was programmed to come here. Is it true?"

"Yes. We set up this facility before we left Nebraska. I couldn't let my star pupil too far from my sight."

"You mean control." Dagger felt numb. Ten years from now he could imagine his head instead of Connie's floating above the desk. He should have never taken the copper necklace off. But then Casey was always here to report back. He looked up from the glossy table top and studied the woman sitting across from him. So calm and cool. So in control, while his fingers were balling into fists. "Who else besides Casey?"

"Only Casey and Violet. With Violet's position compromised, your contact will now be Casey."

"Why do I need him? Why did I need Violet? I have the computer upstairs if I ever need to communicate with you."

"You still don't trust us and you aren't familiar or skilled with your newfound abilities yet. That is why you need Casey."

"And lard ass is going to help with that?"

Mother's hardened gaze softened and the corners of her lips curled. "Since we didn't have the computer system up and running in order to communicate with you, Casey was our eyes and ears."

"Your spy."

She ignored his comment. Too many thoughts cluttered Dagger's head. He had so many questions, yet something didn't feel right.

"Was I programmed to cross paths with anyone else?"

"Like your friends, Simon and Skizzy? No. And not Sara either."

"Sara. It was you. What did you do to her?"

"She was never in any danger. I took a sample of her blood."

"What?" Dagger was ready to launch himself across the table.

"We took four pints so it's understandable that she might be a little unsteady." Mother smiled. It was a grandmotherly smile meant to make people feel at ease. Dagger wasn't buying it.

"And you wonder why I don't trust you."

"I was sure neither you nor Sara would be very receptive to the request. What else could we do?"

"And exactly what would you need it for?"

Mother's eyes traveled the blighted bar. "I'm a scientist.

I'm always curious to understand things I'm not familiar with. Should the Director become aware of Sara's abilities, he would certainly go to great lengths to take more than her blood."

"Which he would never know about if you hadn't kept the video of her shifting."

"He has his ways. Sara makes one slip, someone with a cell phone takes a picture, she has to be careful. One never knows when or where his operatives will appear, so it's a good thing your chip is now functioning. Can you imagine what the Director could do with an army of shifters?"

"So anything he creates, you want to counter. Checkmate."

"Exactly, but I can sense that your anger hasn't subsided. In due time, you will understand why we make the decisions we make."

"Are you telling me all you took was Sara's blood? Because if you planted a chip in her, I swear—"

"Casey only took the blood."

"And what did he do with it?" Dagger's gaze dropped to Mother's pockets. There weren't any bulges, she wasn't carrying a case of any type.

"Samples are already being processed."

Dagger's gaze drifted to the door that led to the kitchen.

"Nowhere near here, Six-One-Seven."

"And why couldn't we have just come to your facility, especially if you claim to be close?"

"Security reasons. Any BettaTec operative could threaten the lives of your friends unless you told them where the facility was. It's for yours and their protection that you not know the location."

There was that feeling again. Something wasn't quite right, but Dagger couldn't put his finger on it. In a way, it was familiar, whether a gesture Mother made or the tilt of her head. "Now that you have Sara's blood, as a show of good faith, you could destroy the videotape of her shifting."

"I could."

That was way too easy. Mother blinked, much the same way Connie would. It was more like an innocent feline with its paw clamped over the throat of a mouse. "You still have the second one from the warehouse. You sneaky bitch."

"You do need to watch your language. We may destroy the second, but the first is leverage. It certainly shows more of her talents. Besides, we need to make sure both of you will continue to work with us. You are too independent to trust. I made you that way, something that I don't regret. However, it does put us at a disadvantage." She pushed her chair away and stood. "Oh, and by the way, if you ever see a green light in your peripheral vision, it means I need to talk to you."

Dagger rose, assuming Mother was ending the meeting. Green light? Now she expected him to be at her beck and call? He looked through the small window in the front door, expecting a black limo to show up to whisk mother back to her bunker.

"So when can I...?" But when Dagger turned his attention back to her, Mother was gone. "What the hell?" He rushed down the hall and opened the back door. Nothing. He checked the kitchen, the restroom. Still nothing. Dagger opened the front door, grabbed Casey's arm, and yanked the big guy back into the bar. "Where the hell did she go?"

Casey didn't look over Dagger's shoulder, which told Dagger the brute wasn't surprised Mother did a disappearing act. And then it hit him. "She was a hologram!"

"Bet you're about ready for a drink now." He moved behind the bar and pulled a cold bottle of Miller Lite from the cooler. Dagger kept staring at him, remembering the holograms he and Sara saw in Nebraska. They had looked so real that Dagger hid behind a pillar waiting for the crowd to leave. When Sara showed up, she saw the slight difference right away. He wasn't convinced until Sara walked right through them. No wonder Mother's stats didn't appear and he had to retrieve them by use of his microchip.

Dagger accepted the beer and took a long swallow. Casey opened a beer for himself and took a long pull. "Where's Sara's blood sample?"

"Like Mother said. On its way to the lab. Mother likes medical histories on everyone, although I'm not sure why she wanted so much of Sara's blood."

Dagger ignored the comment. "I doubt she used the lab down the street which tells me you know where the facility is. And since you're the only Alpha operative in town, I'm betting you have it here somewhere."

"Alpha. I like that name. Kinda like an alpha male."

"I doubt it." Dagger took another long swallow, his mind conjuring images of a mad scientist's lab in Casey's basement. "Makes me wonder why Mother purchased all this property. Maybe there is something below ground level no one can see."

Casey twirled the beer bottle on the highly polished bar surface, seeing the rings of moisture it created. "How long have I known you now? Seven, eight years? Well, I was with BettaTec when you were in diapers. I know what the Director is capable of, and I know what measures he takes to get information. Need-to-know basis. That's the motto to live by. Keeps you safe that way."

"And Violet? Is she back at the facility?"

"Reassigned to another location."

Dagger pointed the bottle toward Casey. "You drove the van that killed the kid. And I bet you were the one who hustled Violet out of town."

Casey said nothing, but his smile spoke volumes.

"And where were you and Violet when the Demko clones came to town? Their mission was to kill a cardinal, of all people. You let me handle them by myself." Dagger was certain if Casey knew about the videotape, he would know why Mother wanted so much of Sara's blood.

Casey chuckled. "And you did a fine job of it. I watched your forensic guy try to scrape up bits and pieces of one of the clones at the bottom of the quarry. My orders were to observe, not interfere. Mine were to watch for BettaTec operatives. Not an easy task since I don't have a chip in my head the way you do."

Dagger finished his beer and slid the empty in front of Casey. "So, what exactly is your expertise?"

"Other than redecorating your office?" Casey said with a twinkle in his eye. "Why, I trained you."

34

"What in tarnation is she doing?"

Sara was sitting on the floor, lotus style, eyes closed, hands on her knees, palms up.

"Doing her own body scan," Dagger said. "Sara is very in tune with her body."

"Shush." Sara took several deep breaths and focused. She started at the top of her head and worked her way down. She would be able to feel for any foreign object, no matter how small, no matter how undetectable to machines. The soft hum from the small refrigerator in the corner of the office didn't bother her. She was able to block out all mundane noises and focus. Even if a tiny transmitter had been inserted under her skin, within a week her body would have pushed the foreign object to the surface.

Finally Sara opened her eyes. "Mother was telling the truth. They only took my blood." Sara rose from the floor and walked over to the desk.

"And why exactly would they want girlie's blood?" Skizzy's one eye leveled on Sara while the other wobbled in Dagger's direction.

Dagger hesitated just a little too long trying to come up with a believable excuse without revealing Sara's shapeshifting abilities.

Skizzy's eyes widened. "Holy shit, Batman. They want to clone her. Right?"

"You obviously took a conspiracy pill today." Dagger

changed the subject by mentioning how Mother appeared as a hologram.

"And she just went whoosh." Skizzy swept his hand in the air. "Just like in Nebraska, huh? Weird shit, man. Weirder shit yet are those paintings."

"Which reminds me, Sara and I are going to Sturgis, Michigan tomorrow morning to look up birth records in the basement of the Fayette Hospital." A flashing green light appeared as if it were floating near his eye. "The boss lady calls."

"Calls?" Skizzy asked.

Dagger logged onto the laptop while he explained the green light to Sara and Skizzy.

"Jeez, I hope the old bat pays you well if you're on call twenty-four seven."

Immediately, a monitor hovered over the desk and a keyboard lit up.

"Wow." Skizzy moved closer, but Dagger raised a hand to stop him. He wasn't sure it was a good idea to have Connie aware that someone other than he and Sara were in the room.

"Six-One-Seven. Something just came up on the Director's computer."

"I didn't see it."

"Perhaps you were too busy trying to pulverize Two-Fifty-Eight." When Dagger gave a puzzled look, Connie added, *"The man you know as Casey."* A photo appeared on the screen. *"We aren't sure who he is or why the Director is interested in him. For some reason this man is targeted. Perhaps you can look into it."*

"No need," Dagger said. "I know him. He's Mark Logan. He just opened an art gallery in Cedar Point."

35

"We need to find out what is so special about Mister Logan."

"The Director has no other information on him?"

"All he has on his laptop are these photos, not even a name. Guess his people are attempting to identify him. We know how the Director works. Logan could possibly be a future curator for an art museum in Paris and the Director plans to use him to steal a priceless piece of art. It sometimes feels as though the Director can time travel and knows what will happen twenty years from now that requires he change the course of action or advance the efforts in present day to achieve his objective."

"So in other words, you want me to be a bodyguard."

"Not necessarily. I'm sure a capable hacker such as your Mister Borden can assist you."

The android face swiveled in direct sight of where Skizzy was sitting in the corner. He scrunched down as if that would help him to disappear. Before Skizzy could utter a word, the android faded and the monitor disappeared.

"Well hells bells. She never said how much she's paying me."

36 He smelled her fear as she ran. Leaves tangled in her hair. Branches clawed at her clothes. He didn't feel as though he was running, didn't hear his feet pounding the earth. It was as though the wind carried him, darting between branches, sailing over treetops. And then he was on her. The wind howled. Or was it him? Her eyes, wild with fear, stared with the stark realization that her life was about to end. A primal scream was cut short as his hands wrapped around her throat. They weren't really hands but hairy, claw-like extensions of his arms.

The full moon muscled its way through thick clouds as though wanting a front row seat to this latest sacrifice. Its rays lit up the forest and all he wanted to do was bathe in its power. But as he lifted his eyes to the skies, he was drawn to a figure on a branch overhead. A grey hawk stared down, its gaze unwavering. An icy breeze chilled him as he looked into the hawk's eyes.

He woke with a start, sweat drenching his clothes. The dream felt so real he found himself checking his hands, expecting to see blood and skin under his nails. But they were clean. He stumbled out of bed and into the studio. He needed to capture the image while it was still fresh in his mind. But it wasn't the victim whose screams he had choked out of her. No, it was the gray hawk he had to paint. The hawk with the turquoise eyes.

37 Skizzy wasn't too happy about hanging around the lobby of a five star hotel waiting for Mark Logan to appear. All Dagger wanted was for Skizzy to get close enough to clone Logan's phone and possibly take a peek at his emails. Skizzy was wearing a suit he forced Dagger to purchase for him so he could blend in as a patron of this fine establishment. Complete with a brown wig and dark shades, he looked more like an aging foreign agent. The shoes gleamed from their morning buffing, but the wig was beginning to itch. He imagined all kinds of microscopic creepy crawlies nesting in it, even though he gave it a good cleaning with Clorox wipes and tossed it in the clothes dryer for ten minutes. He was certain Logan wouldn't recognize him from the grand opening.

Everything on the breakfast menu looked great so he had ordered the most expensive thing on Dagger's dime. Lox and bagels with cream cheese and a five dollar glass of orange juice. Sara convinced him that a restaurant this high class couldn't afford to poison its patrons. Still, Skizzy imagined a stray eyelash in the cream cheese and a slip of truth serum in the O.J. He succumbed to the lox and bagels but couldn't bring himself to drink the O.J. He brought his own thermos of coffee and explained to the waitress that he preferred a blend made special for him by a farmer in Argentina. She was understanding. When Skizzy paid his tab he neglected to see that she still charged him for coffee. Didn't matter. He was spending Dagger's money.

Skizzy paused to read the dinner menu posted outside the restaurant while watching for Logan. The lobby was a cavernous atrium with fountains housing live plants and colorful koi fish. Tall pillars rose from the floor as though holding the weight of the stained glass domed ceiling. Back-to-back seating areas dotted the lobby, each claiming a large Oriental rug that Skizzy was sure cost more than he made in a year. When the gallery owner finally arrived, he took a seat on one of the sofas and set a cup and saucer on the coffee table. The two seating areas were mirror images of each other.

Skizzy strolled over to the sofa butting against Logan's, then set his thermos and briefcase on the table. With his back to Logan, he opened the briefcase, removed a small box and opened it. Inside the box was a drone the size of a mosquito. Next he opened his laptop, tapped a few keys, and directed the drone to the pillar at the edge of Logan's sofa. Now he could watch Logan's movements, even hear whom he might be talking to on the phone. And the minute Logan placed a call, Skizzy would be able to patch into Logan's phone.

38

"Devon Carter, attorney for the Little Shepherd Adoption Agency. I need to examine their storage files in preparation for a legal brief."

Dagger placed the business card on the desk. His appearance hadn't changed much from the Galleria opening other than replacing the tuxedo for a pinstripe suit, black shirt, and gray tie.

The volunteer manning the desk at Fayette Hospital studied the card. Her name tag said Fannie and her frown deepened as she flipped the card over and back again. She handed the card to the woman seated next to her. Forced to toss down the latest rag paper from the checkout line, Matilda sighed as she waved the security guard over while mumbling, "I didn't even know there was a storage room."

Matilda gave a quick once over at the young woman standing next to the attorney and snorted. Sara's hair was in a bun. Her face, overwhelmed by large wire-rimmed glasses displayed, she hoped, a studious librarian look. In Dagger's opinion, there wasn't much Sara could do to disguise her beauty.

The security guard hitched his belt and shuffled toward the check-in desk. His name plate said Henry. Dagger thought he might fall over before he made it to the counter, so he ripped his business card from Matilda's fingers and met the security guard halfway.

Having heard part of the conversation, Henry didn't

bother looking at the card. He curled a finger at the couple. "Follow me. Hope you don't mind getting dirty 'cause the place hasn't exactly been on our list of tourist attractions."

They passed a wall of elevators, rounded a corner, and stopped at what looked like a freight elevator. Henry climbed in and waited for Dagger and Sara to follow. "Do you have to go through this every time someone wants to go to the file room?" Sara asked.

Henry punched a button which read "B". The door closed and the elevator hummed. "No ma'am. The storage room is just what it says. Strictly for storing old files. The file room is on the main level in the office wing. Everything these days is on disk. Nothing has been put in the storage room in twenty years." He opened a small door in the wall of the elevator and pulled out a flashlight.

The elevator rattled their teeth before coming to an abrupt halt. The doors opened and spilled them out into a dark hallway. Henry snapped on the flashlight and led them down a hall. The beam played across the floor and up the wall. A musty odor assaulted their senses as they followed Henry to a panel of wall switches. He flipped each of them on casting the hallway in a dull yellow.

"Cleaning people don't come down here, as you can tell." He crossed the hall and opened two double doors. Racks and racks of shelving units held an assortment of storage boxes. "Here you go. Know what you're looking for?"

"Yes." Although he could cut the dust with a carving knife, Dagger was thankful the racks were labeled. They were standing in front of the "A's."

Henry motioned to a chair next to the door. "I'm gonna take a load off. Let me know if you have any questions."

Exactly what Dagger hoped the old codger would do. "We won't take too long." The way Henry's hooded eyes were drooping, he expected the guard to be snoozing within five minutes.

They moved out of earshot and quickly found the aisle labeled "L." Dagger glanced at Sara. Although she kept up, he didn't like the pale hue to her usual island tan. "You should have stayed home and rested. You still look a little fatigued."

"I slept all the way here, plus ten hours yesterday."

He knew there was no sense arguing with her. She was going to do whatever she wanted to do. Dagger stopped in front of a box. A large sign hung from one of the shelves and each box was labeled with a year. He set his briefcase down and ran his fingers down each of the boxes.

"Can't believe there were so many adoptions." There were shelves of file boxes, all neatly labeled in black magic marker. "Here." Sara pointed at a box on the third shelf.

Dagger hauled it down and set it on the floor. "Not exactly in alphabetical order. I thought nuns were known for being meticulous." Dagger flipped through all the folders starting with "A". He flipped back and started at the beginning. "Could swear all the "Ad's" are missing."

"Maybe we have the wrong year." She checked her notes again and sighed. "Maybe they are filed in the wrong box."

Dagger shoved the box back onto the shelf and pulled out the next one. Sara rechecked each of the boxes just to make sure they didn't miss anything. They heard Henry snoring by the entrance, but weren't sure how long he would sleep.

"Damn." Dagger shoved the last box back on the shelf. "We don't have time to pull out every file for every damn year. I have a feeling someone might have beat us to the punch."

"But who?"

"Take a guess."

* * *

Although they should have headed home, Dagger agreed with Sara that it might be worth the effort to find where the doctor lived. A quick call to Marty Flynn netted them an address for the obstetrician's widow.

Dagger asked Sara to wait in the car, although she insisted she felt fine. He showed his business card to a middle aged woman in a nurse's uniform.

"I'm sorry. Louise is resting. I'm her caregiver. Can I give her a message?" The woman's foot was in the door, obviously not intending to invite Dagger inside.

Dagger handed her a business card for Dagger Investigations and explained he was looking for adoption records Doctor Pushing might have kept.

"I'm sorry. Her memory has been failing for quite sometime. Her daughter will be coming into town later today, I believe. I will have her give you a call."

"That's fine." Dagger figured he wasn't going to get anywhere inside the house so he pulled out a notepad, wrote a quick note, and handed it to the caregiver. "If you could give this to the daughter when she arrives, I would appreciate it."

39

Skizzy didn't know how a man could drink so much coffee. His own thermos was empty but he could swear Logan drank at least a dozen cups already. The drone produced a clear view of Mark's sign-on. Now Skizzy had access to Mark's computer and was happily bouncing from folders to emails without much luck. There wasn't one suspicious email or letter. Either Mark communicated with the artist by snail mail or Mark had another computer.

Mark received two phone calls, and each was from the manager at the gallery. Skizzy's ass hurt from sitting for so long, not to mention that he had to piss like a race horse. It was time to pack up and get the hell out.

Skizzy stood and just as he turned to see what Logan was doing, he saw Sheila Monroe gliding across the lobby toward him. *Oh fuck me.* He turned and sat so fast he almost missed the couch. He kept his head ducked as he slowly packed up his things, hoping not to draw too much attention to himself. Even though his disguise should prevent even his mother, God rest her soul, from recognizing him, he could still imagine Sheila marching up to him and making a spectacle. Skizzy let the drone eavesdrop on the conversation and watched on his own monitor as Sheila kissed Logan on both cheeks.

"Well, hidey hoe," Skizzy whispered. "Wonder if she's going up to his room."

Another man emerged from the restaurant and strode

over to Sheila. Mark Logan stood. In his earpiece Skizzy heard Sheila introduce the man as Alderman Frank Ballard. The alderman had been receiving a number of phone calls from constituents concerned about the type of paintings displayed in Logan's Galleria.

"Daddy hopes to have another casino night benefit for your daughter, Alderman," Sheila said.

"I get it," Skizzy whispered. "Sheila is gonna grease the wheels with the alderman so he doesn't cause trouble for Logan."

"Nice to meet you," Ballard said, then turned to Sheila. "I have a table reserved."

"I'll be right in." She waited for the alderman to leave. "I thought it best that I talk to him alone," she told Logan, "to assure him that the small group of women in the country club who object to some of the artwork in your gallery are just that—a small group and small-minded. I will smooth things over with him and give him the exact words to say to these ladies and to the City Council when they meet next."

"I think I'll stick around the lobby anyway in case I can answer any questions."

Sheila smiled. "Dinner tonight?"

"As long as it isn't at your country club."

"How about Edwardo's at eight."

"I'll meet you there."

"Why you little devil," Skizzy whispered. As he watched Sheila disappear into the restaurant, he waited to see if Logan called anyone, hopefully the artist, to report on Alderman Ballard's concerns. Perhaps the artist would be upset if Logan was forced to remove the exhibit. Perhaps the artist would come out of hiding to retrieve his disgusting artwork. He tapped a few keys and directed the drone mosquito back to the box. He tossed everything into his briefcase, grabbed the thermos, and left.

"So he never called the artist?" Dagger asked. Sara was still asleep in the back seat and he was driving down Interstate 94 toward home.

"Nope, and the artist never called him. No suspicious emails either. However, your fiancée…"

"Ex-fiancee."

"Whatever, she is meeting him for dinner at eight at Edwardo's. Now it's your turn to babysit the guy."

"Did you see anyone suspicious watching or following him?"

"Other than me? Nope. The drone snapped pics of people in the lobby in case the Mother ship identifies anyone. Did you ever stop to think that maybe Logan works with BettaTec?"

"I would have seen stats and I didn't. He isn't in the Director's radar because he is or was an operative. He has him targeted for other reasons."

"How's girlie?"

"Should be back to normal by tonight." Dagger took a quick look behind him. Sara's color did look better. The last time she donated four pints of blood, it took Sara two days to recover.

"You've got night duty on our esteemed gallery owner. You and Sara gonna go out to dinner at Edwardo's?"

"Sara is going to rest. I might go for a drink with Padre. We'll sit in the bar and observe anyone paying too close attention to Logan. You just keep monitoring his computer."

40

"Pretty fancy place to have a drink. Trust you're buying, *mi amigo*." Padre draped his coat on the back of the barstool and took a seat. The bar area was dimly lit by multi-colored pendant shaped lights suspended from the ceiling by thin wires. The blue and tan hues accented the marble bar. Soft music floated from the corner of the lounge where a rail-thin black man sat behind a piano.

"Don't worry. I have an expense account."

"And a fat wallet." Padre checked out the beers on tap. The bartender grabbed an ice cold glass before he even opened his mouth.

"You look like a Coors Lite kinda guy." His too-white smile and arrogant attitude hit Padre all wrong. He reminded Padre of trainee cops who thought they knew it all. And, of course, his name tag said Andre. A made-up name if he ever heard one.

"Hate to burst your bartender bubble, but I'll have a Bloody Mary. Celery salt around the rim, three olives, and save the roughage."

Andre's friendly façade faded. Bartenders hated to mess with salted rims. "Do you want Tabasco added to the Bloody Mary mix?"

Padre imagined Andre getting heavy handed with the Tabasco in order to set his mouth on fire. "No thanks. "

"Feisty," Dagger whispered.

"I've had a rough day." The bar was oval shaped and Padre could see across the bar and into the restaurant where a familiar blonde was having dinner with, of all people, Mark Logan. "So that's why you wanted me to join you."

Dagger lifted his glass and pointed it in the direction of the restaurant area. "I've been hired to watch Logan's back. Supposedly there's a target on it."

"From an art enthusiast who isn't fond of the latest exhibit? That's ironic. Someone wants to kill him for showing paintings of killings." Andre slid the Bloody Mary in front of Padre who motioned to Dagger's stack of bills. Padre raised his glass in Dagger's direction. "Thank you. This is going to taste wonderful." And it did. He popped the olives into his mouth and tossed the toothpick on the bar. "So, who do you think has it in for Logan?"

"Not sure." Dagger played all of his BettaTec cards close to his chest. Padre had been involved in enough bizarre cases. There was no sense adding BettaTec, computer chips, and Alpha into the mix. "Could even be the artist. The fact that he knows so much about those murders makes him Number One on my list."

"And how do you find a recluse?"

Dagger studied his ex, the way her hand rested on Logan's forearm, how she leaned close to whisper in Logan's ear. "Hopefully, our ace reporter can find out something. I think Logan knows more than he's saying. I find it hard to believe that he has all of this mystery artist's paintings but he never once met him. He might slip with a name. Skizzy didn't find anything on his laptop. No emails, no correspondence."

Padre's cop radar clicked on. "Do I want to know how he gained access to Logan's emails?"

"No." Dagger pushed his empty glass toward Andre. "Could have a second computer he uses for confidential correspondence, which makes sense. With the business he's in, he wouldn't want his competitors to steal his artists." Dagger's thoughts went immediately to the Director. His personal laptop is what Dagger was able to access, confidential information that would never be available to the minions working under him.

A woman appeared in his peripheral vision. Her red dress looked painted on and hit well north of her thighs. Dagger's first instinct was to check if she had stats, then to check facial recognition via his embedded chip. She wasn't in his mental file box. Dagger caught a slight nod toward her from Andre. The woman didn't so much slide onto the barstool as slither, causing her dress to ride even higher.

Andre slipped a napkin in front of the woman. Her eyes were smoky, makeup a bit too heavy. Diamond chips were embedded in the blood red nail polish. "What can I get you, ma'am?"

She cast a hungry glance at Dagger. "Is he on the menu?"

Dagger leaned back and gave her a long look. Padre yanked the right side of his sport coat open where his shield was visible. "How about you find another bar to work? And you…" He turned to Andre. "If I see you helping to hook girls up with patrons again, you won't be able to find another job in this town."

Andre backed away. The hooker disappeared so fast, Padre was sure she left a puff of smoke in her stride. "That's why it isn't a good thing to leave a pile of cash on the bar. It's easy to pick out the best marks."

"Thanks for the tip, Dad."

"I'm only saying, fanning a hundred bucks worth of twenties on the bar is a sure giveaway. Use plastic."

"Right. Then Mister Honest Andre will have my credit card number, which he can pass onto the hookers. No thanks."

Out of habit, Dagger started checking the other faces in the bar, whether suspicious of more operatives in town or just stretching his new found talent. Padre, on the other hand, watched Andre give a warning nod to three other women who looked college age. His operation was obviously a lucrative venture. He would have to ask the chief to put an undercover officer in here for a month or so to clean the place out.

"Where's Sara tonight?"

"She did her civic duty and donated blood." He hid the smile behind his drink as he emptied the glass. "She wasn't used to seeing blood that was hers."

"I can understand that." Padre patted his pocket, wishing he could light up. That was the problem with drinking. You always wanted to light up. "Wanted to run something by you. I was thinking of having one of our undercover cops create a Facebook page in order to draw out this killer. The department already has a fake page with fake friends. We change the profile picture and profile information depending on who we're trying to lure."

"Sounds good. I can almost predict Sara was thinking of doing the same thing, using herself as bait. That's something that is not going to happen."

"Great. I can keep peace in your household. Stop by the precinct tomorrow morning and help my tech guy build the profile."

Another figure came into view. Sheila had exited the women's restroom and caught sight of the two men at the bar.

"I'm flattered. Either you two want to make sure I'm doing my job, or Dagger is trying to hide his utter jealousy at my dating another man."

Padre clamored from the bar stool and grabbed his coat. "Three is a crowd. *Adios.* See ya. Good luck. And thanks for the drinks."

"Coward," Dagger said under his breath.

"How nice he wanted to give us alone time." Sheila maneuvered her way between two stools and propped her elbow on the bar.

Dagger picked up the bills from the bar, leaving a five dollar tip. "Word on the street is that Logan's life is in danger. Keep your eyes open."

"Right. Like I should believe anything you say."

Ignoring Sheila was like ignoring a raging pit bull. He had started to wonder when she would direct her wrath toward him after finding out he and Sara were more than just business partners. "What is it you want, Sheila."

"Honesty, which is obviously something you know little about. I suppose you are going to tell me you are madly in love with your little Indian princess, that you fell in love the moment she batted those baby blues."

Dagger stared at her and said nothing. Interrupting one of Sheila's sermons was useless.

"I know you well enough to realize you don't know how to love. You don't have one emotional bone in your body. Sara is a new toy for you to play with until you are bored and ready to discard her." She leaned in close, as if proximity would made the words sink in faster. "Don't think you can come crawling back, Chase Dagger."

Dagger caught a snicker from the other side of the bar. The look in Dagger's eyes removed the smile from Andre's face.

"There's very little chance of that happening." He wanted to tell her that he and Sara were married, anything to discourage the endless attempts his ex tried in order to get back together. It wasn't exactly the truth, but hell, he had a marriage license to prove it, all signed and sealed by the good Pastor Skizzy Borden. In Dagger's mind, he didn't need a piece of paper to know he would spend the rest of his life with Sara. He caught sight of Logan standing near the entrance to the bar. "I believe your date is waiting for you."

41

"I think I was able to convince Alderman Ballard that the Nightfall exhibit doesn't pose a problem. Keeping the French doors closed to the exhibit serves the same purpose as the video stores that have a separate room for adult films." Sheila accepted the glass of Frangelico from Mark. She told herself she was going to go straight home, but after her encounter with Dagger in the bar she thought, screw it. When Mark asked if she would like to have a nightcap at his hotel she accepted, knowing full well the drink would be in his room and not the hotel bar. "The alderman suggested that perhaps the artist could attend a special council meeting to defend his work."

The corner suite was spacious with a view of Lake Michigan from one side of the living room and a view of the harbor from the east side of the room. The décor was Victorian with enough brocade fabric and curved designs to make the Queen of England happy. It was definitely not Sheila's choice of furnishings. Paintings of women wearing pastels and holding parasols hung on the walls. They were a far cry from what hung in the Nightfall exhibit.

"I would never be able to convince him of that and wouldn't even think of asking." Mark set his drink on one of the coasters dotting the coffee table, and took a seat on the sofa across from her. "He made it quite clear that he would remain secluded and absorbed in his work. And by the looks of the finished products, I wouldn't disturb him for the world."

Sheila kicked off her shoes and rubbed her feet. "Not the most comfortable shoes." She watched his eyes travel up her shapely legs and felt a tingling sensation. *Dammit, no. I am not sleeping with him,* she told herself, even though she knew she was horny as hell after seeing Dagger. Her dress was expensive but conservative. She didn't want to give him the impression that she wanted more than dinner.

"Were you able to give the alderman enough ammunition for his meeting?"

"I am a walking list of talking points. I've dealt with these women before. When the Country Club wanted to have a fund raiser by auctioning off dates with the richest bachelors in town, that same group of women almost demanded that the local priest do an exorcism. They're getting to have a very bad reputation, and I assure you, when they show up at the next council meeting, the article in our paper will not be complimentary."

"Good. Hopefully, that will suffice."

"What about his name? Can you give us that much?"

Mark chuckled at that. "Not even that. And I know most artists, know their style. Believe me, I've put out my own feelers hoping he submitted his work to others."

"No luck?"

He shook his head. "Other than the initials on his paintings, I haven't a clue what his name is."

Sheila walked over to the bar and set her drink down. "Did he slip up and tell you what state or city he was born in? Where he went to school? If he had brothers or sisters?"

"No to all of the above." Mark joined her at the bar, a suspicious look on his face about her sudden list of questions.

"I really need to go. I have an early morning and Father is not a happy man when I'm late."

Mark placed his hand on hers. "Are you sure you should

be driving? I do have another bedroom you can use."

She looked into his eyes. Sheila could tell a lot by looking into a man's eyes and it wasn't the second bedroom Mark had in mind.

"Believe me, I didn't have that much to drink." Sheila leaned over to kiss him on the cheek but he turned his head. His kiss was hungry, his hands cradling her face, pulling her closer.

She felt herself respond a little too passionately, but slowly pulled away. "Ummm, tempting but I really have to go."

"Your loss."

Sheila slipped into her heels and grabbed her purse. "I'm sure it is, but don't think I won't take a rain check." Always keep them wanting, was Sheila's motto.

42 Sheila laid on the doorbell. He was taking his sweet time answering. When the door was jerked open she saw sweat glistening on his skin. His granite muscles always sent her head spinning. He was in gym shorts. How like him to be working out before his shift.

"Well, gee. Long time no see." He closed the door behind her. From a side room that he used as a fitness center emerged a woman in a one piece leotard outfit. She was holding a five pound weight in one hand.

"Get lost," Sheila said as she tossed her purse on the couch.

He glanced at the young woman and nodded toward the door. She didn't look too happy as she grabbed her gym bag and car keys and exited the condo.

Sheila lit a cigarette and kicked off her shoes. She knew he hated cigarettes and she knew all the buttons to push.

"To what do I owe the honor of your presence?"

"Doesn't look like you missed me any."

He grabbed a towel and wiped the sweat dripping from his neck. "I needed a workout partner."

"Most people go to a gym."

"I have my own."

"How convenient." Sheila put the cigarette out in a potted plant and walked over to where he was standing. A tangle of dark hair matted his chest. Although his face was scarred from growing up in a rugged neighborhood, he exuded a danger that was electrifying. When they first met, it was his taste in clothes that caught her attention. Detective Sergeant Joe Spagnola looked more like a Sicilian mob family member than a cop. She slid her fingers down his damp chest.

Joe grabbed her hand. "I'm tired of playing games. Every time you run into your ex, you need to take out your frustrations on me. I don't even want to hear what he did this time."

"I thought I was good at picking up on things, but I guess I believed him when he said he and Sara weren't intimate."

"I said I didn't want to hear it." His eyes were as cold as his voice. "You've been drinking. That's usually when you get all weepy eyed. Go cry on someone else's shoulder. I have to go to work." He turned and walked to the bathroom, calling over his shoulder, "You can show yourself out."

He closed the bathroom door. She was tempted to follow him, leaving pieces of her clothing behind, but all she wanted to do was cry. The thought of driving home didn't appeal to her. She needed coffee.

Although a designer at one of the top furniture stores in town helped to accessorize the condo, Joe picked out most of the furniture, preferring dark wood and sleek lines. Accent pieces brought out the variety of rustic hues in the area rug. What happened to the sparsely furnished condo she saw the last time she was here? Were their recent escapades only at her place?

Sheila pulled out a fry pan and set it on the stove. Even she knew how to make an omelet. In her mother's best attempt to prepare her daughter for a life of gourmet dinners for parties of ten or more, Sheila had attended a culinary school. Now here she was, still single, and eating most of her meals in restaurants or at her parents' house. The thought of ten or more people trampling through her castle, much less being married with two and a half kids, never appealed to her.

She found ham, cheese and tomatoes in the fridge. The shower was still running in the master bath. While the coffee dripped, she set two plates on the counter. If Joe wanted some seaweed foamy drink, he would have to make it himself. For a man who ate out a lot, he had a kitchen most women would kill for. The curved counter seated four people on barstools while the island counter provided enough working space for six cooks.

It dawned on her that she never once cooked a meal for Joe. All they ever did was go out to eat or go to bed. He had every right to be angry with her. She did use him. She admits it. Few men would put up with all the shit she dished out.

She checked several drawers before finding a whisk. Even the utensils looked unused. Why would Joe buy such a large condo? For that perfect wife and two and a half kids? Sheila realized she knew very little about him other than he was raised in South Chicago and had a twin sister who was killed in a drive-by shooting when he was fifteen. They never found her killer. Joe became a cop to find other victims' killers since he couldn't find his sister's.

When she heard the shower stop, Sheila poured the eggs into the fry pan. Even though Joe didn't eat every meal at home, he always stocked the fridge with fruit and vegetables, probably for juicing. She found a bottle of V8 and a small juice glass. As she poured the V8 she suddenly had a vision of her condo after the murder. Blood everywhere. She hadn't been able to touch a glass of tomato juice since.

Once the eggs started to set, she sprinkled in the ham, cheese, and tomatoes while visions of the Nightfall exhibit flashed like a slide show. How did the artist get so many of the details correct? Although most of the specifics were kept from the press, she saw what her condo looked like, walked through each room to let the police know if anything was stolen. She saw the overturned furniture, the position of Caroline's body. Even the pattern of spray on the walls had been painted in minute detail.

She flipped the omelet in half and set the glass lid on top of the fry pan. As she was pouring two cups of coffee she heard the door to the bedroom open. The subtle scent of aftershave drifted into the kitchen.

"You didn't have to do that."

"I realized I was hungry." She set the cup in front of him as he took a seat on the bar stool. "And I wanted a chance to apologize for being a bitch, again." She cut the omelet in half, giving him the larger half before garnishing the plate with a piece of cantaloupe and some strawberries.

"I didn't know you could cook."

"There's a lot you don't know about me." And he would probably never find out if she kept screwing things up. She preferred to eat where she stood so they could talk face to face. "Has Padre told you anything about the exhibit at Logan's Galleria?"

"No. What is it and why would I be interested?"

There was no love lost between Joe and Padre. Joe skirted a fine line when working a case and Padre gave that fine line a wide berth in his investigations. Padre once thought Joe might be on the take because he dressed like an investment banker.

Sheila told him about the Nightfall exhibit and how it replicated murders from a few years ago. "I saw the condition of my condo after my assistant was killed. The painting certainly included details that were never made available to the public. I thought, since you worked the case and saw the crime scene photos, that you could take a look at the exhibit. Padre thinks the artist knows way too much about the murders."

"But the killer is dead, right? He committed suicide." He watched her as he ate the omelet. She definitely surprised him. The omelet was better than any he had ever had in a restaurant. "Looking to find an accomplice?"

An involuntary shudder ran through her body. She set her fork down and wrapped her hands around her coffee mug.

"Hey." He reached across and grabbed her arm. "You're really worried about this."

She brought the coffee mug to her lips forcing him to release his grip. His normally cold eyes softened. "You should see the paintings, Joe. I went back to my office and brought up the articles on every single murder. He has details that I hope to God aren't real. I'm finding it hard to sleep wondering if someone is going to sneak in. I've been sleeping with the lights on since the gallery's grand opening."

"Okay. You have me intrigued. I'll pull out my copy of the crime scene photos and stop by after work."

"You may have to call for an appointment first. The Nightfall exhibit isn't open to the public." Sheila walked around to his side of the counter. "I'll clean up the kitchen. Go ahead or you'll be late."

He cupped her face and kissed her on the forehead. "Thanks for breakfast. And don't be a stranger."

She watched him walk out the door. Tears crept from the corners of her eyes and she hated herself. His woodsy aftershave reminded her of Dagger.

After cleaning up the kitchen, she poured herself a tumbler of scotch, found Joe's iPod and scrolled through the songs. "Country music? Really, Joe?" She didn't even know what type of music he listened to. Sheila was just about to pull the earbuds out when she heard the words to a song about a girl crush. She listened to a few verses and froze.

How appropriate. She replaced the words in her head from a woman with long blonde hair to a woman with long brown hair, wanting to taste her lips *because they taste like him.* She could relate too much to the song about a woman who was in love with another woman's man. *I can't get no sleep. I can't get no peace.* It wasn't just the Nightfall exhibit that kept her awake nights. It was imagining Sara *underneath his bedsheets.*

43

The pile of papers at his feet were yellow and dog-eared. It was time. The fireplace cast the only light in the room. He no longer needed to keep all this paperwork. He found the adoption papers after his foster mother died. Which one was she? Number Two? Three? They shuffled him around homes like a bad virus. When he realized that telling grownups he was hearing voices only resulted in a trip to see another in a line of shrinks, he stopped mentioning it. Nothing helped. Voices, images, things no child could understand. Behavioral problems scared some families.

He studied the photo. What were their names? Edna and James? The little white dog was named Scotty, and their five-year-old son was Jacob. He was only eight at the time. When Scotty went missing along with several neighborhood pets, it was Edna who suspected something was wrong with the foster boy they let into their home. She was afraid for Jacob and even told James, "that boy has sick eyes."

He tossed the photo into the fireplace along with reports from doctors and police. Hungry flames licked around the edges, turning the photo black and the reports to ash.

Next was a folder from the Heywood Home for Boys. Ward Chapman, the night supervisor, died from a broken neck after stumbling down a flight of stairs. No witnesses, except for the boy with sick eyes who had waited for him after bed checks and given the pompous ass a little shove to help him reach the pearly gates ahead of schedule. He tossed the entire folder into the fire. Seeing the papers curl and disintegrate gave him as much enjoyment as seeing old man Chapman tumbling down the curved staircase.

A nice Christian couple decided to earn themselves some Godly credits by helping a boy in need. They wanted an older boy seeing that they were a little up in years and not capable of chasing after a toddler. Maeve and Marvin Ames had been a little too Christian for his liking. But he got over it quickly when he saw the four thousand square foot home on a sprawling ranch in Colorado. A mask of deception, he gladly went to church with them twice a week and praised halleluiah with the rest of the congregation. Seems Marvin's family found oil, lots of oil. The Ameses were set for life. But there was only one problem. They gave twenty percent annually to the church. As if that wasn't bad enough, Marvin wanted to bequeath all their wealth and possessions to the church upon his death. Fuck that.

Maeve, though, was malleable. One wing of the house was her art studio. She was a painter and he found that the voices in his head were quiet when he was in that studio. She taught him all about oil and acrylics, pigments and varnishes, low fat and high fat oil contents, and "artists through the ages." Maeve was particularly fond of impressionist artists. Claude Monet, Edgar Degas, and Paul Cezanne, were just some of her favorites. Maeve was a patient teacher and she found him extremely talented. She soon arranged for a tutor so he didn't have to waste time on the long bus trips to and from high school. He was too delicate for sports, according to Maeve.

His love of art didn't stop the voices at night. It was during this time in his life, as he lay in bed and stared past the balcony and out at the night sky, that he realized his urgings and the voices were strongest when the moon was full. The house was too isolated for him to drive off at night without waking his foster parents. As he stood on the second floor balcony, the voice prodded and urged him to jump. And so he did. And nothing happened. He landed as lightly as a cat. It almost felt like flying. And when he ran it was at a speed that was unbelievable.

By morning he couldn't remember where he had been or what he had done, but he knew by the blood on his hands and clothes that he had either done something horribly bad or deliciously wonderful.

Maeve and Marvin never suspected. He would wash his clothes before they awakened. And the front page stories about coyotes going on a rampage was all the talk in town. Some ranchers planned to sit up all night with their shotguns. Not good. Some planned to install cameras. Also not good.

He smiled as he read the newspaper clippings before flinging them into the fire. Next was his sketchpad. He fanned through pages and pages of drawings that, unfortunately, Maeve had found under his bed, the nosy bitch. She was appalled at the images of murder and mayhem. He discovered he had a certain flair for the bizarre, painting dark and depressing images: crows with enlarged talons, pieces of flesh hanging and still dripping with blood; a body hanging from a tree in a dark forest, a slice of moonlight casting an eerie shadow on the dead features; an unusually large moon on the horizon, the bottom half a stark red as though engorged in blood.

There were other artists, he reminded her, like Vincent Locke, Theodore Gericault, H.R. Giger, and Goya who created *Saturn Devouring his Son*. All who painted dark and disturbing artwork, so all he was doing was exploring the various classics, something Maeve taught him to do.

The sketchpad settled on top of the logs. It took much

longer to burn since there were hundreds of sketches. Marvin hadn't cared too much for the drawings, felt Satan was controlling the boy; and tried to convince Maeve to return the teen to the Heywood Home. One day while Maeve was out shopping, Marvin climbed a ladder near the second floor balcony to fix a gutter. One shove was all it took and Marvin was no longer a problem.

After Marvin's funeral, Maeve reviewed the will with their attorney. Although Marvin had left everything to Maeve, she knew he wanted her to leave everything to the church when she died. But she was terribly fond of their foster son. He had promise, and the best art schools cost a lot of money, especially if he wanted to continue his studies in Europe. Those expenses were a drop in the bucket compared to her wealth and investment portfolio. The pastor, though, a shifty guy with groping hands in the choir loft, was starting to make moves toward the widow. The copy of the will was the next item he flung onto the fire.

He convinced Maeve that he wanted to attend a college close to home should she need him. Of course, he had ulterior motives. In his first year in college, the Ames house burned to the ground. No one at college knew he'd made a trip home that night. Maeve had a tendency to use sleeping pills. Ever since Marvin died she found it hard to sleep. The fire started in the studio. With all the chemicals and paint, it spread too quickly, and the house was too isolated for the fire department to arrive in time.

The newspaper article on the fire and Maeve's obituary hit the roaring flames in a burst of sparks. With her death, he became a very wealthy nineteen-year-old.

A few years ago it dawned on him that he wasn't hearing multiple voices, but one annoying, persistent voice. Sadistic images crept into his paint brush. He felt his hand possessed to paint other images that he couldn't explain. One was of a wolf, its coat a myriad of colors whitened by the light from a full moon. But it was the eyes, the turquoise eyes normally seen on an Alaskan husky, that mesmerized him. And then another, a hawk with a broad wingspan, its feathers surprisingly in the same hues as the coat of the wolf, with eyes also identical to the wolf's. Why those images? And why were the voice's demands so urgent? It kept hounding him about someone named Josie Andrews. Why? Who was she? His natural mother? It was then he started his quest to find Josie and to find out his real name.

44 When they entered Padre's office, a young woman was seated in a chair in front of the desk. Her hair was blonde and spiked, her eyes lined heavily in black. She was wearing a spaghetti strap halter and a satin skirt that contained no more than a half yard of fabric. When she stood, they could see she was wearing five inch hooker heels. The stench of cheap perfume trailed like a plume of exhaust. She pumped their hands in a tight grip. "Ellie Gardner," she announced.

"Ellie works vice." Padre gave a half-hearted nod at the exposed skin. "As you can tell." He introduced Dagger and Sara. Sara took a seat next to Ellie while Dagger half perched on the side credenza. "She's working with our I.T. Department to revise a Facebook page to draw out our suspect. We keep a bogus Facebook page that we use for cases such as this. There are a lot of bogus friends on it and we change up the person's profile to fit the case. It tends to look suspicious when a new Facebook page crops up with very few friends or posts."

"He will know it's a trap. Besides, her color is all wrong." Sara studied the female cop from her blonde hair to her brown eyes.

"I would rather have one of my female cops lure the killer than you. She can defend herself." Padre made several notes on a pad of paper. He motioned toward Sara as he spoke to Ellie. "Find a wig as close in color to Sara's as you can."

"Wrong eye color, too," Dagger pointed out.

"I have a variety of colored contacts." Ellie moved closed to Sara. "But definitely not your exact eye color. Yours are amazing." She turned back to Padre. "I'll use the bluest I can find, although it won't be perfect."

"I don't feel right putting someone else in danger," Sara argued.

"Sara, we talked about this," Dagger said.

"Perhaps if you could tell me what this is about." Ellie looked from the couple to Padre.

Padre did his best to explain without getting into the Addison curse. All he told her about the case was that it involved a stalker targeting only women with the name of Sara, Sarah, or variations thereof; and that Padre believed he found his targets using social media.

Ellie digested what little information she was fed. "I see." She studied Sara for several seconds. "And is there a reason you believe the stalker is looking for women who look like you?"

She wasn't dumb. Dagger could say that much for her. However, she was a cop and paid to look at all angles. He shifted his gaze to Padre who was none too happy to be the one to tap dance around the subject.

"We aren't sure. Dagger and Sara have worked a number of cases involving some pretty crazy people. They're looking into those cases now to see if they can pinpoint the man's identity." He looked to Dagger hoping he would save him.

"I don't understand," Ellie interrupted. "If he knows who you are, why is he going after other women? Why doesn't he go directly to you?"

Padre raised an eyebrow toward Dagger and kept his mouth shut. Dagger would have to carry this ball. But it was Sara who saved the day. Padre hoped his heavy sigh wasn't too audible.

"He only knows my first name and what I look like. Many of our cases have taken us to various states." Not quite a lie, but it would have to do. "From the women he has targeted, it appears he remembers the dark hair and the eyes. All of the women he found on social media are single or divorced, no children. He didn't know much more about me. Size and shape doesn't seem to matter to him. He has located women from Arizona to Chicago so he is working his way to Indiana."

Ellie thought about this for another few seconds. "And what happened to the women he assumed was you?"

Now Padre's heavy sigh definitely was heard. "They're all dead," he finally admitted.

45 Sara slammed the door. "Well, that went well. I told you we shouldn't involve anyone else. I won't be able to live with myself if anything happens to her." She tossed her jacket on the loveseat and stormed into the kitchen.

Dagger carried the jacket to the closet and hung it up. It was unlike Sara to leave anything lying around, which was his first hint that she was really pissed. He found her in the kitchen leaning against the counter, her arms crossed in front of her.

"Padre will have eyes on her at all times." He tried to pull her into a hug but Sara pulled away and walked to the sink. "I will even tail her if it makes you feel better."

She drilled him with those ice blues. "Too many tails will spook him. The only person who should tail her is me."

"Out of the question. Besides, you can't be there twenty-four seven. Not one of his other victims was killed at her home. It has always been at night and in a remote location. Padre will have her develop a routine. He already set her up in an apartment under the name of Sara Welsh. She'll be in the gym three days a week. Stop off at the same bar twice a week, shop at the same grocery store. One undercover cop will be nearby, another will be in a van taking pictures and watching for anyone suspicious. Cleaves Jones has given her a job at his restaurant where she'll work nights. Nothing like a roomful of excons to make a killer feel comfortable."

"Excons who would jump at the chance to turn in a cop for the right price," Sara snapped.

"The warden's workers are loyal to him. They owe him their lives for giving them a second chance." The Joint was a favorite of locals and visitors alike. Two of the main features on the menu were the sizzle and high voltage steak.

"Not good enough." Sara turned and walked away, leaving Dagger standing in the kitchen wondering what else he could say to change her mind.

The phone on his desk rang. Einstein flew from the aviary, popped the receiver off, and punched the speaker button. "AWWKK, DAGGER INVESTIGATIONS. YOU BAG 'EM, WE'LL TAG EM. AWK."

"Einstein, get back." Dagger apologized to the caller who couldn't contain her laughter. He pulled a Brazil nut from the desk drawer and held it out. The macaw grabbed it with one claw, and flew up to the railing overhead. "I think I'm going to prepare parrot for dinner."

The caller laughed again. "It seems you have a problem child. Is this Chase Dagger?" The woman's voice was cheerful and a welcome sound after dealing with his unhappy partner. "I'm Geri Moyers, Louise Pushing's daughter. You stopped by my mother's house yesterday."

"Yes. Thanks for returning my call." Dagger took a seat at the desk. He saw Sara slink in from the Florida room and take up a position in front of the desk, her elbows on the wooden ledge.

Dagger told Geri about the missing files from the storage room at Fayette Hospital. "I was told your father kept file copies of every patient. I was hoping you could find Missus Addison's case file."

"I read your note and took the liberty yesterday to go through his files. I pulled out everything he had on Madeline

Addison and mailed it overnight to the address on your card."

"Thanks for being so thorough. Would you happen to know or remember anything your father might have mentioned about the Addison case?"

"Any time Dad talked shop with Mom, it was all beyond my young mind. I can assure you his filing system was meticulous. Even Mom didn't go in his study. He didn't like anyone tampering with his filing system."

"Do let me reimburse you for the shipping charges."

"No need, Mister Dagger. I'm glad you called when you did. I was just thinking of carting everything over to a shredding facility."

46 "Hey, Martinez." Spagnola pulled out a chair and sat down. "Sheila mentioned something about the exhibit at the Logan Galleria. What can you tell me about it?"

Padre saw a file folder in Joe's hands and figured it was from the Caroline Kirby case. "I take it you saw the paintings."

"No, but I called to make an appointment to see them tomorrow."

"Good thing you weren't at the grand opening. They were charging a thousand bucks for a private showing. At least now you can get in free." He leaned back and studied the detective. His suit didn't look wrinkled, yet he was sure Joe was in and out of his vehicle all night long. The detective didn't even look tired after working overtime.

"Sheila said there might be details in some of the paintings that were never made public, according to you. Is that true?"

Joe could be a little abrasive, but Padre knew he would follow a lead until he drained it dry. Like Padre, he detested open cases, much less cold ones.

Padre didn't need to bring out his case files. He practically memorized all of the details. However, he wasn't about ready to admit to all of the gory details omitted in his reports unless he was ready to share details about the Addison family. "The artist was creative on most of the paintings. The media did mention the wild animal attack on the teens so that was no surprise. But the rest?" He showed his palms as though he were as surprised as Sheila regarding the details. Only a handful of people knew talons had lifted Tex Miller's head from his body. "I do admit Sheila has me curious about the homicide in her former condo. Has to be someone familiar with the scene." Joe appeared to be assessing Padre, drilling him with those interrogation eyes. But Padre met his stare with his own and gave a nod toward the file folder in Joe's hand. "Do you trust everyone who worked your crime scene?"

"Of course, but I'll check them out again. To my knowledge, not one person has an artistic bone in his or her body. And what about your friend? He looks like someone who would have a big mouth and sell the information for the right price."

Padre reined in a sharp retort. There was no love lost between Joe and Sheila's ex. "Dagger is more discreet than most of the cops in the precinct. You need to bark up a different tree."

Joe tapped the file folder against his knee while his dark eyes drilled into Padre. "Tell me something, Martinez. Why is it you involved Dagger in all of these cases in the first place?"

Padre expected this question, but how could he explain it without exposing all of the weird cases that had landed on the steps of Cedar Point? "Dagger has a lot of experience with cases involving the—" he searched for the proper word "—occult. Just like some police departments like to work with a psychic, we have someone who deals in the dark side of humanity."

With that Joe stood. But there was a sneer on his face as he gave his parting shot. "Of course he does."

47

He skimmed through the sites quickly. It was as though he were on automatic pilot. His fingers kept tapping, finding the name and checking the profile before moving on to the next one. If any seemed like a good possibility, then he read further. No longer did he need to wander the country. He was where she would be found. HE told him so. This helped to narrow his Internet searches to Cedar Point, Indiana, or at least a close enough proximity.

In his experience he discovered that some women lie. They claimed to be married to discourage perverts. Others claimed to be single when they were actually married but looking for a little action on the side. He would spend days shadowing a target only to abandon her when he saw her picking up a child from day care or a husband from work, yet her Facebook page said she was single. Lying bitches. All of them.

Some days he was too exhausted from lack of sleep, but HE was insistent, said time was getting short. His fingers stopped tapping. "What do we have here? Another possible candidate? Miss Sara Welsh." He scanned her profile, saw she lived in Cedar Point. "YES!" HE screamed in his head. He ignored the voice as he took his time reading each of her posts.

48

"Anything new?" Wozniak collapsed into the chair with a heavy sigh.

Padre finished pounding on the keyboard and took a sip of the tepid coffee. The chief resembled a bull dog whose groomer clipped his facial hairs too close, leaving pink skin in its wake. Every wife of John's had cooked like Julia Child, evident in how the shirt buttons strained across his bulk. "I have checked out Carlton Abrams, the manager of the Logan Galleria. He's clean. No priors. Pretty well known in the art and wine circles. Managed a gallery in Boston for ten years before meeting Mark Logan at an auction in New York City."

"I saw Spagnola in here earlier. What did he want?"

"Sheila told him about the exhibit. He worked the Carolina Kirby case and she wanted him to take a look at the painting, see if it was similar to the crime scene photos. He wanted to get my take on the paintings that depicted my cases."

"So he's going over there?"

"Yep."

Wozniak rubbed a beefy hand across his face and groaned. "He's going to want to follow through on this and we can't have that. He starts digging, Lord knows what he'll uncover. The fewer people know, the better." He wedged himself out of the chair and stood. "How about your undercover girl? Is she ready to go?"

"The Facebook profile looks great. Instead of a waitress at

that restaurant, we made her a manicurist. It's something she did before becoming a cop. And she will work strictly at the Rosen Assisted Living Facility. If a stranger gets suspicious about how long she's worked there, we're sure seniors with short term memory won't know."

"Good. I didn't feel comfortable with her working at a restaurant that only hires ex-cons. Our killer might not think the woman he's looking for was ever in prison."

"I agree."

"Keep me posted."

Padre waited for the door to close before picking up the phone.

"I know who the hell you are, now what the hell do you want?" Skizzy's voice was barely above a whisper.

"I would like an update, and why are you whispering?"

"I don't want *you know who* to hear?"

"Who?"

"You know who." His voice lowered even more. "Big Brother."

"Oh, geez." Padre shook his head. "Need I remind you I AM Big Brother."

"Nah. You're small potatoes. More like Little Brother."

"Will you just give me an update?"

"Nothing to report. Nothing suspicious on either computer or phone. Maybe Logan was telling the truth when he said the guy ships paintings to the shops and leaves notes. If he calls from a burner, can't track it."

"Maybe we're looking at the wrong guy. Maybe I should take another look at Abrams."

"Nah. That cadaver guy is just a worker bee. He manages the shop, displays the paintings, but it's Logan who acquires the artwork."

Padre hung up thinking of how he could confiscate the

packaging the paintings were delivered in in order to dust for fingerprints.

49

Dagger ripped open the brown envelope, pulled out the contents, and set them on the kitchen table. Since Simon was on vacation, he'd stopped by his postal box to pick up the envelope Geri Moyers had shipped overnight.

"Not much there." Sara pulled out a chair and sat down. "Or at least not as much as I expected."

"Pushing's daughter was right. Her father kept meticulous notes." He held up a handwritten sheet. "Legible, too." Dagger let Sara sift through the papers and place them in some type of order. Her hair was twisted up somehow and fastened in place by what looked like chopsticks. Gone was any anger she felt about the undercover cop being used as bait. Sara rarely stayed mad for long. That was one of a long list of things he loved about her.

"Okay, these reports are Madeline's medical history. The second stack is the report on the birth of a baby named Paul." She placed her hand on a third pile. "These are the doctor's handwritten notes concerning the birth of the twin and the mother's request that it be put up for adoption. And these last pages refer to the adoption."

Dagger started with the first stack. Sara started with the last. They read in silence as Einstein filled the air with his endless squawking. They were too engrossed in the task at hand to chase him into the aviary and shut the soundproof door. Hospital reports were easy to read since most were fill-in-the-blank. The handwritten notes took more time.

After thirty minutes, Dagger shuffled his papers into a stack. "No mention on the birth certificate of twins, which is how Madeline wanted it, but Pushing wrote on his copy that there were two boys. One was around six pounds, the other five pounds. His notes also mention that, per the mother's request, the second was to be given up for adoption."

"According to the doctor's notes, Addison Baby Number Two was given to the Little Shepherd Adoption Agency and adopted two weeks later by James and Edna Whitfield." She straightened as she found another passage in the notes. "Look." She held up the page. "Madelyn did give the twin a name. Cliff Addison."

Dagger grabbed the paper and read the words for himself. "C.A. The initials on the paintings and C.A. Holdings where Logan transfers the money. The artist has to be Cliff Addison."

50 She liked working out after ten at night, when the crowds were gone. Michael, her fiancé, complained constantly about her being alone in the gym, but he hadn't seen her kick box the stuffing out of the punching bag. Who would mess with her? Besides, she always stopped by his bar afterwards for an orange juice. It was just a short two block walk past Walker's ghost town, as locals liked to call it. A string of industrial businesses that refused to be dragged kicking and screaming into the tech world had been left in ruins. Japan now made America's nuts and bolts. A business that made parts for typewriters was still hunting for a vowel; a four-color printing business dwindled as PhotoShop enabled anyone tech savvy to create his or her own business cards, posters, and advertising materials. The mom and pop shops just couldn't compete with the big boys.

Eyes could play tricks on you in the dark, which was how Walker's ghost town got its name. Vines appeared to creep around door frames and up cracked walls. Shadows darted behind broken and gaping windows. Damen Walker had been the mayor back in the town's heyday. Refused to sell the property, thinking this new tech stuff was just a fad. He willed the property to the city upon his death with instructions that only comparable businesses be allowed to move in. He died waiting for the return of the horse and buggy days. Kids who played around the decrepit buildings claimed to hear the tap tapping of Damen Walker's cane as he walked the floors.

The moon provided just enough light to see as she crossed the street. A low mist appeared to rise up from the asphalt and snake around the shuttered buildings. It crawled across the road in front of her as though on a lazy stroll. She half expected something to rise out of the fog and take shape. A stone was kicked somewhere behind her. She felt her heart quicken and she turned quickly, her eyes scanning the street and sidewalk. The fog enveloped her and she was suddenly aware of another sound, faint at first, then gradually increasing in volume. Was it someone approaching? But it sounded as though it came from one of the abandoned buildings. Something dark flew from one building to another. The thought of a bat sent a shiver up her spine. Her attention was brought back to the sound. Step-tap. Step-tap. Step-tap.

Had to be her imagination. Without thinking she moved closer to the building, to the entrances concealed by thick plywood. Michael was to blame for filling her head with cautionary words and possible dangers. The gym was only a four block walk from her apartment. She could have gone straight home, but no. She wanted to spend time with Michael so she walked in the opposite direction and took a short cut to the bar where he worked. And what thanks does she get?

Her long ponytail slapped against her back as she turned, thinking it better to just head to her apartment. But her way was blocked by a shadow of a man, and dammit if he didn't appear to rise up from the mist. The only thing she could make out were huge yellow eyes that appeared ringed in red.

51 Dagger thought it was time to touch base with Mother. So the next morning he was seated at his desk in the office above the Hideaway. Once they knew the artist was an Addison, he and Sara thought it was time to educate Mother on the Addison curse.

"You are up early, Six-One-Seven."

"Couldn't sleep."

"What is new on Mister Logan?"

"So far we don't have anything to report. We have checked his computer and phone and don't find anything that would connect him to the Director or even make him of any interest to BettaTec. However, I have a video to show you from a previous case. I'll let you watch first before filling you in."

He uploaded the video Skizzy made when Paul Addison shifted into a winged creature in the coal bin of an aged farmhouse he'd rented. Addison was stealing weapons from a police evidence room and selling them. Skizzy used robot spiders for surveillance in the evidence room, and one found its way to the hat Addison wore, which was how Skizzy was able to track Addison to the farmhouse.

He heard gasps in the background as Addison's body first burst from his clothes like some Incredible Hulk, using his clawed hands to rip off the remaining fabric. When the beast caught sight of the robot spider, it jerked its animal-like face toward the sound of clicking as Skizzy tried to maneuver the insect remotely. Addison's teeth were long and jagged, his fair skin covered with a mat of dark hair. His yellow-slitted eyes were ringed in red and appeared to glow. The creature seemed to know it was being watched and didn't care. With the trapdoor open in the coal bin and the full moon looming in the sky, Addison drew back his bulk, immediately shifted into a winged creature, and flew from the opening.

"What on earth did we just witness?" Mother's voice was barely above a whisper.

"It's not done yet." The continuing film was from the forest the same night they cornered Addison and incinerated him. They could hear Skizzy's voice in the background as he described the weapon he used.

"This is an M-Four Module System machine gun known as a Land Warrior. Has a range finder, video camera, infrared and thermal sighting," Skizzy reported. On the monitor a shot of fire burst from the weapon while Addison tried to shift into animal forms to escape, but the concrete bunker where he was trapped ended up as his tomb.

Dagger tried to determine the number of people in Mother's headquarters as everyone appeared to be talking at once. If he ventured to guess, he would say there were a lot more than in the past. Exactly how many people comprised Alpha?

"Please explain."

"You already know what a shapeshifter is. You have the

video of Sara."

"That certainly doesn't resemble what Sara does. We know about the diary of Lewis and Clark and how they witnessed the Manitou, and still that doesn't appear to be what Sara is."

"No," Sara replied. Connie's face swiveled a one-eighty to face Sara. "There was an elder back on the reservation who was believed to be a Manitou. He was my mentor and taught me how to control my shifting."

"So this Addison is a Manitou?" The android head floating above the desk swiveled back to Dagger.

"This goes back to the early eighteen hundreds, but let me start at the case that was dumped in my lap a few years ago." Dagger reiterated the details of the cases that prompted Professor William Sherlock and Sergeant Marty Flynn to visit Cedar Point. Sherlock witnessed the murder of his entire family by something he said looked like a werewolf. Shrinks thought the young boy was traumatized, not remembering things clearly, but as an adult he became convinced his memories were accurate so he started to research shapeshifting.

"What do you mean by the Addison family curse?" Connie instinctively swiveled to face Sara.

"Nathan Addison was rumored to be a witch, involved in human sacrifices, casting spells, robbing gravesites. It was believed he was rewarded for going to the dark side."

Dagger flicked his eyes toward Sara at the term *dark side*.

He had his, Sara had hers in the form of the wolf that kills any witnesses to her shifting. The fact that Mother did not make a comment when she heard the term proved her theory that everyone had a dark side. However, Addison's was beyond the realm of believability.

"Anyway," Sara continued, "each male in the Addison family who is born during a full moon which falls on a Friday the thirteenth is cursed with this shifting ability and homicidal impulse. There have only been six since Nathan was born."

"Except for Paul's twin, Cliff."

Connie swiveled back to Dagger. He explained how Paul Addison's wife gave birth to a son the same hour that Paul died. "Josie Addison killed her son and then herself. This happened seven months ago. Police say it was a murder-suicide, but we now believe Paul's twin convinced the mother to kill her son and herself. I personally think he was involved. There can only be one. When Paul died, his powers were given to his son. We don't believe Cliff knew he was an Addison, and since only one male in the family can have the powers at a given time, once the son died, Paul started communicating with his brother in order to ensure he carried on the family curse."

"What was it your Mister Borden used to kill this Manitou?"

"Skizzy modified his weapon to shoot napalm. While in his human form, fire is the only thing that can kill him. Any other method would fail since he can just regenerate. Paul was dead. We made sure of it. But he died before he accomplished what he set out to do."

"And what was that?"

Dagger stared across the desk at his partner. How can he protect someone who didn't appear to be the least bit worried about the danger she was in?

"He wants Sara, or at least her abilities. By killing her, he absorbs her abilities."

"But he has the same abilities."

"Not exactly," Sara replied. "I can shift any time I want. Addison can only shift around a full moon. It's only partial, maybe his eyes, talons. He probably has unbelievable strength. Can rip someone's head off. But the full shifting, his full strength and power, are when the full moon falls on a Friday the thirteenth."

"And the next one will be in June," Dagger cautioned.

52 *"June thirteenth,"* Connie sighed, if android faces could sigh. But it was Mother's voice. *"What would you like us to do?"*

"It explains why we don't have time to babysit Logan. There have been seven murders over the past seven months from the West Coast to Chicago. I think, no, I know, they are connected, not so much by the methods used, but because all of the victims are named Sara."

"Good Lord."

"Exactly. Now you understand why this is important. If C.A., the artist, is Cliff Addison, the Director might think Logan can lead him to Addison. Can you imagine what would happen if the Director captured Addison and found a way to create more like him?"

"Dear God," someone murmured from the monitor. *"Logan isn't an operative. You already checked. Is that correct, Six-One-Seven?"*

"Yes. It still doesn't mean he isn't being used by the Director to draw the elusive Addison to him. Perhaps there's something in those hours of downloads that might mention Addison or research on shapeshifting."

"We will check. What have you been doing to locate Cliff Addison?"

"His birth was kept secret by the mother and doctor. Madeline Addison knew her husband would kill the second boy since there can be only one. We have the birth and adoption records and hope to find out the name he is using now. Unfortunately, he could have changed it a number of times. The police are using an uncover cop to draw out the killer. We believe he uses Facebook to research his victims. With any luck, we can find him before he finds Sara."

53 Padre shook his head as he knelt by the body of a young woman. Even before Luther handed him the woman's wallet, he knew her first name would be Sara. And he was right. "Sarah Pearson, 141 Jennifer Drive, Apartment 14. What on earth was she doing in this part of town?"

"According to her boyfriend, she sometimes walked from the gym to the bar where he works. She used this shortcut." The beat cop was swallowing hard and averting his eyes from the body where her torso appeared to have been sliced open, entrails resting on the victim's abdomen. "I checked with the bar owner. The boyfriend was working last night. Never left the building, not even for dinner or a break."

"Thanks. Why don't you go to your vehicle and type up your report. When you're through, contact the boyfriend and ask him to stop by the precinct."

The cop hitched up his gun belt and nodded vigorously before making a hasty retreat to his car.

Padre eyed the blighted surroundings. "Nice out-of-the way place. No cameras, no witnesses." The abandoned buildings didn't look much better in the daylight. If anything, it accentuated the wreckage of broken windows and brick rubble. Even though it had been years since businesses flourished here, people could swear they still smelled ink from the abandoned printing business.

Luther waited for his men to load the body into the M.E.

van before pulling Padre aside. Now that police scanners were as outdated as the Underwood typewriter, messages from dispatch were sent via in-car computers. Luckily, the press was slow in getting to the crime scene.

"I'd say she's been dead around eight hours, probably died around midnight." Luther eyed the leggy blonde reporter making her way toward the makeshift wooden horses where crime scene tape was strewn. Sheila was stepping gingerly around the debris. "We'll talk more at my place."

Padre watched the M.E. vehicles leave. He walked over to the crime tech van where Jason Reese was logging in the few bags of evidence gathered. A newbie to the department, Jason graduated tops in his class and came highly recommended by top forensics and investigative science professors. A fundraiser held several months ago during the holidays offered dinner with the most eligible bachelors in the police and fire departments. Jason garnered the highest bid of three thousand dollars by a socialite widow whom Padre felt was more of a cougar. Only Jason knew if the socialite got her money's worth. He was a strapping six foot two with washboard abs and surfer blonde hair. He could also multi-task because right now he divided his attention between the evidence bags and Sheila Monroe's legs.

"I gather you didn't find a weapon."

"No, sir. Not too many cigarette butts around either so I assume the homeless didn't like hanging around this area. I hear locals think it's haunted." He flashed a dimpled smile at Padre, but his gaze floated toward the blonde reporter on the opposite side of the crime scene tape.

Padre followed his gaze. "A word of caution if you want to continue working in this town. That reporter loves pillow talk. If I read one confidential detail from this case under her byline, I will know who gave it to her. Understood?" He glared at the young man.

"Just admiring, sir."

Padre doubted it.

54 He wasn't sure why the image kept appearing in his dreams, or why it was coming in bits and pieces. All he knew was it needed to be drawn now, to keep it fresh in his mind. He studied what he had drawn so far and waited for…what? Inspiration? The scene was a forest, but there was also a structure containing open stalls. Fifty-gallon drums were scattered around a concrete floor. The image came from inside the building. A faceless figure stood in one of the stalls. Arms were long with claw-like talons jutting from hairy fingers, yet the chest of the man was smooth and human-like. As if on its own, his hand started to draw large wings rising behind the man. He didn't remember seeing this structure, didn't remember being in this forest, yet his hand knew what to draw. It had to be HIM, the voice in his head.

He suspected in his teen years that something wasn't normal. He kept his thoughts from all of the shrinks. It was bad enough he let it slip that he heard voices in his head. Pills that were prescribed ended up in the toilet. HE told him he needed to keep a clear head. Now he knew why. He could never have painted the images without HIS help. While all of these thoughts were running through his head, he hadn't noticed that he'd sketched a beaked face above the figure's head, as if he was wearing some tribal headdress. Not one detail made sense.

He erased the bottom half of one arm and realigned it.

For some reason HE wanted it to look as though the man was warding off some threat.

"What the hell do you want?" he yelled at HIM.

Once he redrew the arm, the pencil made broad strokes from the man's feet up his naked torso. The strokes curled and licked at the hair on the man's arms. The image was beginning to take shape. He stood back and stared at the drawing. Someone had set the man on fire.

55

"I told you this would happen." Sara paced along the side of the examining table. "And he hasn't even set his sights on your undercover cop yet."

Luther flicked his gaze from Padre to Sara. "Would you rather have your picture on the front page of the *Daily Herald* with your home address and a caption 'come and get me?'"

"Just run down the specifics for us so Sara can go home and unleash her vengeance on Dagger." Padre pulled out his notepad and pen.

Sara nailed the cop with her ice blues.

"Okay." Luther pulled the sheet down to the victim's waist. He pointed to the slash mark across her abdomen just below the V-incision. "The injury was definitely not made by a knife. If it was a metal object, I would say a garden tool of some sort. But since we both suspect something else, I would lean more toward a talon. No drugs or alcohol in her system. She hadn't eaten, and as I recall, had just left the gym. The murder was quick. There weren't defensive wounds or skin under her nails. She bled out quickly. I ruled her death a homicide by exsanguination."

"Wonderful." Sara stopped her pacing. "And how many cops do you have watching your undercover officer?"

Padre sighed and faced the young woman. "Ellie is a professional. She can handle herself. I've made sure she has two backups watching her everywhere she goes, but they keep their distance. I don't want to spook this guy."

"That's not good enough."

"Sara, go wait in the office." Dagger used his bastard stare. He was going to pay for it later, but sometimes he had to be an ass.

Sara stormed out of the room, leaving two men staring at Dagger with something resembling pity.

"She'll be fine." Dagger ignored their smirks. "What else can you tell us, Doc?"

Luther cleared his throat. "I compared the injuries to the reports emailed to me from the cities where the other victims were found. It appears our assailant used asphyxiation first, but with enough strength to crush their hyoid bone. I checked the dates of the murders."

"Let me guess," Padre said. "The injuries escalated when the victim was killed around a full moon."

"Right. However, if we go with the theory that he started his rampage seven months ago, that explains why the methods escalated. Not all of the women were killed near or during a full moon. Once he found his target, he killed her. However, if it was near a full moon the killer appeared to possess extraordinary strength and abilities. Certainly nothing like when a full moon falls on a Friday the thirteenth which we witnessed. It's possible he has learned to partially shift, maybe just the talons, maybe an ability to leap tall buildings in a single bound." Luther wasn't receiving the smiles or chuckles he expected. "I thought it was pretty good."

"Ha ha," Padre deadpanned. "You must have been up all night reading Sherlock's notes. Did you read his theory that each generation is stronger and more talented, for want of a better word?" Padre's fingers reached for the gold cross hanging from his neck. "Can't believe we're talking like this. Thought we were done after we killed Addison." He turned to

Dagger and placed a hand on his shoulder. "Go easy on Sara. She has every reason to worry about the lives of innocent women who are being killed because the killer is looking for her. That said, keep an eye on her. She tends to dance to a different drummer."

"How well I know."

56 Skizzy poked his head out of the door. "Where's Dagger?"

"Home." Sara waited for Skizzy to slam all seven locks home. "I wanted to use one of your laptops."

Skizzy cocked his head and eyed her. "And there's something wrong with yours and Dagger's?"

"I need to work on something away from home."

Sara walked around the counter and tapped a key on Skizzy's laptop. Skizzy quickly slammed the lid closed. Sara barely moved her fingers out of the way.

"Uh, I don't think so. If Girlie is coming here, that means she doesn't want Dagger to know what she's working on."

Sara placed her hand on top of Skizzy's with a feigned attempt at adoration. "I need to help someone, Skizzy. Don't you like to help people who are in trouble?"

"Don't go battin' them baby blues at me." He slid the laptop off the glass countertop and clutched it to his chest. "I know what you plan to do. Create a Facebook page that Dagger already said you ain't doin.'"

"Did he call you?"

"No." Skizzy's eyes wobbled in different directions. "But I know he already deleted a page you were creating, trying to bait the killer. Bad idea."

Sara folded her arms. This was going to be harder than she thought. If Eunie was still in town and not on her cruise.

she was sure Eunie would let her use hers or Simon's laptop. "Do you have a key to Simon's house?"

"Yep…uh, nope. You ain't getting the key so you can use their laptop. No sirree, Bob. Besides, if he were here, Simon would tell you the same thing. Nope, no way, no how." He clutched the laptop tighter as Sara made her way to the front of the counter. Skizzy backed away. "You've heard the saying about you can poke a bear once and maybe get away with it, but if you keep poking him, he's gonna get really angry. Well, I ain't about ready to poke the bear."

Sara slammed into the house and marched over to Dagger's desk. "Do you have your hooks into everyone in this town?"

Dagger kept his head down, fingers pounding on the keyboard. "Not everyone. Just a handful of very loyal people." He stopped typing and lifted his eyes. If Sara looked any angrier, he was sure fire would shoot from her eyes. "I'm surprised you didn't try Casey, but then Casey is on your shit list lately." He picked up a file folder and handed it to her. "Something to occupy your mind."

Her glare could have set the folder on fire. Sara turned and marched into the kitchen.

Dagger sighed and followed, folder in hand. He found her leaning against the counter, arms crossed, fingers drumming. "Skizzy tracked down the neighbors of the family that adopted Twin Addison. Thought you might like to give them a call and see if they remember anything about the devil child." He waited several seconds before tossing the folder on the table. "Okay, enough with the daggers, no pun intended."

"I keep thinking how easy it would be to catch this killer if I communicated with him telepathically, gave him a place to meet me."

"No. Besides, you have no way of knowing if he has the ability yet. It isn't a full moon."

"Hear me out, please." She raised her hands as though warding him off. Dagger stepped back. "We could set a trap.

You and Padre would be there, and Skizzy would be waiting with the same weapon he used to kill Paul. No one else would have to die."

"Tell me something, Sara. When we were at the mall, you and I both felt someone watching. I think...no...I KNOW your instincts are stronger than mine. Even when we climbed onto that elevator, you somehow knew something was going to happen. Addison is going to sense the trap. He will know it isn't just you meeting him. And if he has the ability to fully shift, we'd be putting both Skizzy and Padre in danger."

He stepped closer and wrapped his arms around her, but Sara didn't respond. He held her tightly, not giving her a chance to storm off again. "Doesn't it make more sense to find out what name Addison is using? Find the alias, we find the man. And the way to do that is to start at the beginning. If he has been moved from house to house, there is a chance he changed names each time."

"I'm sure he stole the adoption records and knows he's an Addison. Maybe he is using his real name now. Have you checked?"

"Skizzy already did and it netted zip. If Cliff Addison researched his family name, he knows better than to use it. And I'm sure he has done research into the cursed version of the family tree."

Dagger cupped her face and stared into her eyes. Seemed like yesterday that she was a teenager who trembled whenever he came near, who had been as skittish as a kitten. Now she was a self-confident woman who feared nothing. Sure, crowds still sent her into panic attacks, but he understood the cause. No one was more angry about her phobias than Sara herself.

"I love you." And did he ever. Dagger never believed he would ever be capable of loving someone so much.

She placed her hand over his heart, grabbed his hand and

placed it over her heart. She could feel the heartbeats through her fingers. She closed her eyes and listened, how in just a few short seconds, the heartbeats fell into sync.

Sara opened her eyes and looked into Dagger's. Others might see eyes of a killer. She herself had seen Dagger kill with abandon. No second thoughts. No regrets. No sleepless nights. Maybe he never had a gentle side, not until he met her. "Why does love have to hurt so much? I know when I disappeared for two months after Paul Addison died that I caused you a great deal of pain. I won't ever do that again."

"Just this once, don't fight me on it. I need to know where you are and that you're safe. I can't lose you again."

58

Landscapes, fruit, flowers, and everything in between. The only paintings that interested Joe were the naked women. He was certain Sheila knew the names of every technique used by every artist. Joe, on the other hand, could name every ingredient in his Uncle Tito's *parmigiano sformato*. For all the time he and Sheila dated, he never once showed off his culinary talent. Joe had been Uncle Tito's only nephew. He knew everyone in the precinct thought he was on the take. Tailor-made suits, new car every two years, a three-thousand square foot condo. His wealth still paled in comparison to the Monroe family fortune, and still no one knew how Joe amassed such a fat bank account.

"Did you need some help?"

Joe thought Sheila was spot on when she said the gallery manager looked like a mortician. The pasty skin and sunken eyes gave a macabre aura to Carlton Abrams.

"I called about seeing the Nightfall exhibit." Joe reached out a hand and thought if he squeezed a little too hard Carlton's fingers would land on the floor in pieces.

"Of course. Mister Spagnola?"

"That's me." Joe was dressed for work in a suit and tie so it should quell any fears Carlton might have that Joe wasn't a serious buyer. Carlton appeared to admire Joe's taste in clothes.

"This way." Carlton led Joe to the French doors. For being

so crowded during the grand opening, Joe was surprised the gallery was empty.

"Where are all of the art enthusiasts?"

"It's very busy during the day. We're thinking of only being open on Friday and Saturday nights. None of the other shops on this end of the street have late hours except for the weekend."

Sheila was right again. Even the way Carlton spoke sounded like turn-of-the-century Transylvania. The French doors opened and immediately the spotlights on the walls came on. Joe maneuvered around pillars the size of tree trunks. The lit tiki torches looked like a disaster waiting to happen should they ever topple over.

He studied the first piece, which appeared to be the focal point of the exhibit. "Exquisite." And it was. Even though art was on the bottom of Joe's list of knowledgeable subjects, he did appreciate beautiful women. He stepped closer and studied the detail of the two faces. "Why animals?"

Carlton shrugged. "That's why the exhibit is called Nightfall. It depicts things one might see at night." He cleared his throat as his eye caught one of the more colorful pieces on a side wall. "And also things that might happen at night."

"When do you close?"

"In a half hour. Take your time. I do have some work to do by the desk, so if you have any questions, feel free to give a shout."

Once Carlton left, Joe pulled out a piece of paper from the inside pocket of his suit jacket and unfolded it. The artist appeared to use a bright, full moon in each of the portraits. The motorcycle rider. Hit and run. That was one reason why Joe never cared to own a motorcycle. It didn't end well when an eighteen wheeler came in contact with an open mode of transportation, each going at full speed in opposite directions.

The artist probably read about the accident in the paper.

He could swear he caught a movement out of the corner of his eye. He turned toward the French doors to make sure the mortician left and thought he saw someone peering through the window on the far side of the lobby. Joe stepped closer. There wasn't anyone in the lobby. There were only two windows by the entrance and they appeared too high for anyone to see in from the outside. Joe shook it off and returned to the paintings. Looking at all of these dark forest scenes could spook even the strongest.

The way the lights were positioned, each appeared to spotlight the grossest part of the painting. He stopped in front of a painting of two teens. The male was leaning against a tree, appearing to try to hold his guts in. The light was directed on the intestines. Joe may not know impressionists from paint-by-number, but he knew sick when he saw it.

The cop, Lisa. Joe couldn't even remember her last name. Every cop should be pissed that someone would highlight the death of a brother or sister-in-arm so grotesquely. Joe never discussed Padre's cases with him, although there was always talk among the ranks. However, there had been too much talk about her body being wedged in a tree for it to be just rumor.

There was that feeling again. Joe walked toward the doorway. There wasn't anyone there. His gaze roamed to the windows, but he couldn't see anyone. For some reason, his gaze lifted toward the ceiling where a peaked skylight showed the night sky. Was there a shadow that moved? He could swear he saw a face. "Shit," he said under his breath. "This is like a damn house of horrors." He returned his attention to the exhibit, quickly finding the one depicting Sheila's condo, but he couldn't shake the feeling that he was being watched. Slowly, he tilted his head and saw two more skylights in the exhibit room. Was someone on the roof?

He heaved out a long breath. "Must be the goal of the artist—freak everyone out." He held up the picture taken by the crime technician. The blood spray, the position of Caroline's body, the overturned furniture, the opened patio doors, even one of Caroline's shoes found laying under the coffee table had been painted in the exact spot. How could that be? Someone had to have taken the photos from the Evidence Room. Yet, Joe didn't see anyone's name on the Evidence Room log since the case closed. Did someone make a copy of the photos while Joe was working the case?

He pulled out his phone and called Sheila. "I'm here," was all he said. He could sense her bristling at his abruptness.

"And?" She was just as abrupt.

"You were right. Everything is identical. Even every drop of blood splatter. My only guess is someone at the crime scene took his own picture for his own sick album and is now creating his own macabre art show." His voice drifted as he walked past the other paintings.

"Joe, are you there?"

"Yeah." He stopped in front of the painting of the motorcyclist. The Harley was painted as a smoldering twist of metal barely resembling what it was. The headless body was several yards from the bike, the head impaled on a tree limb. He remembered the official report was a traffic accident. But why and how did the female passenger's body end up in a tree on the opposite side of the street? He hadn't heard any rumors about that so the artist seemed to take artistic expression to new heights.

"Joe?"

He noticed Carlton standing in the doorway. "I have to go."

"Did you have any questions? I'm getting ready to close up."

Joe shoved the phone in his pocket. "Yes. I need to speak to the owner of the gallery. I want the name of the artist and any contact information he has."

"Oh, Mister Logan would love that, too. The artist appears to call from an obvious, what do you call it, a throw-away phone? Paintings show up at the galleries."

"Very convenient." For some reason Joe didn't believe one word of it. "Well, I would still like to speak to your boss." Joe handed him a business card. "If I don't hear from him by tomorrow afternoon, I will just park myself in his hotel lobby. I understand he is staying at the Suisse Hotel."

Carlton reluctantly took the card and skimmed it. "So I take it, Detective—," he enunciated each syllable of the word, "—that you have zero interest in our exhibit."

Joe leveled a stare that he usually saved for the interrogation room. "I assure you, I have a great deal of interest in your exhibit."

59 With time to kill, Joe decided to stop for dinner at an out-of-the-way restaurant that served great pasta. He took a short cut down a road that cut through farmland. The BMW six cylinder coasted around curves like a dream. He knew he should knock his speed down a notch but he didn't detect another headlight in sight. Tilled farmland appeared ready for the planting season. This part of the city planted most of the feed corn.

He pulled out a handheld recorder from the center console and pressed record. He stated the date and time and reason for visiting Logan's Galleria. "Upon the suggestion of Sheila Monroe, reporter for the *Daily Herald* and owner of the condominium where her assistant, Caroline Kirby, was the victim of a homicide back in…note to self…check exact date Miss Monroe saw the painting at the gallery and wondered how accurate it was to the actual crime scene, specifically since most of the details in the police report were not released to the public. Having compared the painting to the color photo from the crime scene, Miss Monroe is correct. Everything is identical. Even each drop of blood. The only thing…" He pressed the stop button and thought back to the painting of the motorcyclist. He clicked the headlights on bright and kicked the speed down a few notches. Somewhere up ahead he knew there was a dangerous curve. Joe pressed the record button again. "There were other paintings depicting actual scenes. However, since Sergeant Jerry Martinez was the lead on these investigations, I will have to talk to him further." He pressed the stop button and set the recorder down.

The sky was full of stars tonight. There was an open stretch of hills coming up, which he was sure led to the treacherous curve. Teenagers were known to speed up and down the hills and immediately regret it when they realized mufflers and bumpers had been ripped from their cars.

Joe could feel the BMW lift off the road as he crested the hill. The high beams caught site of the treacherous curve and deep ditch ahead on the right. The guard rail was bent and twisted from other drivers who had taken the hill too fast. From across the road, something flew toward his vehicle and landed with a thud on the windshield.

"What the…" Joe turned the wheel the wrong way. He heard the crunch of metal before the BMW went airborne. His first thought was a deer or some large bird. But he also saw claws, a face, and yellow eyes ringed in what looked like blood. Before he passed out, the SUV rolled end-over-end, careened down the steep slope, and finally came to rest against a tree.

60 "Who found him?" Padre hustled off of the elevator behind his chief of detectives. Wozniak was rustled out of bed at five in the morning by the night shift supervisor.

"A farmer was out with his tractor clearing a field when he saw the SUV. Joe may be an ass sometimes but he has never been a no call, no show. When they couldn't rouse him on his phone, they sent someone over to his condo. Nothing."

The medicinal smells assaulted them as they reached the ER desk. The waiting room looked like a neighborhood sleepover with blankets and pillows on couches and nervous family members huddled in corners. If it were around midnight, the place would probably be packed wall to wall with patients.

Wozniak flashed his shield at the two women behind the counter. "One of our detectives was brought in. Joe Spagnola."

The older of the two stood and motioned for them to join her by the security guard's desk. She wore a dark business suit, and her name tag said she was an RN. "He's still in surgery. At the end of this hall, turn right and follow the signs to the surgical waiting room. I believe an officer is waiting to speak to you." Her smile showed the fatigue in her eyes. The men were well aware of how long nights can take their toll. "I hope everything turns out all right."

"What was his condition? I take it you were here when he was brought in," Padre said. When her smile started to fade, he added, "Please be honest."

"It wasn't good. Head trauma, internal bleeding, possible broken shoulder and ribs. They rushed him to X-ray and then to surgery. He's in my prayers."

They thanked her and made their way down the corridor. "We must have that seminary school odor wafting from our bodies. At least I'm sure you still do, Padre. People look at you and they start confessing or offering up prayers."

"I don't think prayers are gonna help this time. I've got a bad feeling about this, John."

They entered the waiting room and immediately smelled the coffee. Only one person was in the room. A uniformed officer popped up like a jack-in-the-box the moment they entered. Neither John nor Padre recognized him. The two men headed for the coffeepot.

John doctored his cup of caffeine with enough sugar to keep him jacked up for the next three hours. "You were first on the scene?" He glanced at the young cop who clutched a laptop, notepad and pen. "Relax. At ease. Whatever."

"Officer Kevin Buckley, sir."

Padre motioned to a table in the corner. "Why don't you go grab that table and we'll join you as soon as the chief finishes his science project. Did you want some coffee?"

"No. I mean I have a cup, but thanks."

"He's a little nervous. Think it was his first sight of blood?"

John glanced over at the ashen-faced patrolman. "Damn, I feel old. Yeah. Looks like his first rodeo."

They joined Buckley, and after making official introductions, they took a seat. Buckley opened his notepad. "I arrived on the scene at…"

"Just get to the important stuff," the chief said. "What did the accident investigators find?"

"Uh.." Buckley licked his finger and flipped through

several pages. "No skid marks. Pavement was dry, but there's a dangerous curve in that section of the road. The SUV hit the guard rail and went down the embankment. By the condition of the car, it looks as though the vehicle flipped several times. The victim, I mean Detective Spagnola, was wearing his seatbelt. The vehicle is being towed to the tech garage. There wasn't any other paint on the vehicle to point to a collision with another vehicle. And, as mentioned, no skid marks to indicate an altercation with same. The driver was unconscious at the scene and transported via helicopter to Community Hospital."

"Any idea where Joe was headed? That is certainly miles from the precinct and still a couple hours before the start of his shift."

"Luigi's," Padre said. "There's an Italian restaurant about twelve miles south of town Joe has mentioned. He would stop for a carryout or to eat before his shift. He usually took that shortcut through the farmlands. That's probably where he was headed."

A surgeon in green scrubs with a mask hanging around his neck, stepped into the room. He saw the men clustered around the table and walked over. "I'm Doctor Reynolds." Padre introduced himself, Wozniak, and the patrolman. "You're here for Joseph Spagnola?" Wozniak nodded. "He's out of surgery but in critical condition. We will keep him in recovery, then move him to ICU."

Wozniak handed him a business card. "Could you have someone at the nurse's station contact me when he is able to talk?"

"What's the prognosis?" Padre wasn't sure if the surgeon would be forthcoming since they weren't family, but there wasn't a tighter knit family than the police department.

"Hard to tell at this point. He's young and healthy, so that's in his favor. The next twelve hours will tell us more."

Padre felt everyone in the medical field was taught cautious optimism, in their manner, speech, and the stoic facial mask they must have mastered in medical school. The seriousness of a patient's condition, though, is usually more evident when doctors add exactly what Doctor Reynolds said next.

"Does he have next of kin who can be contacted?"

61 "He's too quiet. Not a good sign." Dagger grabbed a cup and made his way to the coffee pot. He had filled Einstein's food bowls and given him another rope toy to play with, but all the macaw did was ruffle his feathers and gaze at the windows.

"I noticed it, too. I checked his vitals. Everything is fine. I think he is just picking up on our anxieties." But Sara knew differently. This was exactly how Einstein acted during the Paul Addison case. He knew there was something different in the world, something not normal in the animal kingdom.

"But you don't believe that, do you?" Dagger carried the coffee pot over to the kitchen table and refilled Sara's cup. A mild breeze drifted in from the kitchen windows, carrying a scent of the impending rain. The forecast called for thunderstorms later in the day.

Sara shook her head. "At night I can sense a change in the creatures. Just after dusk when they should be the noisiest, everything becomes silent. Nature knows something isn't quite right."

He set the pot on the warmer and took a seat. "You were up early." He assumed Sara showered in her bedroom so she wouldn't wake him. Her hair hung down to her waist and contained shades not typical to her Native American heritage. The blackish blue color of a raven was streaked with the brown, auburn, blonde, and gray hues of the hawk and wolf. Her face was void of any makeup. Just the way he liked it. "Find anything new?"

"Skizzy already checked the whereabouts of Edna and James Whitfield, the couple that adopted Cliff Addison. Although he wasn't known as Cliff Addison. Madeline was adamant, according to Doctor Pushing's notes, that any reference to the Addison name was strictly prohibited. So he was named Matthew Barnes. The Whitfields didn't actually adopt the twin. They decided to become foster parents first and wait to see if they wanted to adopt. However, they refused to talk about the boy."

Dagger saw a drawing showing what looked like a genealogy chart with Madeline Addison's name at the top and one line down to Matthew's name. "Did you draw this?"

"I tried to keep things straight in case he was shuffled through several homes. I just got off the phone with Bernie Carson. She still lives in the same house across the street from where the Whitfield's lived in Ohio and remembers them quite well. They kept Matt until he was eight years old. Bernie said the Whitfield's were a nice, loving couple. When Matt was three years old, Edna gave birth to a boy. Although there was the typical jealousy, Bernie claimed there was something not quite right with Matt."

"Let me guess, neighborhood pets started disappearing, the younger boy displayed unexplained bruises."

"You are so devious but correct." Sara cradled her coffee cup in her hands. A vase of fresh cut tulips and daffodils had been shoved to the far end of the table to make room for all the paperwork. She caught him looking at her firm, tanned legs under her shorts. "Is my formal attire too distracting?"

Dagger dragged his gaze to her face and smiled. "You are distracting no matter what you wear."

"Focus and maybe later we can be distracted by a whirlpool, candles, soft music, and wine."

"Oh, hell. Now I won't be able to concentrate on anything."

"And I'll make you wait until nine o'clock tonight."

Dagger groaned. "You do know how to torture a guy."

She set her cup down and returned to her notes. "Back to Bernie. Edna confessed to her that she didn't trust him around her son; and she was sure he was responsible for the disappearance of Scotty, their Scottish terrier. Bernie swore he looked like the boy in the movie Damien. She said when he looked at you he was seeing through you, as though you weren't important and he was thinking of ways to harm you. She said he gave her the chills."

"Where to from there?"

Sara drew a line from the Whitfields and wrote a name. "Heywood Home for Boys in Ohio. That's where he ended up while waiting for another foster home or to be adopted. The home is no longer there. Closed up over ten years ago. So I checked the Internet for any stories about the Heywood Home. I scanned through articles on funding, awards, remodeling, promotions, new hires, and other boring stuff and found something on the death of the night supervisor." Sara handed Dagger a printout.

Dagger quickly scanned it and chuckled. "Freak accident. Fell down the stairs and died of a broken neck. Only witness was a ten-year-old boy who saw it all from the flight above. No mention of the boy's name."

Sara smiled and handed him another printout. "Skizzy found the police report in his usual sneaky way."

"Now who's devious." He quickly found the witness's name. "Matthew Barnes." He handed the report back to Sara.

"From there I am stuck. With the Heywood Home closed, I'm not sure where Matthew ended up."

"Nothing on the Internet?"

"Just an article announcing the closing and that the boys

would be sent to various facilities across the country."

"Search for Matthew's name. If he was Satan's spawn as a child, the adult Matthew might have made news. Have Skizzy troll police departments across the country in search of Matthew Barnes. See if he has a record anywhere."

"And what are you going to do?"

"I'm going to make sure the whirlpool is clean." He gave her a wink and walked out.

62 Sheila pressed Joe's hand to her face. She was sitting beside his bed in ICU and listening to the beeps of all the machines. There were so many wires and tubes taped to his body that he resembled something out of a sci-fi movie. How had this happened? Why did she waste time arguing and being mad at him when they could have been happy? But he was going to get better. She was sure of it. She had a special relationship with the man upstairs. Her gaze lifted toward the ceiling. Of course, the man upstairs didn't have a great track record where she was concerned. How many times did her prayers go unanswered when all she wanted was for Dagger to love her as much as she loved him? Yet the more she prayed, the more the man upstairs appeared deaf. She would have done better to recite some Wiccan ceremony to help with her love life.

There was a flutter in Joe's fingers. She jerked her gaze to see Joe's eyes at half mast. "Joe? Baby? Are you awake?"

Joe slowly turned his face to the beeping machines and settled his eyes on Sheila. He moved his mouth to speak.

"Are you thirsty?" She grabbed a cloth and dipped it in a bowl of ice water. "You aren't allowed to drink anything but I can wet your lips." Joe barely acknowledged the wet cloth. "Does anything hurt? How stupid, of course everything hurts. Do you need another pain shot?"

"I saw…"

"What? What did you see, Joe?"

Tears gathered in the corners of his eyes. Sheila had never seen Joe cry. Was he, too, regretting their argument? She leaned over and placed her ear close to his mouth. "What are you trying to say?"

He was able to get the words out right before the machines went crazy.

"They are taking so damn long they could have taken the whole vehicle apart piece by piece."

"There are two other vehicles in the garage to examine, John. I think drive-bys take precedence over Joe's vehicle."

Padre wished they had found a parking space closer. As it was they were leaving water droplets in the elevator and down the hall. A man in a gray uniform stood guard by the entrance to mop up the water. A large fan was blowing air over the floor to try to keep the area dry. If you were going to slip and break something, you couldn't pick a better place.

"I hate this weather." As though on cue, a clap of thunder cut through the air. "It's always a bad omen, you know, like no sun on your wedding day."

"Guess all three of your weddings were rained out." Padre wasn't sure how John's third marriage was doing. He always avoided pressing John about his personal life.

They headed for Joe's room but caught sight of Sheila sitting in the ICU waiting area. She was staring at the floor, her fingers toying with a ripped tissue.

"Hey, Sheila. Did you get in to see Joe?" Padre sat next to her on the couch. John peeled off his raincoat and draped it over a chair before collapsing in a bench seat across from them.

"He's gone," Sheila said.

"They took him to X-ray?" John asked.

Sheila shook her head and slowly looked at Padre, tears trailing down her cheeks. "He died, Padre. He finally opened his eyes for the first time, and then he died." She covered her mouth and wept quietly. Padre wrapped his arm around her and looked at John.

"Oh, shit." John huffed out a loud sigh. "My sympathies, Sheila. I knew the accident was bad, but the doctor seemed optimistic."

Sheila slowly straightened and dabbed at her eyes. "It's my fault, Padre. I asked him to go to the gallery to look at the paintings."

"Don't blame yourself."

But she wasn't listening. "I thought the painting of my condo was just too accurate, but I wasn't sure. So I asked Joe to take the crime scene photo with him to compare. If he hadn't gone so early before work, he wouldn't have driven out to that restaurant. If I knew he wanted to eat dinner before work, he should have called me. We could have gone someplace local."

"We can *what if* and *if only* all day long. It isn't going to change the outcome." Padre pulled out his hankie and handed it to Sheila. "It's clean." He didn't remember ever seeing her with disheveled hair and streaked mascara before.

"So he never came to at all?" John asked.

"He did, but just for a short time. He said something but it didn't make any sense. I'm pretty sure I heard wrong."

Padre remembered saying some pretty weird things when he was coming out of surgery so it wouldn't surprise him if Joe didn't make sense.

Sheila dabbed at her eyes and proceeded to mangle the hankie. "It sounded like, 'I saw Satan himself.'"

63 The inspection bays in the crime unit garage emitted all the smells of a service station. Oil, grease, chemicals. Exhaust fans overhead sucked out most of the noxious odors. Padre and Wozniak preferred to stay on the opposite side of the glass and watch.

Joe's BMW looked like it had been halfway through a crusher before someone hit the kill switch. The rear door was ripped at the top and resting on the back cargo space. Side doors had either been torn off or the techs had removed them to provide room to inspect the interior. A table set up against a wall held a variety of items the two cops couldn't decipher from where they stood.

A doughy man in a blue jumpsuit grabbed a plastic bag from the table and walked over to the door. His face was pink either from exertion or the sun. He entered the observation area and nodded to the two men. *Al* was sewn onto the pocket of his jumpsuit. "Chief, Sarge." He handed Padre the plastic bag. "So far we've only found maps, discount cards, notepads, pens, typical car stuff." Al nodded toward the bag. "We dusted the recorder for prints."

Padre unzipped the bag and pulled out the recorder. "Any hint of foul play?"

"We're going to hoist it up now and check for any tampering."

"You think the brake lines were cut?" Wozniak looked

from Al to the twisted metal that once was a great looking BMW.

"We'll find out now. Are you going to stick around?"

"Yes." Wozniak waited until Al left, then said, "See if there's anything current on that thing."

They sat down in the plastic chairs. Padre flipped the power button and checked the menu. "Only one entry." He pressed the PLAY button and set the recorder down. They listened as Joe described his visit to Logan's Galleria and his comparison to the actual photo from the crime scene in Sheila's condo and the painting of the crime. The tape was less than five minutes long. Joe hit the stop button so the recorder hadn't been running at the time of the accident.

"What do you think?"

Padre pulled out his phone and dialed Dagger. "Hey. Got about five minutes to spare? I have something for you to listen to."

"Let me put my phone on speaker. Okay. What are we hearing?"

"You'll know soon enough." Padre pressed the PLAY button and let the tape run to the end of Joe's report before pressing STOP.

"Who's there with you?" Dagger asked.

"Just me," Wozniak said.

"Have you spoken to Joe?"

Padre looked across the table at Wozniak. Dagger obviously didn't know. Padre expected Sheila to be crying on Dagger's shoulder by now. "Joe's dead, Dagger." Padre explained the accident and how they were at the tech garage waiting to see if Joe's vehicle had been tampered with."

Sara's voice came over the speaker. "Did he say anything before he died?"

"According to Sheila, the only thing Joe said was, 'I saw

Satan himself.'"

There was silence for several seconds while Dagger digested the information. "Have them check the front windshield for fingerprints."

"The front windshield?" Wozniak asked.

"Yes, do it now."

The two cops entered the inspection area where the BMW now resembled a match car disassembled by a three-year-old. Parts were removed, and what was left of the car had been hoisted up so the brake lines could be inspected.

"Al," John yelled over the noise from the overhead fans. "Where's the windshield?"

Al pointed a wrench to a side wall where a bent and shattered windshield was propped up. "Have at it."

"What am I looking for?" Padre said into his phone.

"Fingerprints would be nice. If they belong to Paul Addison, we'll know he's not dead," Dagger replied.

John brought out a penlight and shined it on the cracked surface. "This is like looking at a jar of cracked marbles. Sure as hell won't find prints."

"Wait." Padre moved John's hand to an area near the driver's side. "What does that look like?" Even through the pebbled surface and spider cracks they could see six deep scratch marks about an inch apart.

"Oh shit," John huffed out in a long breath.

64

"What are you thinking?" Sara followed Dagger into the living room.

"Nothing good. I was hoping the wrong someone saw him at the exhibit comparing the painting to the actual crime scene photo, followed him and forced him off the road."

"You really think those deep scratch marks on the windshield were made by talons?"

"Don't you?" Dagger took a seat at his desk and punched the Skype icon on the keyboard to contact Skizzy.

Sara agreed. If Joe thought he saw Satan, then he saw him through his front windshield; and he wasn't using a vehicle as his mode of transportation.

"Yo, Skizzy at your service."

"Hope you've got something on Matt Barnes." Dagger saw on the monitor that Skizzy was in the shop, not his basement bunker.

"I was just getting ready to ring your chimes." Papers rustled in the background.

"AWWKK, OH SHIT." Einstein pecked at the grated door.

Skizzy laughed. "That my buddy over there?" Skizzy's language over the years had an unwelcome effect on the macaw.

"How do you like knowing that's your name in Einstein's mind?" Sara walked over and tapped Einstein's claw. "Go take a shower."

"OH SHIT, OH SHIT." Einstein flew to the birdbath and pulled the overhead chain to send a shower of water cascading over his body. Sara closed the soundproof door.

Skizzy waved several sheets of paper in front of the monitor. "I let one of my trolls wander through cyberspace. Found scads of Matthew Barnes, but when I filtered for a specific age range and other pertinent poop, I found a Matthew Barnes connected to a couple in Colorado. Maeve and Marvin Ames took in Matthew when he was fourteen. This is where it gets interesting. Maeve was a retired art teacher. Had a studio in their home on acres of farmland. This might be our guy, seeing that Maeve could have taught him everything he knows."

"Were you able to contact the couple?" Dagger asked.

"That's where it REALLY gets interesting. Marvin died in a tragic accident at his home. Was repairing the gutter and the ladder slipped."

"Any witnesses?"

"Matthew was the only one at home. Claims he didn't see the accident, only heard the crash and dialed nine-one-one. Course, being off in the country the ambulance didn't get there soon enough."

"How convenient."

"It gets more interesting. The widow paid for Matthew to go to a pricey college where he could study the arts. During his first year, a fire broke out in the house, killing Maeve. Fire Department chalked it up to all the paint and chemicals in the art studio. And before you ask, Matthew was in his dorm when it happened."

"Was the college close enough for him to get home and back?" Sara asked.

"Close enough. However, police saw no cause to question him more."

Dagger was jotting down notes as Skizzy spoke. He ripped off the page and handed it to Sara to add to the timeline she was making. "How rich were the Ames?"

"Fucking filthy. No relatives, and Maeve left everything to young Matthew. The newspapers estimated their worth at over ten million. But their farmland and house sat on some pretty valuable property. It's now a private country club with six-figure homes. I can't even count that high to tell you how much the developers paid the heir. Certainly enough for Matthew to attend a pricey art institute in Paris and to keep him quite comfortable for the rest of his life. If he had any other occupation I haven't been able to find it. Matter of fact he totally went off the grid after Europe. Didn't make a big splash buying private jets or hanging with the Hollywood type. Preferred a low profile. I can't find him via a tax return, a drivers license, nada. With all that dough he could create a whole new identity if he wanted to and stay below the radar."

"Great." Dagger leaned back and thought about the artist who had created Nightfall. "Certainly confirms in my mind that he is C.A., Cliff Addison. I'm just not sure Logan is being completely honest when he claims that he has never met Addison."

"What about neighbors?" Sara asked. "Someone must know something about the Ames and their foster son."

"No one is around. As I said, the little farming community is now a golf community and shopping center."

"Police reports?"

"Still trolling." Skizzy jerked one eyebrow up and scratched the stubble on his chin. He leaned closer to the screen and they saw his eyes wobble in their sockets. "What else? You've got that crease between your eyebrows when you are about to drop a bombshell."

Dagger told him about Joe Spagnola's death following his

trip to the gallery and his comment to Sheila about Satan. He thought he heard a moan from Skizzy when he mentioned the gouges on the windshield of the BMW.

"No, no no no no no. He's dead. Gotta be another explanation. You sure branches couldn't have caused those gouges? And what about fingerprints? Maybe someone pushed Joe's car over the edge."

"Paul and Cliff are fraternal twins. Identical twins might have some similarity in their prints but fraternal twins would have their own distinct prints."

Skizzy stared, unblinking. For a brief moment, they wondered if he was having a seizure of some type. He looked like he was in a trance. With a couple quick shakes of his head, Skizzy finally blinked. "Well, then. Looks like I need to brush the dust off my Land Warrior."

65 Sheila turned the lights on in Joe's condo. She had never given Joe back the extra key. The kitchen was clean, dishwasher empty. How like Joe to keep things as neat as his appearance. The gym equipment didn't have a speck of dust on it. Maybe his new exercise partner cleaned them off. She tried not to think of him with someone else.

A towel was drying over the shower door. An electric toothbrush was on the counter, electric shaver in the corner. Sheila pulled the towel from the door and the washcloth from the hook. She carried them to the laundry room and went through the hamper. After pouring soap in the washer and fabric softener in the dispenser, she dumped the dirty clothes and towels into the washing machine and turned it on. The ladies at the country club would be shocked to learn that she did laundry.

Sheila went back to the kitchen, grabbed a glass and opened the wine cooler next to the bar. She grabbed a bottle of Shiraz and filled the glass. What she really wanted was a martini but didn't have the energy to make one. One of the bedrooms served as an office. Sheila turned the light on, sat down at the desk, and set her glass down. She should have asked Joe more about his family. She thought he'd once mentioned an uncle who owned a restaurant in New York, or at least used to. Joe might also have mentioned the uncle died. So who was going to take care of Joe's estate, his bills, cleaning out the condo, notifying all the utilities, the bank, broker? Who was Joe's attorney?

Will. Joe should have a will, right? She opened the desk drawers. The few folders she found were neatly labeled, yet not one spoke legalese to her. What about a lock box? Did he have one at the bank? That would be a start, and she was sure Joe's supervisor, or someone in Human Resources was checking into it. The only other visitors to the hospital were Padre and Chief Wozniak. What if Joe didn't have anyone to make funeral arrangements?

Sheila moved to the master bedroom and stood in the doorway. Of course the bed was made, not a crease in the bedspread. Her eyes roamed the crown molding, the dark wood of the furniture, the subtle design in the drapery and headers. Very masculine. So like Joe. The tears fell freely as she set the wine glass down and sat on the bed. She was sure if she ran her hand across the night stand, it wouldn't leave a trail. Had he or has father been in the military? What about his mother? Sheila suddenly realized she knew very little about Joe other than his sexual proclivities. Now she would never get to know more. She swiped at her nose with the back of her hand.

"You are so stupid. When are you ever going to learn?" She opened the nightstand drawer hoping to find a phone book, maybe a family album. Something that would tell her more about the man she loved. Yes, she had loved Joe…in her own way. The drawer only contained a small box and a card. The envelope wasn't sealed. She opened the flap and pulled out the card. It was a simple love you type card. She opened it. There wasn't a greeting card message. Just handwritten words…*be mine.*

This was the side of the bed she always slept on when she spent the night. Had he meant for her to roll over and find it? Her hands shook as she opened the box and gasped at the ring. The pear-shaped diamond was at least three carats. If anyone knew her carats, it was Sheila. She slipped the ring on her finger. It was a perfect fit. Months ago she remembered leaving her ring in the kitchen. That must have been how he found out her ring size. How many arguments ago was that? She could imagine him carrying it in his pocket, planning to spring it on her at dinner somewhere, only for the night to end up in a fight and him probably changing his mind.

"Dammit, Joe." She swiped at her eyes and sniffed back the tears. With the box, card, and drink in hand, she returned to the kitchen, set the drink down, and stuffed the box and card into her purse. What she wanted to do was sleep in Joe's bed tonight. How silly was that?

Her thoughts were interrupted by the doorbell. Sheila opened the door to find a woman, either heavily tanned or of Italian or Spanish descent. Short dark hair, nice figure. But what caught her attention was the floral print jersey shirt. Sheila was sure it was Versace and cost over five hundred dollars. This was worn over skinny cream-colored leather pants. Vince Camuto maybe? A Gucci navy, soft leather bucket bag was flung over one shoulder. And, could it be? Christian Louboutin cream colored studded sandals with four-inch heels? Oh my God, Sheila thought. I'm looking at an Italian version of myself. Definitely not the cleaning lady.

"I'm sorry. Is this Joe Spagnola's place?"

"Yes, it is. And you are...?" She left that comment hanging in the air.

"I'm his wife."

66 Ellie Gardner nursed her wine while she checked her phone. She took her job seriously, to the point that she died her blonde hair brown so it matched the dark wig she was wearing. A voice interrupted her game of *Words with Friends* that she was playing with the cop who was shadowing her. Jumpin' Joe's was not exactly a jumping place. She mentioned it on her Facebook page as a local hangout where she liked to go to unwind. There were a number of office buildings several blocks away so it wasn't unusual to see business types mingling with construction workers. At least it wasn't a cop hangout. Those bars were on the other side of town.

"At your three o'clock," the voice from her earbud said.

Ellie casually checked the mirror behind the bartender and saw the young man sitting at the end of the bar eyeing her over his beer glass. "Got him. He's been checking out all the women. I'm going to finish my drink. You hang back and see if he follows." Ellie left a two dollar tip, gave a wave to the bartender, slipped into her jacket, and walked out.

She purposely picked a bar four blocks from her house so she could walk. According to Sergeant Martinez, Sarah Pearson had taken a short cut to meet her boyfriend before she was killed. Padre eluded to possible other homicides in other states, but had not shared the details with her. The department wasn't sure if Sarah's murder was connected.

The air was crisp. Lightning could be seen in the distance,

and Ellie purposely did not bring her umbrella. Some kind soul might offer to give her a ride, and he just might be her target.

"He's not your guy," the earbud said. "Looks like a girlfriend just came in. They are all smiles and kisses."

"Does she have dark hair?"

"Blonde. Cute ass, too."

"Nice, Kellerman. You do know this is being recorded, right?"

"Hey, just giving a description."

"Can you be more specific?" This voice was deeper. John Billings was in a cargo van parked down the street. Kellerman was now off duty and Billings would be taking over as Ellie's new shadow.

"Great. Trying to catch a killer and being shadowed by two perverts." Ellie stopped at the end of the block and took time to light a cigarette. It was after eleven o'clock and traffic was light. If anyone was going to make a move, it would be in a less busy area, according to Padre.

Ellie enjoyed undercover work. Four years in the high school drama department taught her how to become a different person, how to change not just her hair and dress, but to actually become someone else. Just by spending twenty minutes with Sara Morningsky, Ellie knew she needed to make a mental switch from a skank to a timid girl next door. The hardest part was changing her language. Fuck, ass, shit, dammit, had to be cleansed from her vocabulary. Sara also didn't smoke. Oh well. Although Sara appeared shy when Ellie met her, there was an underlying intensity in the way she carried herself, her self-confidence and demeanor. Something told her Sara was more of a chameleon than Ellie. Padre relied heavily on her opinion as well as the P.I.'s. What a hunk. He seemed to be fiercely protective of Sara.

"Who's a hunk?" John said.

"Shit, did I say that out loud?" She obviously hadn't done a good enough job cleansing her vocabulary. She closed her eyes and pressed fingertips to the lids. "These contacts are drying out my eyes." And she forgot her eye drops.

She had taken a picture of the hamburger she had eaten at the bar and posted it to her Facebook page. She also posted pictures of Miss Lily at the assisted living facility at her birthday party. Ellie gave her a free manicure for her one hundredth birthday. Now all of her Facebook friends knew where she worked and where she hung out.

The street ahead was dark. She heard the cargo van start up and expected John to keep his distance. A low rumble in the distance was followed by a flash of lightning. Street lights were scarce on the side streets. The canopy of trees made it hard to see the sky as leaves rustled overhead. Ellie took one last puff, then flicked the cigarette away.

"Should have brought a flashlight."

"Want me to follow with my headlights on?"

"No, Billings. Stay where you are. Anything happens, you can be here in a split second."

"Ten-four, good buddy."

More leaves rustled and branches swayed. "Is it raining?"

"Negative."

The movement of the branches appeared to keep in time with her steps. Ellie slowed to a stop and listened. The swaying and rustling overhead stopped. She pulled out her phone and pressed the flashlight app.

"Nice. Now I can see you, or at least your location," Billings said.

"My turn is up ahead," Ellie whispered. "Just one more block of underbrush and woods and I'll be in my neighborhood. I can see the streetlights from here."

Shadows moved up ahead on her right. Now that her eyes were getting used to the dark, pockets of shadows appeared everywhere. A flash of lightning made her stop. She could swear she saw a car and two men leaning against the front bumper. Were her eyes playing tricks on her? A soft thud sounded to her left. The rustling of branches was replaced with the crunching of dried leaves.

A dot of yellow could be seen in the direction of the car. She knew when a cigarette was being sucked on. She did see someone.

"Think I've got a live one," Ellie whispered.

"Where?"

"Hold back for now. Looks like two guys. I can smell pot. Could just be some teens enjoying a smoke."

She slowed her pace and kept to the center of the street. The shadows moved away from the car while the crunching of leaves grew louder. Were there three men? Ellie's flashlight timed out. She pressed the power button, and shined the light in the direction of the car. The two men were advancing.

"Hey, doll. Whatja doing out on this fine night?" They separated. One stayed on her right, the other moved to the left side of the road.

Ellie stopped. "Just getting home."

"Might start raining. We can give you a ride."

Both men were tall. She could probably take the skinny one, but the other looked like a linebacker gone to seed. Slow and dangerous. Ellie slowly slipped her hand into her jacket pocket and grabbed her taser. Did the killer act alone or did he have a partner?

The linebacker moved closer. That was when the van came creeping down the street, its bright light spraying over the two men. The window rolled down.

"Hey, Sarah," Billings said. "Thought that was you. Need

a lift?"

"You do know you are blowing my cover," she whispered.

"No." Billings nodded to the car as its tires skidded on wet leaves in an attempt to hightail it out of the woods. "They were blowing your cover. Get in. I'll give you a ride home."

Several yards away and forty feet above them the gray hawk watched the van drive off. Although it doubted the two pot smokers posed a serious threat, a chill continued to wash over its body. Ten minutes after the hawk lifted off for its return home, a figure emerged from the woods. The man stood for several minutes contemplating his next move. There was no need to get any closer to the van or the woman to hear what they were saying. His hearing was exceptional.

67

"Can you believe that? All this time I didn't have a clue he was married."

"Maybe she lied." The bartender wiped the bar for the third time, hoping to give her the hint that it was past closing hour.

"No. Her lawyer came with and had a copy of the will." Sheila pulled out another cigarette. He immediately flicked a lighter for her, ignoring the No Smoking rule. "Here's the best part." She downed her drink and shoved it toward the man. Ernie was a fixture at the Cedar Point Country Club, having been the bartender for twenty years. Trim and fit, Ernie's hair was flicked with more silver than black; and his voice was as smooth as a radio announcer's.

Sheila whispered as though there were other patrons in the bar. "Joe met her in Vegas by the pool, and they were married in one of those tacky Elvis chapels. He had no idea she was the daughter of LeMeers, the diamond guru. LeMeers is worth billions." Her laugh was forced and she made no attempt to check her face in the mirror. Mascara sketched lazy trails down both cheeks. "Course, Joe wasn't good enough for his daughter. Their drunken weekend was one of those, 'what the hell have I done' vacations. She never told her father she was married until she turned up pregnant."

"Joe has a child?"

Sheila snorted, a very unrefined sound her mother would be embarrassed to hear. "Angie LeMeers had an abortion.

Daddy was going to disown her, strip her of her inheritance, you name it. Joe was furious. His signature on the divorce papers came with a price. Ten million bucks, which was a drop in the bucket to the LeMeers. And here everyone in the police department thought Joe was on the take." She brought the glass up to her lips, stopped, and set it down again. If it didn't taste strong enough, it was because Ernie neglected to add vodka to the last two drinks. He was a popular bartender because he remembered what every member drank and was an excellent listener.

"So Joe was divorced."

Sheila waved the cigarette back and forth. "Angie never signed the papers. Told her father she did. Her father spent most of his time in New York City. She was given two of the diamond stores in Chicago to manage. She knew where Joe worked. Tried to keep in touch. Unfortunately for her, Joe could not forgive the abortion."

She admired the rock on her left hand. A LeMeers diamond. When Angie's stuffed shirt lawyer asked what she was doing in Joe's condo, she turned back to the kitchen counter. That was when she slipped the ring off and dropped it in her purse. She handed the key to the attorney and told the two she stopped by to return it and to check if he had any contact information in the desk.

"Before leaving I told Angie there was a load of wash that needed to go into the dryer." Sheila laughed at the thought of Angie folding towels. She probably made the attorney do it. She held both hands up, palms facing her. "How do you like that? An engagement ring on each hand. I wonder how many I can collect before I'm fifty."

"Is that what you want? A white picket fence and three kids hanging on your skirt?"

"Good question," Leyton bellowed from the doorway.

"Goodbye Gucci shoes and fur coats. Breast milk on fur is tough to get out. Ask your mother." Leyton hoisted his bulk onto a barstool and pointed at Sheila's drink. "I'll have one of those."

"Go ahead. Tell me 'I told you so.'"

"No sense beating you up. You're doing a great job on your own." Leyton gave his daughter a closer look. "You look like hell."

"Thanks."

Ernie caught Leyton's eye as he poured vodka into the glass. He gave a slight shake of his head which Leyton understood. Sheila was drinking straight tonic.

Leyton grabbed her left hand and studied the three carat diamond. "LeMeers? Great taste. Did he buy it or steal it?"

Sheila admired the stone. "I don't know and I don't really care."

Ernie slid the drink in front of Leyton. Leyton asked the bartender, "How many of our fine members do you think married for true love?"

Ernie laughed. "I can probably count on one hand."

"Right," Sheila scoffed. "You trying to say the majority of them were arranged marriages?"

"Not arranged, but married for social status," her father said. "Or what each could bring to the table. Your mother's family wasn't rich. I could probably have married any debutante I wanted in my younger, thinner days. Your grandmother, God rest her soul, was like Martha Stewart on steroids. That woman could throw a party and decorate like nobody's business. People clamored to be invited. And she taught your mother everything she knew. I needed someone who could entertain prospective business investors. I may be an ass to deal with, but your mother could sugarcoat them with that sweet southern drawl and have them eating out of her hand. Sex was inconsequential. With you young people today, sex seems to be the only thing. You equate sex with love. You'll learn when you are older, although that may be too late."

Sheila slid off the stool and pushed her glass toward the bartender. "Thanks for listening, Ernie, but you make a lousy drink."

Leyton stood, pulled out his wallet, and fanned five one hundred dollar bills on the bar. "Thanks, Ernie." He knew Ernie didn't have to keep the bar open. Leyton appreciated the call that Sheila was there and knew Ernie would keep his mouth shut, even if Leyton hadn't paid for his silence. "Come on, apple of my eye. You are going to spend the night with your mother and me, enjoy a wonderful breakfast, and cry on your mother's shoulder."

68 Sara came up behind Dagger, wrapped her arms around his neck, and kissed him on the cheek. "Thank you."

Dagger turned his head and caught the second kiss on the mouth. "Happy now?" Sara wanted to see Ellie for herself, confirm that she had enough backup in case Addison showed up. Dagger had to admit that no matter how hard he tried, he couldn't keep Sara from worrying about the undercover cop. Last night he agreed to let her see for herself.

"What are you working on?"

"Padre's on his way over. In the meantime, Skizzy found a photo of Matt from his post graduate days. There was some art exhibit in Paris." Dagger tapped a few keys.

"Cute." Sara winced at Matt's appearance. She ran a hand down Dagger's hair. His reached past the collar and could be pulled back in a ponytail. But there was some natural curl to it, like a perm that was growing out. Women found it sexy. Matt's was spiked blonde on top and long and scraggly on the bottom. His beard made him look more like a mountain man.

"Cute doesn't describe his artwork."

Dagger was right. The painting was of devils devouring babies. "I do hope he didn't win."

"It seems the art critics weren't too fond of his talent, either. Where he went from there, Skizzy can't tell. Matt went off the grid after that embarrassing weekend. No credit card activity. No drivers license or tax returns. Skizzy and I both think Matt changed his name. He's going to try some software to age Matt, clean him up a bit, try different hair colors. He wasn't an identical twin so we can't look for someone who looks like Paul."

The buzzer from the gate sounded. Sara walked over to the panel by the front door and checked the monitor. "It's Padre." She pushed the button to open the gate.

Dagger printed out the photo Skizzy sent him and gathered his notes. Curious about their visitor, Einstein clamped onto the grated door and leveled one yellowed ring eye on their visitor as Padre entered.

"AWKKK, UP AGAINST THE WALL." His screech echoed in the spacious room.

"Good morning to you, too, Einstein." Padre set his briefcase down and walked over to the grated door. Einstein pecked at his finger. "You know, I could shoot you."

"Go to your tree, Einstein." Dagger closed the soundproof door. "Let's go in the kitchen."

They walked in to find coffee and pastries on the kitchen counter. "I love coming here." Padre doctored a cup of coffee and placed several pastries on a plate. While Sara and Dagger followed suit, Padre filled them in on Sheila and Joe Spagnola's wife. One of the clerks in Human Resources made sure all of the details were floating around the precinct the first thing that morning. Padre called Sheila earlier to express his sympathies and got an earful.

"It seems Joe wasn't too forthcoming about the ten million or the wife. And the uncle he supposedly inherited the restaurant from was in debt. So the story he told Sheila about inheriting from a rich uncle was a lie." Padre noticed the worried look on Dagger's face. "What are you thinking?"

"When something blows up in Sheila's life, she throws

herself into her work. Is she suspicious about Joe's accident?"

"Not yet. She did press me on whether the other paintings compare to the actual homicides and whether Tex Miller's death was actually a hit and run. I was as vague as possible, said it was a vehicle accident and the other paintings with the disemboweling of Tex Miller's wife and Officer Lisa Cambridge were grossly fabricated. I think she bought it."

"I hope so. She isn't above paying to have someone dig into your file drawer."

"I'm keeping the actual files in my home. The doctored ones are in my office and I'm conveniently leaving them on my desk should she stop in to snoop."

"Good."

"More coffee, Padre?" Sara held up the carafe.

"Sure." He raised his cup. "Hear from Simon?"

"Yeah. Got a postcard from Hawaii. After the cruise they flew back to Los Angeles, rented some sports car and drove to Vegas. They plan to drive it all the way home on some one-way drop-off rental deal."

"Eunie is having a ball. She sent me a text from the casino," Sara said.

Padre reached into his pocket and pulled out several sheets of paper. "I changed up some parameters in my search for other homicides through the U.S. It's possible Sara's name hadn't popped into his head yet. So this time I asked for female, date range between eighteen and thirty. Knowing our guy has a penchant for weird, I looked for unusual or unknown causes of death or unclaimed bodies. Don't ask me why. I was just trying to narrow it down to the most bizarre. And guess what?" He unfolded one of the pages and laid it on the table. It was a picture of a woman on an examining table, skin tinged blue, hair brown and shoulder length. Her neck was bruised and there were large claw marks on both sides of her neck. "A victim in Austin, Texas. She was killed about six months ago, they estimate."

"She looks like a candidate," Dagger pointed out. "Anything else unusual?"

"Yeah. Before the M.E. could do the autopsy, someone stole the body."

"Why do you keep staring at her photo?"

Long after Padre left, Dagger was still sitting at the kitchen table staring at the photo of the young woman whose body disappeared from the morgue in Austin, Texas.

"I'm not sure. There's just something familiar about her. Can't quite put my finger on it."

"Old case you worked?" Sara stood in front of the opened freezer and studied the contents.

"No. I don't think so."

"Do you feeling like grilling tonight?"

"Not sure if we'll be home. I should check in on Mother. Her green light has been pulsing in my peripheral vision since this morning. Maybe she found something."

"Okay." Sara closed the freezer door. "Looks like takeout again or nuking leftovers."

"Or I can take you to dinner."

"That sounds better."

Dagger's cell phone rang. It was Padre. He put the phone on speaker. "What's up?"

"Ellie stopped at a Starbucks on the way to the assisted living facility. When she got to work, she noticed someone dropped an envelope into her tote bag. Someone took a picture of the cop who was tailing her in the bar and of Billings, who was in a cargo van down the street outside of her apartment. I don't know how he found the tails. I just came from Starbucks and looked at their video footage. Not one customer stood close enough to slip them into Ellie's tote. She does remember a young boy bumping into her on the sidewalk. Just puzzling that Addison would expose himself by letting us know he is onto us, the cocky sonofabitch."

"He must have heard Ellie talking to the cops who were tailing her," Sara said. "You said Ellie wore an earbud so she could talk to the two cops anytime. She may have thought she was whispering, but Addison doesn't have to be close to hear." Sara knew all about enhanced hearing.

"You are just a wealth of good news today," Padre said. "I'm headed over to Logan's hotel. That ass knows something. He might be protecting Addison. Hell, he might even be staying in his hotel suite. Catch up with you later." The call ended.

Dagger checked his watch. "The best time to catch Addison is now. I don't want to wait until June thirteenth."

"There is one sure way."

Dagger stared at her, but she could sense him wavering. "It may come down to that. But we do it together. Are you prepared for that?"

"Yes. I want this over with."

"You do need to be a bit more punctual, Six-One-Seven."

"Sorry. Got a bit distracted. Would be much easier if you could just call me. I do have a photo I want you to see." He held up the photo of the victim Padre had shown him. "She was murdered six months ago in Austin, Texas. Strange thing is, her body was stolen from the morgue. Seems only you and the Director have the talent for pilfering morgues. Does she look familiar? Our police department ran her photo through the database and came up empty."

"We just now made a copy and will run it through the Director's database."

"Great. Now what do you have for me?"

"We have been picking up a lot of interoffice emails between the Director and his research facility. Naturally, the facility still cannot be located since the emails appear to bounce from the Soviet Union to Chili and the Arctic and even New Zealand in an attempt to keeps its location secret. What caught our attention is that they keep referring to Project Transformation. The Director is of Greek descent. Transformation is a pretty benign word, but when you look at the translation to Greek, it..."

"It means metamorphosis," Sara said.

"Of course. We believe the Director already has a plan in place, possibly to capture this Mister Addison."

70

"I'm not waiting around the damn hotel, and I have no cause to get a search warrant. Logan may think he found the next Michelangelo, but if he's harboring a killer, he's just as guilty as Addison." Padre draped his trench coat over the suit of armor. "Hang onto that for me."

"Hey, that ain't no dang coat rack," Skizzy barked.

"I kinda like it. Might buy it for my office." Padre surveyed the items in the pawn shop with a cop's eye, searching for anything that looked stolen.

"It's yours for two hundred bucks."

"I'd pay fifty."

Skizzy's mouth gaped. "That is a relic. An heirloom. Fifty bucks would only buy you one arm."

"Can we get down to business?" Dagger yawned, feeling as though he wasn't going to get a good night's sleep until this whole Addison case was over.

"Where's Girlie?"

"I left her back at the office. She's waiting for an I.D. on the Austin victim."

"All righty then. What's our next step?" Skizzy leaned his elbows on the glass display case and shifted his eyes from Dagger to the cop. "All full of ideas, huh?"

"Other than knowing Addison is in town, we have zip." Padre pulled out his notepad and slapped it on the counter. "We have no way of knowing where he will strike next. Our undercover cop was a bust. Unless we put out an ad with Sara's picture in it, I haven't a clue how to lure the guy out."

"That is not going to happen." Dagger had to admit, though, that it might be their next step. He may have to go with Sara's suggestion to let her communicate with Addison. It was better than spinning their wheels.

Skizzy snapped his fingers. "Addison has to be staying somewhere. Have some cops who are sitting on their butts doing nothing call around to realtors and check recent rentals. It would have to be a house, not an apartment. Something out of the way, maybe a cave somewhere."

Dagger slowly straightened with a feeling of finally having something solid to go on. "We don't have to do that. Paul Addison was renting a house before. Maybe the farmhouse is still there."

The farmhouse where Paul Addison had lived with his pregnant wife, Josie, was a thirty minute drive from Cedar Point. It was in the middle of an unincorporated area north of Valparaiso. The horizon lost its grip on the last of the sun's rays by the time Skizzy's Humvee crept up the drive, headlights off. There weren't any lights on in the house, but that wouldn't stop a shifter who could see in the dark.

"What's the plan?" Padre asked. Skizzy was already out of the vehicle and pulling his M-4 weapon from the back.

Dagger climbed out of the passenger side and stared at the square block of cinder and clapboard. All he did was think the words thermal imaging and he immediately saw the interior of the farmhouse. "I don't think he's home. No car in the driveway."

Skizzy hoisted his weapon over his shoulder. He was ready to use it on the first thing that moved. "Do you hear that?"

The men stopped. "Hear what?" Padre asked.

"He's right," Dagger replied. "Nothing. There isn't a sound. Not a bird call, no frogs, not even a firefly."

"Yep. Just like before."

"Front or back?" Dagger whispered.

"Skizzy and I will take the front." Padre looked at Dagger's hands. "Where's your flashlight?"

"I'm fine. I was a bat in a past life."

"Funny."

Dagger peered through windows as he made his way to the back of the house. Sara was right. Nature was in hiding and Addison was on the prowl. An uneasy feeling swept over him. While they were hunting Addison, what if Addison was closing in on Sara? Whatever they found here, they had to get in and out quick. The longer he was away from Cedar Point, the more uneasy he felt.

The stairs in the back were wooden. The creak as he stepped on the second stair sounded like it echoed across the fields. When he reached the top step, he stole a glance through the glass pane. He could see a Formica table, chairs, faded linoleum flooring, but no sign anyone was occupying the house. If the door was locked, he wasn't about ready to take the time to pick the lock. His pick gun was useless on a lock system this old. He would just break the glass. Fortunately, whoever was living here trusted his fellow man. The door was unlocked.

Dagger stepped inside and let the screen door quietly click shut. On the kitchen counter were a half loaf of bread and a bag of potato chips. He could hear the refrigerator humming in the corner. If the only occupant was an elderly woman, she was definitely going to have a heart attack when he hovered over her bed.

A beam from a flashlight cut into the kitchen and landed on his chest. "Jeez, I almost shot your ass," Padre said. "How the hell did you get in?"

"Door was unlocked. Find anything?"

"Wait til you see it."

Dagger followed Padre into the living room. A couch and two chairs were pushed against one wall. Duct tape held a painter's drop cloth in place on the floor. And on an easel in the center of the room was what looked like a pencil sketch.

"Holy shit." Dagger stepped closer as Padre's flashlight

illuminated the image of Paul Addison when they killed him in the storage building. The actual event was fresh in all of their minds, and there didn't appear to be one detail out of place.

"It's almost as though he were right there. How the hell did he get the details so perfect?" Padre almost sounded in awe of the brother's talents.

"Someone is obviously giving him the details." Skizzy adjusted the M-4 weapon, as if he were ready to blast the artwork out of existence.

"According to Sherlock's notes, it could be his brother, Paul." Dagger couldn't believe he was even agreeing with what Sherlock wrote. "The family curse is strong. Would it be that far of a stretch to believe that Paul was communicating with his twin? Cliff wasn't around when Paul was on his rampage so he'd have no idea about the murders. Paul had to be the one who gave him all the details needed to create the Nightfall exhibit." He walked over to a fireplace where the brick facing was black from years of use.

Padre's light beam followed him. "What did you find?" The light hit a mound of ashes on top of charred wood.

Dagger jabbed a poker into the pile. "Smells recent. He obviously found a need to get rid of a pile of papers. And he did a good job of obliterating any information that might give us a clue as to what exactly he burned."

"Maybe he sacrificed a feral cat." Skizzy was met with two blank stares. "Only saying."

Padre's hand went instinctively to his gold cross. His flashlight found a set of stairs. "Let's see what's upstairs. I just hope it isn't a pile of bones from previous victims."

"I'll stay down here and guard the front door," Skizzy said. He looked at a door near the kitchen. "Wait. There's a basement. I remember the coal bin from the last case."

"You aren't going down there on your own." Padre pulled out his gun and headed to the door.

Dagger pulled out his Kimber. "I'll check the second floor."

"Hey. Take my flashlight." Padre held his out to Dagger.

"I'll be fine." Dagger pointed his Kimber 9mm at a wall. A beam of light shot out from the tactical light guard attached to his weapon. His vision in the dark was so good he had to keep reminding himself to keep his newfound talents to himself. "Meet me upstairs when you're done."

The second floor led to one large room on his right and a bathroom straight ahead. Wooden flooring squeaked under his weight. He guessed the farmhouse to be over fifty years old just from the siding used and the outdated appliances. The beam splashed over an unmade bed against one wall. Other than a chair and a desk, the room, like the rest of the house, was sparsely decorated. His eyes took in the full scope of the room. Footprints in the dusty floor were definitely recent. The wooden stairs squeaked, and within seconds Padre and Skizzy joined him. "Find anything in the basement?"

"Mouse droppings, dust, water leaks from a broken tile outside."

"No body parts," Skizzy said, almost with disappointment in his voice.

"What about you?" Padre flashed his beam around the room. "This guy needs an interior decorator." His beam hit another door. "Maybe all the bodies are in the closet." He opened the door to a rack of shirts, pants, and sport coats. "Well, well. What have we here?"

They crowded around the doorway. Padre lifted one of the shirtsleeves. The initials ML were embroidered on the cuff. "Sonofabitch. Logan has been here so he does know where Addison is hiding."

Dagger flipped through the rest of the clothes. The

pants were all the same length and the dress shirts all had embroidered cuffs. "No. Logan doesn't know Addison. Logan IS Addison."

72

Sara checked her watch. It was dark out and the monitor above the desk still showed a floating screensaver. She wasn't sure how much longer she cared to wait for Dagger to call so she didn't know if they found anything at the farmhouse. Was he out of cell phone range? She was giving Connie five more minutes to show her android face or she was leaving.

There was a knock on the door. Sara moved to the window and spread the blinds. "Come in," she called out.

Casey stuck his head in. "Sorry to bother you. Computer glitch. Mom lost the connection, and since you don't have Dagger's thumbprint, you can't sign back on. She wanted me to tell you she found something on the woman whose body disappeared in Texas. She was a BettaTec operative. The reason he had that Logan guy's photo in his computer is because he was the last person to see her alive."

Sara grabbed her purse and headed for the door. "I don't know how to turn that thing off."

"No problem."

"Can you lock up when you are through?"

"Need my help?" he called out, but Sara was already down the steps and headed to her car.

"Did you have dinner?"

Sheila looked up from her computer. "I'm not hungry,

Dad." The truth was, she had been burying herself in work since Joe died. That was a better alternative than burying herself in a bottle of vodka every night.

"You gotta eat, hon. Your mom and I are worried about you."

Sheila smiled at her big bear of a father. Being an only child did have its advantages. The love and care he showered on her since the day she was born overshadowed the pain in the ass he could be at times.

"Just seeing my old condo again in full color has tamped down my appetite a bit. I think once I figure out a way to expose this artist, I'll sleep better."

"Okay, sweetheart. I'm going to have one of the security guards come up here and escort you to your car when you're ready. Don't stay too much longer."

Sheila waited for her father to climb onto the elevator. She couldn't leave yet. Sheila paid three hundred dollars to a maid of questionable legal status to check Mark Logan's hotel room. Sheila thought he might be sheltering the artist. She didn't believe for one minute that Mark knew nothing about the artist or that the paintings mysteriously showed up at the gallery. The maid had already checked the registry to see if Logan reserved more than one room, but he hadn't. It was just the one. Sheila knew Mark stopped by the gallery every day after six so the maid should have no fear of running into him.

Sheila's cell phone rang. She checked the number. "Finally." She pressed the phone icon. "What did you find out?"

"He no here."

Sheila sighed. "I know he isn't in. That's why I wanted you to check when I knew he'd be gone."

"No, I mean he no here. Nothing. No clothes. No suitcase. Shower has not been used."

That was puzzling. She'd been to his hotel room. She knew he was staying there. "Did he check out?"

"No, ma'am. Not according to front desk. He always leave privacy sign on door knob so no one has even been in to change bedding or give fresh towels."

Something didn't feel right. Sheila's reporter nose smelled a cover up. Why would Logan rent a room and not stay there? Did he reserve a room at more than one hotel just to throw off snoopy reporters? No, she already checked the other five star hotels in the area.

"Thanks anyway. You did good." Sheila hung up and grabbed her purse. There was one place she was sure to find Logan.

73

Sara wandered into Logan's Galleria ten minutes before closing. The place smelled of paint and cleaning solvents. After leaving Dagger a voicemail, she shoved her hair up under a baseball cap and left her cell phone, purse and keys in her car.

The family crest in mosaic tiles was highlighted by an overhead can light. Now that she knew what to look for, she could clearly see the vine weaving between the letters. Only the A, D, O and N were visible. But if you filled in the blanks, it clearly spelled Addison. The triple moon symbol in the crest she knew was sometimes called the Triple Goddess and represented the three phases of the moon. How appropriate.

Sara stepped toward the doorway to the Nightfall exhibit. The three tiki torches sprayed dancing shadows on the walls. There was a change in the painting on the wall directly in front of her. The painting of the woman with her face half wolf and half hawk was wearing a white dress. But something was added—red blood stains on the woman's hands and splattered down her dress. She stepped closer. The paint glistened and as she touched her finger to the dress, it left a red stain on Sara's finger. She brought it up to her nose. It smelled like blood.

A chill swept up her spine and she sensed an evil presence. She took a deep breath and focused on keeping her heart rate normal. Why give Addison the impression that she feared him.

"Can I help you, miss?"

"Did you know nyctophilia is the love of darkness? Some people find comfort in the dark." She didn't so much hear his footsteps as sense his close proximity.

"I'm not sure I understand."

"The paintings. I believe the artist loves the dark."

"I guess you could say that."

Did his pulse just quicken? Did he sense she was a danger to him? Sara slowly pulled off her baseball cap. Her dark hair tumbled down her back. "I believe you've been looking for me." She turned to face Mark Logan.

Mark's eyes widened, his eyes shifting from amber to normal. "You!" His head tilted as though listening to a voice in his head.

"I'm sure your brother is confirming that I'm the one you seek. But you have to wait until the thirteenth, when the moon is the fullest, or you won't absorb all of my abilities." Now that she faced him, Sara could see a slight resemblance to Paul in Mark's eyes, or was Paul's image somehow bleeding through? "It must hurt that you were shunned by your family."

Mark took a step closer and smiled. It was anything but a friendly smile. If he'd hoped to corner her and reduce her to a frightened victim, his disappointment showed. Sara turned back to the painting. "Is there a reason you painted blood on my picture?"

"Isn't it obvious? You and your friends have blood on your hands. You killed my brother."

Sara again forced her pulse to slow, certain that Mark would be able to hear any change in her heartbeat or breathing. "Paul was a bloodthirsty killer. Have you been killing for yourself, or for him?" She could sense him moving closer. "You made one major mistake, Mark, or should I call you Cliff?" Sara turned to face him. "You killed a woman in

Texas who has ties to some very powerful people. They won't rest until they have you locked in a concrete room where they can study you. Where you won't have any contact with the outside world."

"I fear no man. They are mere mortals."

Sara waved her arm toward the walls of artwork. "Even these paintings aren't yours. They are Paul's. He told you what to paint, told you who to kill, manipulated you for his own benefit. Do you really think he is going to let you live? He's been taking you over piece by piece."

Mark could feel his hands starting to claw and tried to rein in the impulse to kill. "NOT YET," the voice in his head screamed.

Sara looked down at his hands. "Feeling the urge, Mark? Little hard to wait until the thirteenth, isn't it?"

"SHE'S TAUNTING YOU," HE cautioned.

"SHUT UP!" Mark screamed at the voice in his head. There was a click as Mark's talons shot out.

"Mark?" Carlton took a cautious step back, his eyes riveted on the sharp talons. Neither Mark nor Sara heard him enter. Carlton looked up sharply, confusion on his face, but his next word caught in his throat as Mark turned quickly, the talons ripping through the gallery manager's neck.

Before his body hit the floor, Sara shoved the heavy pillar with all her strength. The tiki torch toppled over, splashing hot oil onto both men. She was a blur as she raced to the other two tiki torches and shoved them over like dominoes. The hot oil splashed against the walls, setting the paintings on fire.

She turned back to see Mark charging at her, his body in flames, his face contorting from Mark to the image of Paul. She ran for the door, but Mark's arm shot out sending Sara sprawling against a far wall. Flashes of light sparked in her eyes, and she struggled to remain conscious. She slowly moved her head toward Carlton's prone body. She didn't see his chest rising, didn't hear his pulse. The flames were licking at his body while Mark turned in circles trying to put out the flames. Sara pushed herself to a sitting position, trying to escape the pool of flames running toward her. Mark continued to dance in a circle, flopping his arms like a bird trying to take flight. She wondered if Mark ever learned to fully shift. Did he not realize his full potential or was it something Paul kept hidden from him?

Mark slumped to his knees, but his eyes never left her. A laugh, vile and victorious spewed from a mouth that didn't appear to be Mark's. It was as though there were two faces interchanging as he spoke. "You're too late. Our family curse will live on." Then he fell face first onto the marble floor, his clothes still in flames, his skin charring. Sara suddenly realized that when Mark struck her, some of the hot oil was transferred to her jacket and now her clothing and hair were on fire. The smoke and noxious odors were making it difficult to breathe. The two bodies on fire brought back vague memories of the fire that killed her parents. She'd waited at the top of the stairs to the attic as the mob pelted the house with torches. Her mother had screamed for her to hide, but six-year-old Sara wasn't sure where to go. It was a scene no child should ever experience and one Sara could not forget.

"OH MY GOD."

The scream came from the lobby. Sara forced her head to turn from the carnage and saw Sheila, her hands over her mouth, her eyes taking in the scene. Sara managed to reach an arm up. Her throat was raw from the smoke and the words wouldn't come out. Sheila stared at her, screamed again, and ran out of the gallery.

74 The Humvee skidded to the curb just as Sheila ran out of the gallery. The three men rushed out of the vehicle. Smoke trailed behind the reporter as she threw herself into Dagger's arms.

"He's dead. Oh my god oh my god."

Dagger pulled her arms down and shook her. "Who's dead? Who's in there?"

"Mark and Carlton. There's blood, and, and, someone stabbed Carlton and the fire. Everything is on fire." Sheila started coughing and taking gulps of air.

Dagger gripped her shoulders and shook her. "Is there anyone else in there?"

Sheila stared for several seconds until he shook her again. "No. Only Mark and Carlton. There isn't anyone else in there."

They leaned Sheila against the Humvee and ran for the door. Heavy smoke was pouring from the gallery. It forced the men back just as they saw Sheila tearing away from the scene in her Jaguar.

"We gotta make sure he's dead." Skizzy pulled the M-4 from the back of the Humvee.

"Hey." Padre pointed across the street and down several darkened storefronts. "Isn't that Sara's PT Cruiser?"

Dagger jerked his head back to the gallery and screamed, "SARA!"

Padre grabbed his arm. "You can't go in there."

"I'll try the back door." Dagger raced around the building

to the back, screaming Sara's name in his head in case she had shifted to escape. *"SARA!"* He screamed in thought only.

"Thakoza, grandchild, you must awaken."

Sara blinked and slowly pushed away from the seared wall. Who was calling her? She thought she heard her grandmother's voice. She looked down at her left arm. The sleeve of her jean jacket was burned away. She thought she could see blisters on her skin. The left side of her neck and face felt hot and the jeans fabric on her left leg was in flames. Sara was mesmerized by the colors. She slowly moved her face to the wall and watched the flaming portraits drop like dominos.

"Thakoza, please."

The voice again. And was that Dagger's voice calling her? The smoke was thick and the room was so hot. There were two bodies across from her. Visions of her family home and her parents being burned alive in their house continued to play like a slide show in her mind. But her grandmother's voice and Dagger's screams shook her from her nightmare. She staggered to her feet, her body numb with pain. She took one last look at Mark's charred remains before shifting. The gray hawk blasted through the skylight and into the night air where it landed on a branch.

She could see him by the back door to the gallery. *"Dagger."*

Dagger looked up. *"Sara? Are you all right?"*

The hawk shook its body, trying to rid it of burnt feathers. Smoke drifted from its wings and it flapped continuously, drifting down to a lower branch.

"I don't have any photos."

"What?"

"Photos of my parents. They all burned in the fire."

Dagger didn't like the sound of Sara's voice. Was she in shock and stuck in the past when her parents' died? *"Sara, think. What happened in the gallery? Is Mark dead?"* He waited, looking up at the hawk whose attention seemed to be on something in a tree across from the parking lot. *"Sara!"*

The hawk turned its head, looked down at Dagger, and back to the gallery.

"Mark killed Carlton. I set the gallery on fire. I had to."

"You are sure he's dead?" He saw the hawk's attention riveted on the flames shooting from the skylight. The second skylight burst from the heat sending glass shards flying. *"Sara?"*

"I have to... I need to get home. Now."

He could hear the panic in her voice and wanted nothing more than for Sara to be far away from here. *"Go, sweetheart. I'll drive your car back and meet you there."*

Dagger watched the gray hawk leap from the branch and take off. He returned to the street without seeing the hawk fall to the ground, shift to the wolf, and limp away.

"Did you find her?" Padre asked.

Dagger nodded. "The fire reminded her of the home fire where her parents died. She panicked and ran off. I know where to find her." That was the best excuse Dagger could come up with on the fly. "She said Mark killed Carlton. Sara set the gallery on fire, probably using those tiki torches. How the fire department ever approved those torches around paint I will never know."

"So, no need for my baby?" Skizzy almost looked disappointed.

"I want to stick around and make sure he's dead." Padre looked down the street. He doubted any fire trucks would be coming anytime soon. The gallery was the only business open this time of night.

Skizzy patted his toy. "I'm staying with you."

"Good. Let me know what you find." Dagger shoved his hand in his pocket and pulled out a set of keys. He kept a spare to Sara's car. There were still three weeks left before the thirteenth of the month. How lucky could they be to have finally ended the Addison curse?

75 Dagger tossed his jacket and keys on the kitchen table and made his way up the stairs. He saw Sara's bedroom light on from the driveway and assumed she was washing the smoke out of her hair.

The bedroom door was open. He entered and stopped abruptly when he saw her. Sara was lying on the bed wearing only underpants and a thin-strapped tee. "Oh my god," he whispered. The skin on her left arm was singed and covered in raised welts and blisters. The damage ran up the side of her neck to the left side of her face and ear. Hair was missing from above her ear and back three inches. "Sara!"

"Don't come near. Please. It hurts just to touch the sheets." She didn't move her head but her gaze shifted to him. She could see tears pooling in his eyes. "I'll be fine by morning. I didn't want the dead skin to fall onto your sheets so I came up here."

Dagger carefully sat on the bed, his hand hovered over her arm as though he expected to magically remove the damage. "What can I do, Sara?"

"I think some pain pills would help," she said with a laugh.

"I can do that. What about ice? Can I put ice on the burns?"

Sara gulped in a shaky breath. Salty tears running from her left eye stung when they touched the blistered skin. Dagger dabbed at the tears with his shirt. "Grandmother kept jars of berry root paste, but I can't remember where she stored them. Maybe the greenhouse?"

"I'll check." Dagger tore down the stairs taking them two at a time, rushed through the kitchen and opened the door to the greenhouse. He checked the cabinets above the counter, shoved aside the bags of plant fertilizer, watering cans, and pottery. Nothing. He opened the cabinets below the counter and checked behind coiled hoses, stakes, and larger pots. He didn't find any jars of strange paste.

"Shit." He left the greenhouse and opened the door to the laundry room. Soap, fabric softener, cleaning supplies and an iron filled the cabinets. Still, no berry root paste. Did he even know what it looked like? He never asked Sara what type of container or jar it might be in.

He left the laundry room, walked through another entrance into the living room and entered the second bathroom. He didn't bother turning on the lights, relying on his eyesight to illuminate the room. There wasn't a cabinet above the sink, only below. He opened the cabinet and in a white container he saw several jars which looked like jelly. He grabbed one and read the label. Berry root paste. He grabbed two jars and a bottle of Tylenol and ran back upstairs.

"I found them. How do I put it on? Do I heat it first?" He set the jars on the nightstand, rushed to the bathroom, and filled a glass with water.

"Use your fingers."

"It's going to hurt, won't it?" He handed her the glass, then shook out two Tylenols. The pills also contained a sleeping aid. They may not take the pain away, but at least she'll get some sleep. He helped raise her head as she swallowed the two pills.

"Can't hurt much more than it already does." Sara handed the glass to Dagger.

Dagger went downstairs and returned with a glass of scotch and an ice bucket.

"I don't think I should drink with the pills."

"It's not for you."

Sara laughed, the first time Dagger saw a light in her eyes since he came home. It didn't last long. He tried to be quick applying the paste and could see the pain in her eyes. The damage ran from above her left ear, down her neck, left arm, and left leg. Her body started to shake. She should be in a hospital, Dagger thought, even if it was the last place she wanted to be. By the time he finished she was sobbing. Dagger rinsed his hands in the bathroom, wet a washcloth, and returned to the bed.

"Why did she do it?" Sara whispered.

"Who?"

"Sheila. I thought she was going to bring help."

"Sheila saw you in the gallery?" Anger started building. Dagger could imagine Sheila standing in the doorway weighing her options. Could she really be that vindictive, or had she been in shock, too? He felt rage pulsing through his veins. Sheila claimed only Logan and Carlton were trapped in the gallery.

"She looked right at me." Then Sara saw Dagger's dark side emerging. She had never seen his eyes turn black so fast. Her good arm shot out and grabbed a fistful of Dagger's shirt. "NO!" She stared into his eyes, as though addressing only his dark side. "Think about it. Tomorrow I will be fine, no scars. Even my hair will have grown back. You accuse Sheila, you even bring it up, and she's going to wonder why I don't look injured. She saw my jacket on fire. She will know I was injured."

"You could have died." But it wasn't Dagger's voice. It sounded more like an enraged growl.

"Let her think she imagined it. Better that than my trying to explain why my skin isn't burned. She has been questioning her sanity since the haunting of the Sebold mansion." Sheila's overnight stay with a group of ghost hunters led her to an excursion into an alternate time period resulting in the return of a serial killer from a century ago. Dagger and Padre had convinced Sheila that she had been trapped in a panic room under the staircase and imagined it all after suffering a concussion.

"Dagger!" Sara saw the smoky black of his eyes start to retreat. "Please. We would never be able to explain my miraculous recovery."

He closed his eyes and forced back the rage. Sara was right. A green light started flashing in his peripheral vision. Mother would have to wait. He planned to sit in a chair and watch over Sara all night. He leaned over and kissed her forehead. "Okay. It makes sense. I don't like it, but we'll do it your way."

He dipped the washcloth into the bucket which contained ice water, then pressed the cloth against her forehead, face, and neck in an attempt to cool her body. She was already drifting off to sleep.

Dagger's phone rang. It was Padre.

"He's definitely dead. I slipped a few bone fragments into a bag and will have Luther do a DNA test to confirm. Your buddy wasn't satisfied until he blasted the room with napalm. Fire investigators will have fun trying to figure out what incinerated Logan's ass so completely. I'll get in touch with Marty Flynn and give him the good news."

"That's great."

"How's Sara?"

Dagger looked over at the love of his life as her legs writhed in pain and she softly moaned. "A little smoke inhalation. She didn't get much farther than a couple steps through the back door when she saw the fire. But she'll be fine."

"Wonderful. We did good. Got rid of the bastard with three weeks to spare."

Dagger hung up wondering why it didn't feel like it was over.

76 As Sara predicted, by morning all signs of her burns were gone. Her burned hair had repaired and grown to the length of the rest of her hair, all overnight. When Dagger's dark side came out last night, Mother saw the condition of Sara's body. Today Sara dressed in shorts and a sleeveless blouse to show Mother how her body repaired itself.

"That is unbelievable." The android's eyes widened in disbelief. She blinked several times as she took in Sara's current appearance, proof of her remarkable recovery.

"I thought since you have my blood, perhaps you can figure out how it can be duplicated to help burn victims." Sara wanted to convince Dagger that there could be other advantages to Mother having her blood.

"You are absolutely right. I will get on it right away." Connie swiveled to face Dagger. *"Something is bothering you. We can see it in your heart rate and the worry in your eyes."*

Dagger hadn't discussed his fears with Sara or Padre. "I'm wondering where BettaTec has been. They knew about Logan, knew he killed their operative, probably even saw the way he killed. The Director's operatives never work alone, so there had to be a witness to Logan's partial shifting, his strength. I expected some unmarked, lead-lined semi to swoop in and cart him away. Have you seen anything on his computer that could tell us more?"

"We are looking into something. There is another woman whom the Director is focused on. She isn't an operative and may have nothing to do with this Mister Logan. When we find something out, we will be in touch." With that the screen disappeared.

**77** "Dagger!" Sheila was all smiles as she spotted her ex at the marina restaurant three days after the fire. "I haven't seen you since that night."

"I'm sorry about Logan. You two were dating weren't you?"

She placed her hand on the back of a chair across from him. Dagger didn't doubt for one second that she wanted to join him. "My track record isn't very good lately. First Joe, then Logan, although I wouldn't say we were an item. Thank God. Doesn't say much for my reporting skills when I start dating a serial killer."

Dagger let her ramble. Had she been scouring the papers looking, or hoping, that three bodies instead of two had been found at the gallery? Had she been waiting for him to call her with news of Sara's horrible injuries?

"All those women. It still doesn't explain how he knew all those details about Caroline Kirby's murder. It's puzzling." Sheila slowly pulled the chair out.

Dagger wasn't ready to help her connect the dots with Paul Addison, nor had Padre even mentioned in his report that Mark Logan had been an Addison. Luther confirmed that the DNA were matched to Logan and Carlton. Dagger could see Sheila swallow and look around the room. Was she nervous? Feeling guilty about something? He wanted desperately to tell her exactly what he thought, to reveal what he knew about that night.

"Hi, Sheila. How are you?" Sara wore a sleeveless top over shorts, exposing her healed skin. Her hair, straight and shiny, was full and hung straight down her back, not one hint of singed hair. She pulled out a chair and sat down.

Dagger knew what day and where Sheila met her father once a week for lunch. He asked Sara to wear something sleeveless so he could see his ex's reaction. Sara thought he was making too big a deal out of it. In typical Sara fashion, she had already forgiven and forgotten.

Sheila took a step back and tried to make a quick but subtle check of Sara's body. She quickly returned her attention to Sara's face. "I'm fine. You're looking good, as usual."

Dagger watched Sheila closely. Was that disbelief Dagger saw? Or disappointment? And did her face just lose all color? Her eyes seemed to linger over Sara's bare arm and leg a little too long. When Sara first told him she saw Sheila at the gallery, he wanted to give his ex the benefit of the doubt. Maybe because of the smoke she didn't see Sara on the floor in the Nightfall exhibit. Maybe the shock of seeing two bodies on fire sent her fleeing from the scene.

"We were just talking about the fire at the gallery," Dagger said. Were those tears in Sheila's eyes?

"Never saw bodies that charred before." Sheila shivered at the memory. "I didn't know if I was going to puke or pass out. I thought seeing my assistant's body was bad, but that…"

Dagger wanted to soak in her discomfort. How cruel was that? "I'm sure if there was anything you could have done, you would definitely have done it."

"Of course." Her eyes settled into a vacant stare. Was she questioning what she saw? Her eyes strayed back to Sara's arm and hair. Sheila looked puzzled for a brief second, but with a shake of her head she forced a smile.

"Would you like to join us?" Sara's offer was sincere.

Sheila shoved the chair back into place. "I already have a table. Thanks anyway. Have a great lunch." She turned and walked away.

"You enjoyed that way too much," Sara said.

"Guess we'll never know if she was shocked you're alive or if she is starting to question her sanity. I'm sure she has her shrink on speed dial." Dagger cast a glance across the room to where Sheila was sitting with her father. Her face was still the color of the ashes left on the floor at the Logan Galleria.

78 The days and weeks went by. Sara cut back on the amount of vegetables she planted having, in the past, always planted more than needed. Orchid trees and azaleas were in full bloom as were all of her potted plants. She and Eunie set aside Wednesdays to go to lunch together. Simon already planned another cruise for next year. This time they were going to Alaska. Eunie convinced him the scenery would be worth it, even if the weather would be chilly.

Dagger was working on a new project. He wanted to screen in the back yard patio, and Sara was already picking out patio furniture. They kept an eye on Einstein. His previous signs of anxiety were gone. Dagger and Sara, on the other hand, kept their eye on the calendar. Skizzy was expecting some weird magnetic force to somehow combine the ashes of the Addison twins to create a gruesome offspring.

Mother either had nothing to report or was keeping them in the dark. For now, Dagger and Sara spent their time trying out different restaurants, shopping, and sitting by the stream on the same bench where Sara cut off Dagger's black cord necklace.

On June 13, they met Padre for lunch at the Joint. The place was becoming quite the tourist attraction as gawkers took pictures of the wait staff in prison garb and the beer spigots shaped like hypodermics.

"So…" Padre drummed his fingers on the table. "This is

the big day."

"Hopefully, not too big." Dagger's pulse had been on overdrive for the past few days.

"What time again?" Padre asked this question almost daily for the past week.

"A little past eleven tonight," Sara said.

"Thought it was midnight."

Dagger shook his head. "That's eastern time zone."

"Right." Padre lifted the menu and studied the meat selection. "I'm having the sizzler. Don't care if it's lunchtime or not. I probably won't have an appetite later, so may as well make my last meal now."

"I'll have the same." Dagger set his menu down. "Have you talked to Marty Flynn?"

"He considers the case closed and isn't going to think about it."

"Smart man."

A burly guy in prison stripes lumbered over to the table. "Are you ready?"

The men ordered their steaks. Sara ordered a lobster roll and salad. "I haven't read anything else in the paper on Logan. Hopefully, no one is asking questions."

"Nope. We found a laptop in the farmhouse and our tech guys were able to determine the different Facebook pages he was researching. He has been tied to all of those women's deaths. Cases closed and tied in a nice ribbon."

"What about the gallery?" Sara asked. She hoped that the clothes she shifted out of had burned completely. Since Padre made no mention of it, she could only assume the investigators hadn't found evidence that someone other than Logan and Carlton were in the shop that night.

"Fire investigators ruled out arson. We believe there was an altercation between Logan and his manager and they somehow knocked over the torches. The only good thing out of this disaster, besides Logan, aka Addison, being dead, is that every one of those horrible paintings was destroyed."

79 They didn't bother going to bed until well after eleven o'clock. They listened for a phone call, fire trucks, and police cars. But nothing happened. No calls from Padre other than the one at eleven-fifteen to say, "We survived." They had even stepped out onto the back patio to see if nature was awake. The silence was gone and replaced by all the chatters of the animal kingdom.

At one o'clock in the morning, Dagger's eyes snapped open. How was it, even when he was asleep, he could see that damn pulsing green light? He sat up and dragged his legs over the side.

"What's wrong?"

"I'm being summoned."

Sara ran up to her bedroom while Dagger used his bathroom. They were dressed and out the door in fifteen minutes. "I don't like the idea of Mother contacting us so soon after the bewitching hour."

They sped through red lights. There were few cars on the road and not one police car. Dagger figured they were all in the downtown district where the restaurants and late night bars catered to the young crowd.

Once in the office, Sara hit the light switches on the wall while Dagger closed and locked the door. Dagger pressed his thumb to the indent and Connie's face immediately appeared. He didn't know androids could look flustered. Mother always seemed so calm and in control. Suddenly, shelves in the bookcase rearranged themselves exposing the satellite monitor in its full color. Sara pulled a chair around to Dagger's side of the desk and took a seat.

"We have a situation." A photo of a woman appeared on the screen.

"Isn't she…?"

"Yes, Six-One-Seven. She is the woman the Director appeared most interested in. We have identified and located her. We wanted to be certain of the details before sharing it with you. Her name is Callie Rodak from Tucson, Arizona. She and Mister Logan dated for a brief month. He obviously targeted the woman. She came from a Catholic family. Her uncle is a priest so, naturally, abortion was out of the question."

"Oh shit." Dagger knew where this was going.

"She delivered a baby boy just after ten o'clock last night at Tucson General Hospital."

"Which would have been after eleven our time," Sara said, her voice barely above a whisper. "That's what Logan meant when he was dying. Now I remember. He said, 'It's not over. The family curse will live on.'"

Dagger washed his hands over his face. "Let me guess. It was stolen from the Maternity Ward."

"Correct."

"Great."

"Fear not, Six-One-Seven. The Director may have had someone pose as a nurse to steal the baby, but we had an obstetrician who delivered it."

"Remind me to never doubt you again."

"Oh, I will be certain of that."

Sara asked, "So you have the infant?"

"Oh, no. We let the Director's people keep it but not before our physician implanted a completely undetectable microchip on the infant's right shoulder. Undetectable to him, but not to you."

"What do you mean?"

"Its frequency can only be detected by you, Six-One-Seven. Wherever the baby was taken, you can be sure it will be to his most secure research facility. I believe he has abandoned any thoughts of underground facilities, given the unstable fault lines. He is clever so knowing him it will be hidden in plain sight."

"What am I supposed to look for? How will I know if my chip has located the baby?"

"First, don't refer to it as a baby. I can see Sara's reaction already at the thought of eliminating what is supposed to be an innocent child. He is anything but innocent, Sara. You have seen what he will become. We wouldn't have believed it ourselves if we hadn't seen your videotape. It's a creature which, if left to the Director's devices will, in time, expand

to an army."

Dagger glanced at Sara. He could tell she was still having a problem not seeing Logan's baby as a cute newborn.

"So you aren't just after the baby," Sara said. "You are looking for the new research facility."

"Right. Once his operatives get the infant to this concealed research lab, he will give it a complete physical and body scan. They didn't have the time at the hospital and they don't have the facilities on the plane, as I'm sure that will be their mode of transportation. They may think all they are doing is examining the infant. However, what they will be doing is turning on the chip we implanted. That is when you should see a pulsing red dot, Six-One-Seven."

"What do you plan to do when you locate the facility?" Sara asked.

Connie blinked slowly. There was a hush that seemed to last for several minutes. "Anything you need my help with?" Dagger asked.

"Actually, everything. We need you to stay there and tell us the moment you see the red dot. Retrieve your global map, then we will also be able to see the map and red dot on our end. All you have to do is watch the monitor in the bookcase."

80 It was another hour before the red dot appeared in Dagger's peripheral vision. He called up the global map and it appeared to drop in front of his field of vision. Immediately the identical map appeared on the monitor, replacing the image of Connie.

"Now what?"

Sara sat forward, focused on the red dot that appeared to float in the Atlantic Ocean. "Zoom in."

All Dagger did was think it, and suddenly he had a close up of Florida, then Miami. However, the red dot was still further east. His gaze trailed east, past Nassau, farther east and north of the Turks and Caicos Islands. He zoomed in closer. The area was halfway between Bermuda and Puerto Rico.

"I don't get it. Unless some volcanic disturbance pushed a rock up to the surface, I don't see an island anywhere near the demon child."

Sara peered closer, knowing the hawk vision could see more than Dagger's could. "It's a ship. They used camouflage paint of some type."

"Of course!" Although they didn't see Connie's face, they did hear the android's excited voice.

"As you said, Mother. Hidden in plain sight." Now Dagger wondered what Mother was going to do with the information.

"We can only divert the satellite for a few seconds without arousing suspicion."

"Satellite?" Sara asked.

Dagger raised his gaze to the monitor in the bookcase. Sara did the same. Mother was manipulating one of the BettaTec satellites. They heard voices in the background uttering what sounded like longitude and latitude coordinates.

Suddenly, a light appeared on the satellite screen. Dagger and Sara held their collective breaths as a bright light shot out from the satellite. It appeared to be in slow motion. Did Mother slow down the image to make sure it hit its target? A split second later a large explosion could be seen on the screen.

Sara's hand drifted to her mouth. "All those people," she gasped.

"They weren't innocents, Sara," Mother said amid cheers. *"How clever he was to put the new facility in the middle of the ocean."*

"That certainly explains the Bermuda Triangle. Ships and planes that got a little too close for comfort were never seen or heard from again." Dagger chuckled. What would Skizzy think of that scenario? He would never go for the logical explanation. After all, boats and planes have been lost in that area since man started flying.

"It certainly encouraged today's airlines and cruise ships to avoid the area. All the Director had to do after he shot a plane down was to instruct the crew to move the facility away from the area until the authorities were through searching for debris."

"Won't he suspect that you were the one who destroyed his ship?" Sara asked.

"He will know someone is onto him. Can't be me since he believes I'm dead. It should keep his operatives away from Cedar Point for a while. Matter of fact, he has already moved the second satellite and sent it in another trajectory. Now he has a larger threat and he doesn't know who it is or where it is coming from. It will take him a while to figure out it was his own satellite that destroyed the facility. For now, he will look for a traitor or espionage." The map disappeared and the android face reappeared.

"Wait." Dagger eyed the android as though he were speaking to Mother directly. "That was far too easy. The Director always had a backup plan." Dagger sat back and thought of what he would do if he were the Director. "He would anticipate three moves ahead. If I consider that scenario, I would think he would want a sample of the baby's blood, just in case something happened to the infant. It could die on the way to the facility."

"They would take several dried blood spots," Sara offered.

Connie remained silent.

Dagger shook his head. "No. A newborn only has one cup of blood. I think he would have wanted the entire cup."

"You can't be serious. They would kill it for its blood?" Sara couldn't believe someone would be that cold-blooded. "No. He would do a blood transfusion."

"Correct," Connie said. *"Falsified medical reports necessitated a total blood transfusion."*

"But he still took the baby."

"To throw off anyone who might be onto them, they claimed the baby died in the hospital."

"And the mother?" Sara asked. "Is she dead?"

"Affirmative."

Sara didn't want to know whose operative did the killing.

"Checkmate." Dagger wasn't sure whether to admire Mother or revile her. "You were always three steps ahead of Father. That's why you took Sara's blood. You knew he would need more than a spot of blood, which is the normal amount taken from a newborn. Now he has a cup, but you have four pints."

"Not quite. As you have said before, Six-One-Seven, it is all a big chess game. For now, I think we are in a stalemate. He will regroup, probably determine who the traitor is, and I wouldn't doubt that he moved the one satellite into a different trajectory to throw us off. My guess is he will focus on Tucson. That is where Logan was first sighted and where the baby was born. We will need to focus on the location of another research lab. He will need complete privacy to do his research on the baby's blood.

"Do you have any thoughts on where that might be?"

"This one will be far more advanced and again, in plain sight. The challenge may not be that hard. He already tried a lab in a remote area in the middle of the Atlantic. I don't think he will try that again. It would have to be somewhere in North America. There are too many variables in other parts of the world, not to mention wars and unrest. It can't

be near any areas prone to disaster which really narrows it down. Just about every part of the United States has some type of disaster. Hurricanes, tornadoes, earthquakes, forest fires. And I doubt he doesn't already have it constructed and up and running. A new construction would garner too much attention. My guess, he would have taken over some existing facility."

"You didn't find anything?"

"We are still searching his files. I would gather the research will take sometime. Shapeshifters are new to all of us. He will be careful for now. Probably won't trust anyone around him. That plays to our advantage. We will have time to search out this facility."

"About thirty-five years' worth," Sara said. "The next full moon on a Friday the thirteenth won't be until August 2049."

EPILOGUE

He ran a hand over the face of his Jaeger-Lecoultre watch as he stood at the window of his hotel suite overlooking the waterfront in Vancouver, British Columbia. A shimmer of light could be seen to the east as the sun made its slow ascension.

Behind him his trusted assistant had just hung up the phone. Fredrik Hensen had been roused from a deep sleep when the call came in about the research ship blowing up. While his hair was still pressed flat by the pillow and he hadn't had time to change out of his silk pajamas, his boss was dressed for a board meeting, every wisp of salt and pepper hair in perfect position. Fredrik gulped the remains of his coffee, wishing he could inject it.

"Did the specimen make it to the lab?"

"Yes, sir. As you had suspected, someone targeted the research vessel."

"It is a pity the small crew we left onboard, as well as the infant, were eliminated, but at least we have the specimen."

"Unfortunately, we still don't know what caused the explosion or if the threat has been eliminated." Fredrik coughed and shook the sleep from his eyes. He stood on shaky legs and fought the feeling of vertigo. What was wrong? He had been on ships before that never made him this queasy.

"We have a traitor or two in our midst, Fredrik. Don't know who to trust these days." He took a sip of his own coffee as he heard a sound behind him. Fredrik had been the only other person with access to his laptop. The discovery of the drone insect on Fredrik after the botched sale of the vaporizer had been his first clue that his assistant might have been compromised. There was no telling how much information his assistant had divulged.

He pulled out his cell phone, scrolled through the contacts, and pressed a button. "This is Director Keyes." He turned from the window and stared at his assistant. Fredrik was sitting on the floor, his back against the couch, a confused look on his face. The trusted assistant looked at his boss and shook his head no, pleading his innocence with his eyes. "I have a suspect ready for interrogation." He hung up the phone and calmly took a seat on a chair in front of Fredrik. "Of all the people, Fredrik, I trusted you the most. You only have a few minutes before they come to get you. Do you want to tell me who you were working for?" Again Fredrik shook his head. "No, you won't tell me or no, I have it wrong? I know it's difficult to talk with the drug, but surely you can give a first name, can't you?"

"Not me," Fredrik whispered while his eyes jerked, seeing the walls come to life, imaginary insects crawling over his body. The drug had that kind of effect.

"You know me better than that, Fredrik. I am rarely wrong." He patted his assistant's cheek as the door to his suite opened and two men rolled in a large metal crate. "You will talk. They all do eventually." Tears fell from Fredrik's eyes which were wide with fear. He continued to shake his head no as the men lifted him into the container and fastened the lid.

Once the door closed again, the Director returned to the window and stared at the sun cresting over the water. He had the sample. That was the important thing. Although it was currently in the lab, it would be moved soon to the new facility. For now, Jonathan Keyes, the Director of BettaTec, was aware of a posing threat. He had a new adversary.

Or was it the same one?